ALMOST A QUEEN

Book One of The Three Graces Trilogy

LAURA DU PRE

ESCAPE TO THE COURT

Join Laura's mailing list now and get a copy of the sequel, *Safe in My Arms*.

ABOUT ALMOST A QUEEN

Travel back to the court of the French Renaissance..

Almost a Queen: Book One of the Three Graces Trilogy

Who wouldn't want to be Queen?

Cousins to the King of Navarre, the Cleves sisters witness the glamour and danger of the French royal court firsthand. Youngest sister, Marie is trapped in an unhappy arranged marriage with her cousin, Henri, Prince de Conde. Determined to make the best of her situation, she awaits the wedding of the King of Navarre in Paris.

Paris of 1572 boils with religious war, and few will make it out of the wedding celebrations alive. Those that do survive face an impossible choice: convert or die. Will Marie and Conde make the decision to abandon their Protestant faith in order to save their lives? Will it cost them their souls?

Along with the threat of death comes a change for true love with the king's younger son, the Duc d'Anjou. Yet Marie promised to love honor and cherish her husband till death did them part. Will death part them soon? Is it possible to find love in the midst of tragedy?

Based on a true story

The Cleves sisters' story starts with Marie, the youngest sister introduces you to the world of court politics in France of the 16th Century. Like most great noble families of the period, the web of intermarriages and alliances made enemies out of blood relatives. It also meant that the stories of the people who served the Valois monarchs were as intertwined and as complicated as their marriages.

Led by the ever-vigilant Catherine de Medici, Queen Mother of France and a force of nature, the members of the court shaped the political and religious future of France of the Sixteenth Century. In upcoming novels, you'll meet the often- derided Charlotte, Madame de Sauve, and enough royal mistresses to satisfy your need for scandal.

The Three Graces Trilogy continues with eldest sister, Henriette and will conclude with middle sister Catherine's story. Why did I choose that order? You really will have to read to to find out for yourself. I'm available 24/7 at www.lauradupre.com. **Stop by there for a free book and make sure you'll be the first to hear about new releases and special discounts.**

❧ I ❧

L ouvre Palace, Paris, 1572

I CANNOT KEEP THE RIBBONS FOR THE QUEEN'S DRESS FROM tangling as I walk. It is as if they are conspiring to knot and defy me. Amused at my predicament, the Queen's guards nod at me and try to suppress a smile. I try to hurry to my mistress' chambers, but the extra effort sends a wave of air and what progress I had made tangles into a loose braid.

Entering the Queen's antechamber, I bob into a curtsey, "I'm sorry, Madame, they seem to have gotten the best of me." Like the guards, she cannot suppress a giggle at my frustration. Recovering herself, she shrugs her petite shoulders.

"Perhaps it wasn't meant to be, Marie." She answers me in Latin, our shared language. Since coming to the French court, Elisabeth of Austria has attempted to speak French, but she has as much difficulty as I have found in maintaining her wardrobe this morning. "If you would, please fetch my gown."

Thankful for the reprieve, I place the ribbons on the nightstand

and quickly forget them. As Queen of France, we would usually expect Elisabeth to rule over the court, but we all know that the true Grande dame is her powerful mother-in-law, Catherine de Medici. A quiet, pious and studious young girl, this arrangement suits Elisabeth well and she appears at court whenever the circumstances warrant it.

This hot August morning, her presence is certainly justified in court, as is mine. My cousin Henry, the young King of Navarre, is about to be married and we are eagerly awaiting his arrival in Paris. The bride to be is the king's sister Margot, the Princess of France and one of the most celebrated beauties of Europe. At first glance, their match seems perfection, but as the bride and groom do not share the same faith, the betrothal has been fought with difficulties. The largest hurdle the two have faced, was the lifelong hatred between their mothers. Their hatred is due in no small part to my Aunt, Jeanne, the formidable Queen of Navarre.

I should not speak ill of my aunt; she took me in after my mother's death and my father's inability to raise his youngest daughter, a girl of nine. Married to my mother's brother, Antoine of Bourbon, Jeanne of Navarre did not hesitate to send for me and offer to bring me up within her home. Of course, life with my aunt came with certain conditions, amongst them the requirement that I follow her Reformed faith. Unable to imagine what to do with me on his own, my father readily agreed, and I was packed off before my tenth birthday to an unfamiliar home with its odd and alien faith.

So I was raised, like my cousin, the King of Navarre, as a Protestant, although little of the Reformed faith appealed to me. My loyalty to my aunt meant that I followed her religious instruction, and I have spent my life as a Protestant. My older sisters, Henriette, who is eight years older than I and our middle sister, Catherine, five years older than I, were raised in the Catholic faith. As a result, my family feels very alien to me sometimes. After ten years with my aunt, I returned to the French royal court to become a lady-in-waiting to the new Queen, whom I found an easy mistress to serve.

I had not seen my aunt in months when she traveled with my cousin, Catherine to Paris to negotiate the marriage between Henry of Navarre and Margot of Valois. Our reunion was tense, as I felt she judged me for falling from the faith she had instructed me in since childhood. Within weeks, however, my aunt died I had lost the second mother I had known in my short life. Aunt Jeanne was determined to see her children married well and safely, while furthering the reformed faith and that included not only her son's marriage to a Catholic princess. My aunt had seen that I also married well and married within her faith.

My aunt chose my other first cousin, the Prince of Condé, to be my groom almost a year ago. Condé's Christian name was "Henry" in honor of the king's father. I had known my cousin since I came to the Navarrese court, as he also came to court as a motherless orphan adopted by Jeanne of Navarre. Many people criticized her for being harsh and calculating, but one could never say Jeanne of Navarre abandoned a child in need of a motherly figure. Rather than hold her generosity over our heads, she seemed to relish her opportunity to be the mother of more than the two children of her body.

Because of her generosity in taking me in, I felt obligated to go along with the match she had made for me. Protestant princesses were rare in Europe, Save the foreign ones from German principalities. It was a foregone conclusion, therefore, that I would marry and become the Princess of Condé as we forged a new Protestant dynasty. Despite any misgivings I might have about our marriage and mourning the death of my surrogate mother, I went ahead with our ceremony this past July and Condé and I married according to Protestant rites.

Now, almost a month later, I struggled with adjusting to married life. My royal mistress, herself, married for less than two years, became a genuine friend and a source of support for me. Elisabeth was in the final months of her first pregnancy and as her stomach expanded, we worked to expand her gowns. As I placed the rose-colored one she had selected for the evening's reception on the bed, my wedding ring hung on the silk of the bodice.

"I'm sorry, Madame," I grimaced and looked at her helplessly.

"It's all right; you aren't used to wearing it. It will become second nature to you, eventually."

"It feels heavy," our time together had taught me that I could be honest with her without fearing her judgment.

"I miss wearing mine. It's been months since I've been able to get it on my finger." Her hand went to her belly absentmindedly. All of France eagerly awaited the birth of the royal heir. Like any other woman, Elisabeth only hoped for the birth of a healthy child.

"I suppose it won't be long before I'm in the same situation." I tried to keep the edge out of my voice, but looking at the expression on her face, I knew that I had not succeeded in doing so.

Elisabeth smiled at me, the compassion showing on her face. Like me, she had no control over the man she married. She fulfilled her duty as a royal princess and her current condition was a fulfillment of her obligation to supply an heir. Unlike me, she accepted her role without complaining, a choice I secretly envied.. Although officially separated by our religious beliefs, the devoutly Catholic Elisabeth never held my faith as a strike against me. We were inseparable most of the time, except for the times we worshiped our Lord. The Queen accompanied the king to Mass daily while I attended sermons from the leading Protestant preachers who were allowed to remain at court.

AS SOON AS I ENTERED MY PRIVATE APARTMENTS WITHIN THE VAST Louvre palace, I removed my hood and attempted to smooth my brown hair. I had wanted a few quiet moments alone, but as I entered the bedchamber, I saw that my husband was already sitting beside our bed. Since going from cousins to husband and wife, our interactions had been awkward. Every new bride must take some time to adjust to married life, but I felt as if my adjustment period took me more time than most.

I was determined to work to make our marriage a success, but the truth was that my husband and I were very different people. Like my Aunt Jeanne, he had taken to the Protestant religious with relish and embraced the dour and restrained nature of the most ardent followers. As a result, his character was often dark and brooding, which made it difficult for us to connect with one another. A life stripped of the gaiety and spontaneous nature of most Frenchmen seemed an empty life to me. I was determined, however, to do my duty to make our marriage work, if not for our shared for faith, then for our family's sake and to honor the memory of my Aunt Jeanne.

"I've just come from the Queen's rooms; we've done all we can to prepare for Navarre's arrival. If he decides to come at all."

I raised an eyebrow, "Do you think that he will back out of his mother's promise?"

"If he knows what's good for him, he will. None of the Papists can be trusted to keep their word."

I held my tongue, choosing not to remind him that my closest friend at court was a Papist. I had no desire to pick a fight that moment, exhausted as I was from the continual preparations for the upcoming wedding.

"We are expected to be at the Admiral's house this evening to hear the Reverend Challoit." His imperious tone grated on my nerves and this time, I chose to say something.

"When have I failed to join you for a sermon at court? Do I not come faithfully as a believer and as your wife?"

He shrugged, and I imagined that he got some thrill out of bating me. "I sometimes feel as if you are not as sincere about our faith as I am. One might think that the Catholic flavor of the court is rubbing off on you."

Would that be so bad? In my mind, toleration was better than the extremism that my husband seemed doggedly determined to display. The king himself was willing to allow those of both faiths to worship without molestation at court. Both the king and his mother had encouraged toleration amongst the two groups of Christians within France and within the court. Still, men like my husband seemed determined to provoke hostility between themselves and the moderates of the court. Sometimes I felt as if my fellow Protestants only wanted to play the part of the persecuted party to garner sympathy abroad. From what I had seen so far, my countrymen enjoyed an unusual degree of religious freedom.

"We both serve at the pleasure of the king and his mother; we cannot forget that. Attempting to incite hostility between the Catholics and Protestants does nothing to help either side."

He snorted, "Now you sound like Catherine."

I shrugged, weary of his baiting. "Perhaps she is right."

LOUVRE PALACE, PARIS, 1572

I CANNOT KEEP THE RIBBONS FOR THE QUEEN'S DRESS FROM tangling as I walk. It is as if they are conspiring to knot and defy me. Amused at my predicament, the queen's guards nod at me and try to suppress a smile. I try to hurry to my mistress' chambers, but the extra effort sends a wave of air and what progress I had made tangles into a loose braid.

Entering the queen's antechamber, I bob into a curtsey, "I'm sorry, Madame, they seem to have gotten the best of me." Like the guards, she cannot suppress a giggle at my frustration. Recovering herself, she shrugs her petite shoulders.

"Perhaps it wasn't meant to be, Marie." She answers me in Latin, our shared language. Since coming to the French court, Elisabeth of Austria has attempted to speak French, but she has as much difficulty as I have found in maintaining her wardrobe this morning. "If you would, please fetch my gown."

Thankful for the reprieve, I place the ribbons on the nightstand and quickly forget them. As Queen of France, we would usually expect Elisabeth to rule over the court, but we all know that the true Grande dame is her powerful mother-in-law, Catherine de Medici. A quiet, pious and studious young girl, this arrangement suits Elisabeth well and she appears at court whenever the circumstances warrant it.

This hot August morning, her presence is certainly justified in court, as is mine. My cousin Henry, the young King of Navarre, is about to be married and we are eagerly awaiting his arrival in Paris. The bride to be is the King's sister Margot, the Princess of France and one of the most celebrated beauties of Europe. At first glance, their match seems perfection, but as the bride and groom do not share the same faith, the betrothal has been fought with difficulties. The largest hurdle the two have faced, was the lifelong hatred between their mothers. Their hatred is due in no small part to my Aunt, Jeanne, the formidable Queen of Navarre.

I should not speak ill of my aunt; she took me in after my mother's death and my father's inability to raise his youngest daughter, a girl of nine. Married to my mother's brother, Antoine of Bourbon, Jeanne of Navarre did not hesitate to send for me and offer to bring me up within her home. Life with my aunt came with certain conditions, amongst them the requirement I follow her Reformed faith. Unable to imagine what to do with me on his own, my father readily agreed, and I was packed off before my tenth birthday to an unfamiliar home with its odd and alien faith.

I was raised, like my cousin, the King of Navarre, as a Protestant, although little of the Reformed faith appealed to me. My loyalty to my aunt meant that I followed her religious instruction, and I have spent my life as a Protestant. My older sisters, Henriette, who is eight years older than I and our middle sister, Catherine, five years older than I, were raised in the Catholic faith. As a result, my family feels alien sometimes. After ten years with my aunt, I returned to the French royal court to become a lady-in-waiting to the new queen, whom I found to be an easy mistress to serve.

I had not seen my aunt in months when she traveled with my cousin, Catherine to Paris to negotiate the marriage between Henry of Navarre and Margot of Valois. Our reunion was tense, as I felt she judged me for falling from the faith she had instructed me in since childhood. Within weeks, however, my aunt died I had lost the second mother I had known in my short life. Aunt Jeanne worked to see her children married well and safely, while furthering the reformed faith and that included not only her son's marriage to a Catholic princess. My aunt had seen that I also married well and married within her faith.

My aunt chose my other first cousin, the Prince of Condé, to be my groom almost a year ago. Condé's Christian name was "Henry" in honor of the King's father. I had known my cousin since I came to the Navarrese court, as he also came to court as a motherless orphan adopted by Jeanne of Navarre. Many people criticized her for being harsh and calculating, but one could never say Jeanne of Navarre abandoned a child in need of a motherly figure. Rather than hold her generosity over our heads, she seemed to relish her opportunity to be the mother of more than the two children of her body.

Because of her generosity in taking me in, I felt obligated to go along with the match she had made for me. Protestant princesses were rare in Europe, save the foreign ones from German principalities. It was a foregone conclusion, therefore, that I would marry and become the Princess of Condé as we forged a new Protestant dynasty. Despite any misgivings I might have about our marriage and mourning the death of my surrogate mother, I went ahead with our ceremony this past July and Condé and I married according to Protestant rites.

Now, almost a month later, I struggled with adjusting to married life. My royal mistress, herself, married for less than two years, became a genuine friend and a source of support for me. Elisabeth was in the final months of her first pregnancy and as her stomach expanded, we worked to expand her gowns. As I placed the rose-colored one she had selected for the evening's reception on the bed, my wedding ring hung on the silk of the bodice.

"I'm sorry, Madame," I grimaced and looked at her helplessly.

"It's all right; you aren't used to wearing it. It will become second nature to you, eventually."

"It feels heavy," our time together had taught me I could be honest with her without fearing her judgment.

"I miss wearing mine. It's been months since I've been able to get it on my finger." Her hand went to her belly absentmindedly. All of France eagerly awaited the birth of the royal heir. Like any other woman, Elisabeth only hoped for the birth of a healthy child.

"I suppose it won't be long before I'm in the same situation." I tried to keep the edge out of my voice, but looking at her expression, I knew that I had failed in doing so.

Elisabeth smiled at me, the compassion showing on her face. Like me, she had no control over the man she married. She fulfilled her duty as a royal princess and her current condition was a fulfillment of her obligation to supply an heir. Unlike me, she accepted her role without complaining, a choice I secretly envied.. Although officially separated by our religious beliefs, the devoutly Catholic Elisabeth never held my faith as a strike against me. We were inseparable most of the time, except for the times we worshiped our Lord. The queen accompanied the King to Mass daily while I attended sermons from the leading Protestant preachers who were allowed to remain at court.

◎◦◎

As soon as I entered my private apartments within the vast Louvre palace, I removed my hood and attempted to smooth my brown hair. I had wanted a few quiet moments alone, but as I entered the bedchamber, I saw that my husband was already sitting beside our bed. Since going from cousins to husband and wife, our interactions had been awkward. Every new bride must take time to adjust to married life, but I felt as if my adjustment period took me more time than most.

I was determined to work to make our marriage a success, but I could not ignore the fact my husband and I were very different people. Like my Aunt Jeanne, he had taken to the Protestant religious with relish and embraced the dour and restrained nature of the most ardent followers. As a result, his character was often dark and brooding, which made it difficult for us to connect with one another. A life stripped of the gaiety and spontaneous nature of most Frenchmen seemed an empty life. I was determined, however, to do my duty to make our marriage work, if not for our shared for faith, then for our family's sake and to honor the memory of my Aunt Jeanne.

"I've just come from the queen's rooms; we've done all we can to prepare for Navarre's arrival. If he comes at all."

I raised an eyebrow, "Do you think he will back out of his mother's promise?"

"If he knows what's good for him, he will. We can trust none of the Papists to keep their word."

I held my tongue, choosing not to remind him that my closest friend at court was a Papist. I had no desire to pick a fight that moment, exhausted as I was from the continual preparations for the upcoming wedding.

"They expect us to be at the Admiral's house this evening to hear the Reverend Challoit." His imperious tone grated on my nerves and this time, I said something.

"When have I failed to join you for a sermon at court? Do I not come faithfully as a believer and as your wife?"

He shrugged, and I imagined that he got a thrill out of bating me. "I sometimes feel as if you are not as sincere about our faith as I am. One might think the Catholic flavor of the court is rubbing off on you."

Would that be so bad? In my mind, toleration was better than the extremism that my husband seemed doggedly determined to display. The King himself allowed those of both faiths to worship without molestation at court. Both the King and his mother had encouraged toleration amongst the two groups of Christians within France and within the court. Still, men like my husband seemed determined to provoke hostility between themselves and the moderates of the court. Sometimes I felt as if my fellow Protestants only wanted to play the part of the persecuted party to garner sympathy abroad. From what I had seen so far, my countrymen enjoyed an unusual degree of religious freedom.

"We both serve at the pleasure of the King and his mother; we cannot forget that. Attempting to incite hostility between the Catholics and Protestants does nothing to help either side."

He snorted, "Now you sound like Catherine."

I shrugged, weary of his baiting. "Perhaps she is right."

2

I fidget in the room, as always, feeling uncomfortable. In front of me, another "preacher", whose name I struggle to remember is droning on and on about "atonement" and other lofty concepts that I have heard since childhood. These meetings and prayer nights are a stripped-down version of the Mass that the Catholics attend daily and officially, they are meant to encourage discussion and personal understanding of the word of God. I have never confessed this to anyone, but for me, these meetings are more like being scolded for being a naughty child. The men who run them seem angry and spiteful, and I rarely feel the presence of God during them. Instead, I feel as if I were watching a performance or lecture. After the man designated as the "minister" concludes his sermon, the congregation is encouraged to speak of their sins openly and confess them to one another. I am far from a shy woman, yet the idea of having my privacy violated in front of virtual strangers horrifies me.

The entire experience feels more like an excuse for a gossip session like those that run rampant amongst the lords and ladies of the court, except this is supposedly sanctioned by God. My bit of rebellion is to list demurely some shallow "sin," such as loving my shoes too much or feeling as if I am unable to return my husband's love that he gives me. This ploy seems to satisfy the overbearing men who run the meetings and for a few moments at least, I am left alone.

Still, I long for an hour of solitude to be alone with my thoughts and for the blessed quiet to hear God's voice, not that of a preacher whose performance is scheduled for a given night. I wonder what it would be like in the hushed halls of a Catholic mass. But of course, as a Protestant princess, I am not allowed to know. I am not allowed to confess even that I am curious to learn. If I were to ask the Queen to allow me to accompany her during Mass, she would leap at the opportunity to bring her dear friend along, but she is wise enough to never put me in the position of "violating" my professed religious beliefs. Without any other options, I am forced to wince as the noise and din around me swirls until the meeting is over.

CONDÉ AND I TAKE OUR PLACES IN THE MASSIVE THRONE ROOM OF the Louvre palace. Navarre and his gentlemen have finally arrived in Paris safely, and to our relief, the formal betrothal will be held as planned. The ceremony demonstrates the tangled web of relations and religious preferences across the country; while the groom is Protestant, his cousin is the very Catholic Cardinal Bourbon, who will conduct the betrothal ceremony and the strange wedding ceremony that is to come. In deference to Navarre, they will be wed on a platform erected outside of Notre Dame Cathedral. After their vows, the new Queen of Navarre will be escorted by her brother the Duc d'Anjou, known as "Monsieur," who will stand in the groom's place for the Catholic Mass that will follow the ceremony.

I cannot help but flash back to my wedding ceremony a month earlier, as Condé and I were wed in a thoroughly Protestant ceremony in the formidable Chateau Blandy near the village of Melun. Navarre had stood nearby while I was wed and now I would watch as he likewise was united in matrimony. Like the ring on my finger, our marriage had failed to settle upon me, being more of an intrusion than a comfort. I hoped that as time passed, this would no longer be so. I wished the same for Navarre.

The appearance of so many new people in Paris had also meant that the court had been reshuffled in our housing arrangements. My husband and I were allowed to move out of the Louvre and lodge in my sister's home with her husband, the Italian Duc de Nevers. Henriette was the heiress of our family, our elder brother having died a few years earlier, and her husband took her title, but not the management of her finances. Thanks to Henriette's wily use of her financial assets, she was fast becoming one of the most important creditors in France.

Perhaps every new groom is uncomfortable being lodged with his new wife's family, but I sensed that my husband tried little to integrate himself with mine. Henriette and her husband, Louis were devoted Catholics, like our other sister, Catherine and that brought no small amount of scorn from my husband. I would have thought that the idea of having so many fellow Protestant allies in Paris weeks after meeting for our ceremony would make Condé happy, but he seems so dour and determined to be quarrelsome that I doubt anything could make him happy. Even during our shared meals, he took the opportunity to criticize my sister and her studious husband.

"Must we sit here while the two of them continue crossing themselves?"

"Husband, it's simply in thanksgiving of their food. We should all be grateful for the bounty of God's providence," I quoted a minister's lecture from a few weeks earlier, hoping that he would use the parallel to find some common ground with Louis and my sister.

"It's idolatry," he sneered, poking at his fish.

"Making the sign of the cross is not creating an idol. We all revere the cross as the instrument of our Lord's torture and resurrection. Surely we can all agree on that?"

"I will be glad when this spectacle is over and we can get back to our regular lives."

"And back to our rooms at the palace?"

He shrugged, "As far away from Paris as we can get."

My husband's sulky attitude notwithstanding, we all felt the uneasiness surrounding the two factions stuffed into Paris that hot August. The stifling heat, bereft of any rain or wind to bring us relief, and the overcrowded streets turned the city into a tinderbox. I waited on Queen Elisabeth as best I could, but the crowds and our continual obligations to attend banquets, fetes, masquerades and dinners meant that I rarely had time to speak with her. I had hoped to be with her when her child came and like me, she had hoped to go into confinement in quiet.

The Queen's quiet descent into confinement was not to be; her sister-in-law's marriage demanded her attendance and despite their different natures, the two women were close friends. No matter how many demands pregnancy or decorum placed on her body, Elisabeth was determined to attend as many events surrounding her Margot's marriage as possible.

As I had suspected, the wedding ceremony was odd, to say the least. The platform gave the half-Protestant half-Catholic wedding a cobbled and confusing flair, and the fact that it was held outside meant that the atmosphere was more like an open market than a solemn rite. We held our breath as the vows were said, Navarre readily agreeing to the marriage and Margot holding her tongue. The King in his anger pushed her head forward, forcing her to give her assent to the marriage. In a typical wedding, this would have been suspect, but this was far from typical. Rumors abounded that Catherine had resorted to trickery and bribes to attain the dispensation from Rome for the close cousins to marry and few, if any of us, had seen the supposed letter from the church.

At last, the Cardinal Bourbon pronounced his kinsman and the Princess of France man and wife, and Navarre stepped aside to allow his new wife to celebrate the marriage mass. Dressed even more splendidly than the bride, the Duc d'Anjou led his sister into the cathedral and out of propriety, we Protestants in the assembly waited outside until the mass was over.

"Let the pompous boy take her inside. That's half an hour that I won't have to spend looking at him." My husband mumbled in my ear and I turned to glare at him.

"This is hardly the time to resurrect old quarrels."

He looked at the Duc de Guise, whose eyes were on Margot instead of my sister, his wedded wife. "Tell that to Guise."

After the ceremony, we all sighed a sigh of relief that the feared violence that could stop the wedding from happening had not occurred. The streets of Paris stayed blissfully quiet through the following evening. Perhaps the Protestants were silly to worry that they were in danger.

I FIDGET IN THE ROOM, AS ALWAYS, FEELING UNCOMFORTABLE. IN front of me, another "preacher", whose name I struggle to remember is droning on and on about "atonement" and other lofty concepts I have heard since childhood. These meetings and prayer nights are a stripped-down version of the Mass that the Catholics attend daily and officially, designed to encourage discussion and personal understanding of the word of God. I have never confessed this to anyone, but for me, these meetings are more akin to being scolded for being a naughty child. The men who run them seem angry and spiteful, and I rarely feel the presence of God during them. Instead, I feel as if I were watching a performance or lecture. After the man designated as the "minister" concludes his sermon, he encourages the congregation to speak of their sins openly and confess them to one another. I am far from a shy woman, yet the idea of having my privacy violated in front of virtual strangers horrifies me.

The entire experience feels more like an excuse for a gossip session like those that run rampant amongst the lords and ladies of the court, except this is supposedly sanctioned by God. My bit of rebellion is to list demurely some shallow "sin," such as loving my shoes too much or the fear I am unable to return my husband's love that he gives me. This ploy seems to satisfy the overbearing men who run the meetings and for a few moments at least, I am left alone.

Still, I long for an hour of solitude to be alone with my thoughts and for the blessed quiet to hear God's voice, not the droning voice of a preacher whose performance is scheduled for a given night. I wonder what it would be like in the hushed halls of a Catholic mass. But of course, as a Protestant princess, I may not know. I may not confess the scandalous idea that I am curious to learn. If I were to ask the queen to allow me to accompany her during Mass, she would leap at the opportunity to bring her dear friend along, but she is wise enough to never put me in the position of "violating" my professed religious beliefs. With no other options, I am forced to wince as the noise and din around me swirls until the meeting is over.

CONDÉ AND I TAKE OUR PLACES IN THE MASSIVE THRONE ROOM OF the Louvre palace. Navarre and his gentlemen have finally arrived in Paris safely, and to our relief, the formal betrothal will go on as planned. The ceremony reflects the tangled web of relations and religious preferences across the country; while the groom is Protestant, his cousin is the very Catholic Cardinal Bourbon, who will conduct the betrothal ceremony and the strange wedding ceremony is to come. In deference to Navarre, they will be wed on a platform erected outside of Notre Dame Cathedral. After their vows, the new Queen of Navarre will be escorted by her brother the Duc d'Anjou, known as "Monsieur," who will stand in the groom's place for the Catholic Mass that will follow the ceremony.

I cannot help but flash back to my wedding ceremony a month earlier, as Condé and I wed in a thoroughly Protestant ceremony in the formidable Chateau Blandy near the village of Melun. Navarre had stood nearby while married and now I would watch as he likewise unites in matrimony. Like the ring on my finger, our marriage had failed to settle upon me, being more of an intrusion than a comfort. I hoped that as time passed, this would no longer be so. I wished the same for Navarre.

The appearance of so many new people in Paris had also meant that the court had reshuffled in our housing arrangements. My husband and I moved out of the Louvre and lodge in my sister's home with her husband, the Italian Duc de Nevers. Henriette was the heiress of our family, our elder brother having died a few years earlier, and her husband took her title, but not the management of her finances. Thanks to Henriette's wily use of her financial assets, she was fast becoming one of the most important creditors in France.

Perhaps every new groom is uncomfortable being lodged with his new wife's family, but I sensed that my husband tried little to integrate himself with mine. Henriette and her husband, Louis were devoted Catholics, like our other sister, Catherine and that brought no small amount of scorn from my husband. I would have thought of having so many fellow Protestant allies in Paris weeks after meeting for our cere- mony would make Condé happy, but he seems so dour and determined to be quarrelsome that I doubt anything could make him happy. Even during our shared meals, he criticized my sister and her studious husband.

"Must we sit here while the two of them continue crossing themselves?"

"Husband, it's in thanksgiving of their food. We should all be grateful for the bounty of God's providence," I quoted a minister's lecture from a few weeks earlier, hoping that he would use the parallel to find some common ground with Louis and my sister.

"It's idolatry," he sneered, poking at his fish.

"Making the sign of the cross is not creating an idol. We all revere the cross as the instrument of our Lord's torture and resurrection. Surely we can all agree on that?"

"I will be glad when this spectacle is over and we can get back to our regular lives."

"And back to our rooms at the palace?"

He shrugged, "As far away from Paris as we can get."

MY HUSBAND'S SULKY ATTITUDE NOTWITHSTANDING, WE ALL FELT the uneasiness surrounding the two factions stuffed into Paris that hot August. The stifling heat, bereft of any rain or wind to bring us relief, and the overcrowded streets turned the city into a tinderbox. I waited on Queen Elisabeth as best I could, but the crowds and our continual obligations to attend banquets, fetes, masquerades and dinners meant that I rarely had time to speak with her. I had hoped to be with her when her child came and like me; she had hoped to go into confinement in quiet.

The queen's quiet descent into confinement was not to be; her sister-in-law's marriage demanded her attendance and despite their different natures, the two women were close friends. No matter how many demands pregnancy or decorum placed on her body, Elisabeth attended as many events surrounding her Margot's marriage as possible.

As I had suspected, the wedding ceremony was odd. The platform gave the half-Protestant half-Catholic wedding a cobbled and confusing flair, and they held it outside meant that the atmosphere was more like an open market than a solemn rite. We held our breath as the couple repeated their vows, Navarre readily agreeing to the marriage and Margot holding her tongue. The king in his anger pushed her head forward, forcing her to give her assent to the marriage. In a typical wedding, this would have been suspect, but this was far from typical. Rumors abounded that Catherine had resorted to trickery and bribes to attain the dispensation from Rome for the close cousins to marry and few, if any of us, had seen the supposed letter from the church.

At last, the Cardinal Bourbon pronounced his kinsman and the Princess of France man and wife, and Navarre stepped aside to allow his new wife to celebrate the marriage mass. Dressed even more splendid than the bride, the Duc d'Anjou led his sister into the cathedral and out of propriety, we Protestants in the assembly waited outside until the mass was over.

"Let the pompous boy take her inside. That's half an hour I won't have to spend looking at him." My husband mumbled in my ear and I turned to glare at him.

"This is hardly the time to resurrect old quarrels."

He looked at the Duc de Guise, whose eyes were on Margot instead of my sister, his wedded wife. "Tell that to Guise."

After the ceremony, we all sighed a sigh of relief that the feared violence that could stop the wedding from happening had not occurred. The streets of Paris stayed blissfully quiet through the following evening. Perhaps the Protestants were silly to worry that they were in danger.

3

The Sunday evening following the wedding we were all invited to a banquet given by the King. Given the Reformed faith's belief that to be joyous on the Sabbath was disrespectful, none of the Protestants accepted the King's invitation. Yet to decline the invitation was to insult the King himself. When I heard that they had planned to risk offending the King, I was horrified.

"You cannot just refuse to go," I trailed after my husband as he stumbled around our bedchamber, looking for last minute items before he left. I shoved his hat and shoes into his hand, impatiently waiting for him to finish dressing himself.

"We have gone above and beyond in our willingness to be polite to the King and we have the right to attend our services. This debauchery is against our beliefs and we will not compromise on them in fear of offending an earthly monarch."

I exhaled a sigh. King Charles had been more than accommodating towards his Protestant guests and now they were thumbing their noses at him. As one of the Queen's ladies-in-waiting, I could ill afford not to attend the banquet. As far as I was concerned, my husband was acting rude and downright childish.

"I will attend the banquet while you attend the service at the

Admiral's house." Compromise seemed better than continuing the argument. My husband was intransigent as always.

He snorted in response, raising my ire even further. "Absolutely not —you will not attend an event without me there beside you. I will not have it said that my wife is a wanton woman."

"And I am to offend both the sovereign and my mistress?"

"You are to explain that your husband commanded you to accompany him, as any dutiful wife would."

❦

AT THE MEETING, I SEETHED AND DID MY BEST TO AVOID CONTACT with my husband. What would the King think of our absence? I was sure that his arrogance would place both of us in danger. During the seemingly endless sermon, I turned over in my mind what I would say to the Queen to explain our absence.

Afterward, Admiral Coligny took my elbow and asked to speak with me. Despite his decision to become a firm Protestant, unlike my husband, the elderly admiral was willing to work towards reconciliation between the two faiths. In fact, the King considered the Admiral to be a close friend and mentor, calling him "father" after the death of the King's actual father. It was difficult not to like the admiral; while he was an accomplished soldier, he was also a fair and kindly man. He was one of the Protestant leaders I had always had respect for, going back to my days as a child in Aunt Jeanne's court when the Admiral would visit.

"I hope that all is well between you and the Prince of Condé." Such an innocent question, spoken without malice, caused me to wince. Unwilling to upset him, I chose to lie. "I think that we are still getting used to one another. We'll take time to settle into married life."

He nodded, whether out of an understanding of what I meant or simple kindness, I could not tell. "It was your aunt's fondest wish that her family remain united in marriage. She had high hopes for both of you and your marriage was one of her triumphs. I'm sure she is looking down from Heaven, smiling with pride at both of you."

Guilt coursed through me. Had I been acting with ingratitude and judgment towards my husband? Was it just as difficult for him to adjust to married life? Was a being disloyal to my Aunt in my constant unhappiness about my marriage? After all, few women were allowed to choose to marry for love and perhaps I was also being unreasonable.

I looked at the admiral who in turn looked at me without a hint of judgment in his eyes. "I think that I am asking too much of my marriage so far. Perhaps I'm being too harsh on Condé."

"Ah, we are all sinners with a multitude of faults. Thankfully, we can ask our Lord for forgiveness." He winked at me, "Even for a Bourbon princess."

I laughed at his joke, thankful to have a moment of levity. "Still, I worry that our absence today is going to be seen as a sign of stubbornness and disrespect. The King has been a close friend to you and as Protestants, I fear that we are trying the limits of his goodwill."

He nodded, "King Charles has proven to be a generous monarch towards us and it could be that we are acting paranoid at the supposed threat in Paris towards those of our faith. His mistress is a devout Protestant, and he willingly gave us the freedom to worship two years ago."

"Shouldn't we be doing all that we can to work towards reconciliation?"

"I will speak with the King and assure him that we meant no insult by missing the banquet." He squared his shoulders, "As an elderly man; I can attest that I am almost worn out from the endless fetes surrounding the King and Queen of Navarre's wedding. Perhaps the Catholics have more stamina than we do."

That evening, I resolved to be more generous towards my husband. Motivated in part by the shame I felt in neglecting to appreciate what my aunt had done for me, I thought of ways to repay her. After all, those acts were motivated out of concern for my welfare. Also, I had neglected to show compassion for my husband who felt as ill at ease in our marriage as I did. We had one another to depend on upon and perhaps I should try harder to be his helper in our marriage.

THE FOLLOWING WEDNESDAY EVENING, THE COURT HELD ANOTHER ball and masque and this time, the Protestants had no objection to attending. Mindful of the strain the event would place upon her in the late stages of her pregnancy, the Queen had decided to sit by her husband and preside over the banquet. "I'm pleased to see that our Protestant guests will be here tonight," she squeezed my hand and for the moment, I was assured that the King had not felt slighted by our absence.

Still, despite the King's efforts to bring the two sides together, most of the Protestants sat in a corner, dour and grimacing at the celebrations laid out before them. They seemed poised to find insult and offense at every corner, and I had no doubt that they would eventually find it. Perhaps it was the influence of those angry, brooding men in black who had influenced my husband in his dark nature. If I put my mind to it, perhaps I could use our time at court to show my husband that life could be brighter by moving him away from their heavy influence.

Despite the Queen's assurance that she and the King bore me no anger for missing the ball on Sunday, I felt as if I should do everything that I could to tend to her, particularly since she had two scant months before her child and the heir to the throne was born. I resolved to remain seated beside her and attend to her every need. I was accompanied by Madame de Sauve, the wife of the King's chancellor, who had been called out of town for state business. As married women, we enjoyed a bit more freedom in our movements than the unmarried girls who formed the Queen's household.

"Princess, you should take a break and enjoy the masquerade. I can sit with the Queen." Although Madame de Sauve's offer was made without a hit of artifice, I was reluctant to go. I still felt that I had to make up for my earlier absence.

"Yes, do Marie. While I am barely able to move and Madame sits here in Paris bereft of her husband, there is no reason why you should not enjoy yourself."

Unwilling to offend the Queen for the second time in a week, I rose and made my way to the dance floor. As this was a masquerade, I wore a masque depicting the Queen of Hearts. Scanning the ballroom,

I looked for my husband to ask him to dance. After several minutes, however, I realized that he was not to be found in the cavernous ballroom. Feeling foolish, I decided to return to the Queen.

"Madame, you must do me the honor of a dance." The lilting voice beside me caused me to turn. I saw a man richly dressed and sporting Lion's head for a mask.

"I must return to the Queen, Sir; she will be expecting me." Embarrassment mixed with annoyance at my inability to find my husband when I most needed him. I had no intentions of fighting off unwanted attentions from another man to add to my problems of the night. I looked desperately at the Queen to try to catch her eye; to my horror, I found that she was being attended to quite sufficiently by her other ladies. My heart sank as I failed to come up with another excuse.

"Ah, I see that the Queen is well taken care of. Excellent, you must dance the next dance with me." Taking my hand, he led me to the center of the ballroom where the couples were already lining up to begin the next dance. I was trapped.

THE SUNDAY EVENING FOLLOWING THE WEDDING WE WERE ALL invited to a banquet given by the king. Given the Reformed faith's belief that to be joyous on the Sabbath was disrespectful, none of the Protestants accepted the king's invitation. Yet to decline the invitation was to insult the king himself. When I heard that they had planned to risk offending the king, it horrified me.

"You cannot just refuse to go," I trailed after my husband as he stumbled around our bedchamber, looking for last-minute items before he left. I shoved his hat and shoes into his hand, impatiently waiting for him to finish dressing himself.

"We have gone above and beyond in our willingness to be polite to the king and we have the right to attend our services. This debauchery is against our beliefs and we will not compromise on them in fear of offending an earthly monarch."

I exhaled a sigh. King Charles had been more than accommodating towards his Protestant guests and now they were thumbing their noses at him. As one of the queen's ladies-in-waiting, I could ill afford not to attend the banquet. As far as I was concerned, my husband was acting rude and downright childish.

"I will attend the banquet while you attend the service at the Admiral's house." Compromise seemed better than continuing the argument. My husband was intransigent as always.

He snorted in response, raising my ire even further. "Absolutely not —you will not attend an event without me there beside you. I will not have it said my wife is a wanton woman."

"And I am to offend both the sovereign and my mistress?"

"You are to explain that your husband commanded you to accompany him, as any dutiful wife would."

⁂

AT THE MEETING, I SEETHED AND DID MY BEST TO AVOID CONTACT with my husband. What would the king think of our absence? I was sure that his arrogance would place both of us in danger. During the seemingly endless sermon, I turned over in my mind what I would say to the Queen to explain our absence.

Afterward, Admiral Coligny took my elbow and asked to speak with me. Despite his decision to become a firm Protestant, unlike my husband, the elderly admiral worked towards reconciliation between the two faiths. In fact, the king considered the Admiral to be a close friend and mentor, calling him "father" after the death of the king's actual father. It was difficult not to like the admiral; while he was an accomplished soldier, he was also a fair and kindly man. He was one of the Protestant leaders I had always had respect for, going back to my days as a child in Aunt Jeanne's court when the Admiral would visit.

"I hope that all is well between you and the Prince of Condé." Such an innocent question, spoken without malice, caused me to wince. Unwilling to upset him, I chose a lie. "I think we are still getting used to one another. We'll take time to settle into married life."

He nodded, whether out of an understanding of what I meant or simple kindness, I could not tell. "It was your aunt's fondest wish that her family remain united in marriage. She had high hopes for both of you and your marriage was one of her triumphs. I'm sure she is looking down from Heaven, smiling with pride at both of you."

Guilt coursed through me. Had I been acting with ingratitude and judgment towards my husband? Was it as difficult for him to adjust to married life? Was a being disloyal to my Aunt in my constant unhappiness about my marriage? Few women married for love and perhaps I was also being unreasonable.

I looked at the admiral who looked at me without a hint of judgment in his eyes. "I think I am asking too much of my marriage so far. Perhaps I'm being too harsh on Condé."

"Ah, we are all sinners with a multitude of faults. Thankfully, we can ask our Lord for forgiveness." He winked at me, "Even for a Bourbon princess."

I laughed at his joke, thankful to have a moment of levity. "Still, I worry that they will see our absence today as a sign of stubbornness and disrespect. The king has been a close friend to you and as Protestants, I fear that we are trying the limits of his goodwill."

He nodded, "King Charles has proven to be a generous monarch towards us and maybe we are acting paranoid at the supposed threat in Paris towards those of our faith. His mistress is a devout Protestant, and he willingly gave us the freedom to worship two years ago."

"Shouldn't we be doing all that we can to work towards reconciliation?"

"I will speak with the king and assure him we meant no insult by missing the banquet." He squared his shoulders, "As an elderly man; I can attest that I am almost worn out from the endless fetes surrounding the king and Queen of Navarre's wedding. Perhaps the Catholics have more stamina than we do."

That evening, I resolved to be more generous towards my husband. Motivated in part by the shame I felt in neglecting to appreciate what my aunt had done for me, I thought of ways to repay her. Her actions were motivated out of concern for my welfare. Also, I had neglected to show compassion for my husband who felt as ill at ease in our marriage as I did. We had one another to depend on upon and perhaps I should try harder to be his helper in our marriage.

THE FOLLOWING WEDNESDAY EVENING, THE COURT HELD ANOTHER
ball and masque and this time; the Protestants had no objection to
attending. Mindful of the strain the event would place upon her in the
late stages of her pregnancy, the queen had sat by her husband and
preside over the banquet. "I'm pleased to see that our Protestant
guests will be here tonight," she squeezed my hand and for the
moment, it assured me that the king had not felt slighted by our
absence.

Still, despite the king's efforts to bring the two sides together, most
of the Protestants sat in a corner, dour and grimacing at the celebrations laid out before them. They seemed poised to find insult and
offense at every corner, and I knew they would eventually find it.
Perhaps it was the influence of those angry, brooding men in black who
had influenced my husband in his dark nature. If I put my mind to it,
perhaps I could use our time at court to show my husband that life
could be brighter by moving him away from their heavy influence.

Despite the queen's assurance she and the king bore me no anger
for missing the ball on Sunday, I felt as if I should do everything I
could to tend to her, particularly since she had two scant months
before her child and the heir to the throne was born. I resolved to
remain seated beside her and attend to her every need. Madame de
Sauve, the wife of the king's chancellor, sat on Elisabeth's other side.
As married women, we enjoyed more freedom in our movements than
the unmarried girls who formed the queen's household.

"Princess, take a break and enjoy the masquerade. I can sit with the
queen." Although Madame de Sauve's offer came without a hit of artifice, I was reluctant to go. I still felt I had to make up for my earlier
absence.

"Yes, do Marie. While I can barely move and Madame sits here in
Paris bereft of her husband, there is no reason you should not enjoy
yourself."

Unwilling to offend the queen for the second time in a week, I rose
and made my way to the dance floor. As this was a masquerade, I wore
a masque depicting the Queen of Hearts. Scanning the ballroom, I

looked for my husband to ask him to dance. After several minutes, however, I realized I could not locate him in the cavernous ballroom. Feeling foolish, I returned to the queen.

"Madame, you must do me the honor of a dance." The lilting voice beside me caused me to turn. I saw a man richly dressed and sporting Lion's head for a mask.

"I must return to the queen, Sir; she will expect me." Embarrassment mixed with annoyance at my inability to find my husband when I most needed him. I had no intentions of fighting off unwanted attentions from another man to add to my problems of the night. I looked desperately at the queen to catch her eye; to my horror, I found that she was being attended to sufficiently by her other ladies. My heart sank as I could not think of another excuse.

"Ah, I see that the queen is well taken care of. Excellent, you must dance the next dance with me." Taking my hand, he led me to the center of the ballroom where the couples were already lining up to begin the next dance. I was trapped.

❧ 4 ❧

Despite my initial misgivings, my partner turned out to be a welcome diversion. We spent the dance in amiable conversation and he even managed to get a few laughs from me. By the time the dance had ended, I was sorry to see him go. With a courtly bow and a chaste kiss on my hand, he reluctantly left my side. I began to scan the room again for my husband and eventually, my eyes alighted on him. Stalking towards him, I grabbed his hand and pulled him away from the men he had been speaking to earlier.

"I believe that we should spend at least one dance together tonight."

"Now? I am in the middle of a conversation with the Seignior--"

"Henry, we both have duties to perform and I think that one dance is not too much to ask of my husband." I could hear the angry edge in my voice and no doubt the men he had been speaking with earlier could hear it as well. I cared little for their opinions, however, as our standing at court was more important than whatever he was talking about with them.

He gave a heavy sigh, "Very well. Gentlemen, if you would excuse me." I gave a coquettish courtesy and allowed him to lead my out onto the ballroom floor. As he methodically led me through the dance, I noticed the man in the lion mask dancing in the corner with his part-ner. He gave me a slight nod which caused me to blush. I tried to cover it, but not before my husband noticed it.

"What is the ass doing now?"

"Who?

"Anjou. He's taunting me, just as he did with my father."

Thankfully, my mask hid my surprise. I had no idea of the identity of the man I had danced with earlier. Part of me enjoyed the mystery of not knowing who my gallant partner was. Now I knew that it was the King's younger brother who had partnered me. Despite myself, I felt a thrill that he had chosen me out of all the ladies at the masquerade for a dance.

"Stay far away from him; there is no telling what kind of mischief he is up to."

"At a ball? I hardly think that he is plotting as he dances."

My husband snorted, "There is talk that he is plotting an assassina-tion of one or more of the Protestants in Paris."

I rolled my eyes, weary of the plotting and paranoia. "You have been convinced that there is a plot going on for days and we have seen no evidence of it. I am growing tired of all of this." My husband said nothing, choosing to end our argument at the point. We spent the rest of the dance in silence and he returned to his place with the black-clad men for the rest of the evening.

I, however, marched straight to the Queen and sat beside her, determined not to leave her side for the rest of the night. Waiting on the Queen could hardly lead to any trouble, or cause my husband to object to my behavior. I would play the part of the respectful matron to perfection. My resolve lasted for about an hour until I saw a tall figure walking towards the raised dais and straight towards the Queen. My heart sank as I noticed the lion's mask covering his face.

"Your Majesty," he sank to his knees before the Queen, giving his sister-in-law a courtly bow that would put the most ardent actor to shame. When he rose, I noticed the wide grin splitting his face. To my horror, he plunked down beside me, taking the seat that Madame de Sauve vacated eagerly. I was trapped and decorum dictated that I could not ignore the King's brother.

The Duc turned to the Queen and began a lively conversation that made her smile. Perhaps he was not there merely to speak with me or to cause mischief, which caused me to relax in his presence. "Sister, you are at quite a disadvantage. How do you feel?"

The Queen fanned herself and exhaled a long breath. "I feel unwieldy, waddling and sitting constantly. The heat is not helping my discomfort; I would be happy once my condition is over, to be truthful."

He crossed himself and took her hand tenderly. "Would be to God that your son is born soon and all of France can rejoice in his birth."

I was touched by his kindness and concern for the gentle Queen. I was in the midst of deciding that I had misjudged the Duc when he suddenly shot to his feet and bowed again to the Queen. "You look parched; I will get you some wine." He bounded off and for a quarter of an hour, we had a respite.

"Majesty, do you feel up to staying? I can help you back to your apartments." If I could convince the Queen to retire early, my problem would be solved. To my chagrin, however, she simply patted my hand and fixed a smile on me.

"Absolutely not. I will remain here to support my husband. And as you were deprived of the opportunity to attend the last ball, I will not force you to leave early."

I opened my mouth to protest, but the Duc appeared suddenly in front of us, cutting off my response. In his hands, he carried two cups, one for the Queen and another for myself. Once again, decorum dictated that I could not be rude to the Duc. "Thank you, Sir," I replied, trying to keep my voice as level as possible.

"Madame, I don't believe I have had the honor of introducing myself." He once again settled next to me and by his behavior, it was obvious that he was determined to carry on a conversation with me.

"You have been on the battlefield for the King, your brother, is that not so?' The rivalry between my late father-in-law and the Duc was an open scandal and I hoped that bringing it up might cool his enthusiasm. Anjou led his armies against Protestant strongholds, including the city of La Rochelle, against my family members. One of those armies surrounded and fatally wounded Louis, the previous

Prince de Condé. To be fair, Anjou did not do his duty purely out of bloodlust. Despite the King giving us freedom to worship across the kingdom, some Protestant enclaves like La Rochelle were unwilling to bow to royal edicts. We were on very different sides and I hoped that chasm would discourage him from attempting to continue to flirt with me. Earlier, I had the excuse of ignorance of his identity, but now I could not claim to Condé that I was unaware of who I consorted with as I sat beside the Queen. I hoped that my husband would storm to the dais to reclaim me and remove me from this awkward situation, but once again, my husband was nowhere to be found. For all I knew, he was out planning a counter strike to answer the feared attacks by the Catholics.

"Yes, we have been dealing with rebellions against the throne for some time and my brother has entrusted me with putting down any insurgents. It would seem that no matter how many concessions the King makes towards the Protestants, they are determined to show no loyalty to their King."

That had my ire up, I may not be the most dedicated to the Reformed faith, but his casual retelling of the royal attacks on Protestant strongholds was going too far. "I beg your pardon, Monsieur. Some of those 'insurgents' are my kinsmen." Ignoring decorum, I glared at him, daring him to say anything more offensive.

He was immediately contrite, "Forgive me, my lady. It is the extremists that I am talking about. And the Protestants are not the only ones who suffer from extremists." His gaze alighted on the Duc de Guise, my other brother-in-law, who held a view that rabid Catholicism was the only way to unify France. Guise and my husband continued to circle warily around one another, but Catherine and I had no idea how long their uneasy truce would last. Or when Protestant would decide to attack Catholic.

Still, I refused to concede any point to Anjou. Snapping my fan open, I began to wave it wildly, moving his flowing golden brown hair out of place. "I take it that you agree with your mother that moderation in both faiths is the best way for all Frenchmen."

"Aye, I do." He said it with such a soft voice that I could not help but look at him. His expression was contrite and gentle. His bravado from a moment earlier was gone. I immediately felt guilty myself for being so harsh with him.

❦

THE DUC D'ANJOU WAS DETERMINED NOT TO LEAVE HIS PERCH beside me, although he took pains to appear as if the reason was that he was loath to leave the King's pregnant wife without a male champion to take care of her. He kept her plied with wine and sweetmeats, feeding her from his own plate. From all appearances, we were simply seeing to the Queen's needs and her comfort.

The truth was that the more time I spent with Anjou, the more I grew to enjoy his company. He was solicitous and kind to both of us, seeing to our every need as if he were a suitor. Despite my earlier reservation, I found myself laughing at his quick jokes. Perhaps it was the mulled wine that went to my head, but in his presence I relaxed more than I had in the previous months. Unlike my husband, the Prince of Condé, Anjou was a lively and quick-witted man, one more than capable of flattering a young girl looking for attention and appreciation. The longer we sat together, the more I began to resent my husband in his treatment of me. I had brought some prestige to our marriage and unlike Condé, my family was well connected at court. My position as a lady-in-waiting to the Queen furthered our position at court. If my husband were unwilling to appreciate me, perhaps other members of the court would be willing to do so.

"Heavy thoughts, Madame?" Anjou cut into my reverie and I blushed at the thoughts that had been going through my head.

"No, I was thinking about how difficult it would be to make it to her majesty's chambers early tomorrow morning after tonight's festivities." I smiled at him despite myself and I was rewarded with a laugh from the Queen.

"You are dismissed until tomorrow afternoon, Marie. I could not ask for a more attentive servant tonight."

"And what am I? Simply a decoration?" Anjou's mock offense caused both of us to laugh and the Queen rolled her eyes at him in mock disgust.

"Well, you did get us some refreshments, so I believe that you have been somewhat useful. But not as useful as my ladies."

"Perhaps I should visit your rooms more often, Sister, to learn how to serve you better. It appears you have the best attendants in France." The meaning of his words was clear, and I felt a sharp sense of foreboding. I would do nothing to encourage the King's brother to visit me on such a pretense, but once again, I was trapped and had no means of extricating myself from the situation.

We spent the rest of the evening in easy companionship, as I tried desperately to downplay Anjou's obvious ardor. Finally, at two in the morning, the musicians played their last dance, and we were all instructed to remove our masks. The moment was quite anticlimactic for me and I used the end of the festivities as an excuse to find my wayward husband.

I found him once again scowling, but this time deep in conversation with the King of Navarre. While my cousin took pains to greet me, my husband barely spared a glance at me. "Well, I see this bit of frivolity is finally over."

"I am glad—attending the Queen in her condition is quite challenging. She was kind enough to allow me to join her later in the afternoon." I motioned for my husband to place my cloak on my shoulders and as he spun around, he caught the eye of Anjou.

Anjou inclined his head as if the gesture were for my husband, but I knew it was intended for me. I balled my hands and drove my fingernails into my palms as I waited for his Condé's ire. "I wonder what Anjou is up to now." His comment, made so casually, made me realize that he had not noticed the hours that we spent in each other's company. For now, at least, I was safe.

"I have no idea," I tried to appear as disinterested as possible.

"We'll find out soon enough; I'm sure of it."

DESPITE MY INITIAL MISGIVINGS, MY PARTNER TURNED OUT TO BE A welcome diversion. We spent the dance in amiable conversation and he even got a few laughs from me. By the time the dance had ended, I was sorry to see him go. With a courtly bow and a chaste kiss on my hand, he reluctantly left my side. I scanned the room again for my husband and eventually, my eyes alighted on him. Stalking towards him, I grabbed his hand and pulled him away from the men he had been speaking to earlier.

"I believe that we should spend at least one dance together tonight."

"Now? I am in the middle of a conversation with the Seignior—"

"Henry, we both have duties to perform and I think one dance is not too much to ask of my husband." I could hear the angry edge in my voice and no doubt the men he had been speaking with earlier could hear it. I cared little for their opinions, however, as our standing at court was more important than whatever he was talking about with them.

He gave a heavy sigh, "Well. Gentlemen, if you would excuse me." I gave a coquettish courtesy and allowed him to lead my out onto the ballroom floor. As he methodically led me through the dance, I noticed the man in the lion mask dancing in the corner with his part-ner. He gave me a slight nod which caused me to blush. I tried to cover it, but not before my husband noticed it.

"What is the ass doing now?"

"Who?"

"Anjou. He's taunting me, just as he did with my father."

Thankfully, my mask hid my surprise. I did not guess the identity of the man I had danced with earlier. Part of me enjoyed the mystery of not knowing who my gallant partner was. Now I knew that it was the king's younger brother who had partnered me. Despite myself, I felt a thrill he had chosen me out of all the ladies at the masquerade for a dance.

"Stay far away from him; there is no telling what kind of mischief he is up to."

"At a ball? I hardly think he plotted as he danced."

My husband snorted, "There is talk he is plotting an assassination of one or more of the Protestants in Paris."

I rolled my eyes, weary of the plotting and paranoia. "You are convinced that there is a plot going on for days and we have seen no evidence. I am growing tired of all of this." My husband said nothing, choosing to end our argument at the point. We spent the rest of the dance in silence and he returned to his place with the black-clad men for the rest of the evening.

I, however, marched straight to the Queen and sat beside her, determined not to leave her side for the rest of the night. Waiting on the Queen could hardly lead to any trouble, or cause my husband to object to my behavior. I would play the part of the respectful matron to perfection. My resolve lasted for about an hour until I saw a tall figure walking towards the raised dais and straight towards the Queen. My heart sank as I noticed the lion's mask covering his face.

"Your Majesty," he sank to his knees before the Queen, giving his sister-in-law a courtly bow that would put the most ardent actor to shame. When he rose, I noticed the wide grin splitting his face. To my horror, he plunked down beside me, taking the seat that Madame de Sauve vacated eagerly. I was trapped and decorum dictated that I could not ignore the king's brother.

The Duc turned to the Queen and began a lively conversation that made her smile. Perhaps he was not there merely to speak with me or to cause mischief, which caused me to relax in his presence. "Sister, you are at quite a disadvantage. How do you feel?"

The Queen fanned herself and exhaled a long breath. "I feel unwieldy, waddling and sitting constantly. The heat is not helping my discomfort; I would be happy once my condition is over, to be truthful."

He crossed himself and took her hand tenderly. "Would be to God that your son is born soon and all of France can rejoice in his birth."

His kindness and concern for the gentle Queen touched me. I was about to decide that I had misjudged the Duc when he suddenly shot to his feet and bowed again to the Queen. "You look parched; I will get you some wine." He bounded off and for a quarter of an hour, we had a respite.

"Majesty, do you feel up to staying? I can help you back to your apartments." If I could convince the Queen to retire early, it would solve my problem. To my chagrin, however, she patted my hand and fixed a smile on me.

"Absolutely not. I will remain here to support my husband. And as it deprived you of the opportunity to attend the last ball, I will not force you to leave early."

I opened my mouth to protest, but the Duc appeared suddenly in front of us, cutting off my response. In his hands, he carried two cups, one for the Queen and another for myself. Once again, decorum dictated that I could not be rude to the Duc. "Thank you, Sir," I replied, trying to keep my voice as level as possible.

"Madame, I don't believe I have had the honor of introducing myself." He once again settled next to me, his tone showed his determination to carry on a conversation with me.

"You have been on the battlefield for the king, your brother, is that not so?"

The rivalry between my late father-in-law and the Duc was an open scandal, and I hoped that bringing it up might cool his enthusiasm. Anjou led his armies against Protestant strongholds, including the city of La Rochelle, against my family members. One of those armies surrounded and fatally wounded Louis, the previous Prince de Condé. To be fair, Anjou did not do his duty purely out of bloodlust. Despite the king giving us freedom to worship across the kingdom, some Protestant enclaves like La Rochelle were unwilling to bow to royal edits. We were on very different sides and I hoped that chasm would discourage him from attempting to continue to flirt with me. Earlier, I had the excuse of ignorance of his identity, but now I could not claim to Condé that I was unaware of who I consorted with as I sat beside the queen. I hoped that my husband would storm to the dais to reclaim me and remove me from this awkward situation, but once again, my husband was nowhere to be found. For all I knew, he was out planning a counter strike to answer the feared attacks by the Catholics.

"Yes, we have been dealing with rebellions against the throne for some time and my brother has entrusted me with putting down any insurgents. It would seem that no matter how many concessions the king makes towards the Protestants, they continue to show no loyalty to their king."

That had my ire up, while I was hardly the most dedicated follower of the Reformed faith, but his casual retelling of the royal attacks on Protestant strongholds was going too far. "I beg your pardon,

Monsieur. Some of those 'insurgents' are my kinsmen." Ignoring decorum, I glared at him, daring him to say anything more offensive.

He was immediately contrite, "Forgive me, my lady. It is the extremists I am talking about. And the Protestants are not the only ones who suffer from extremists." His gaze alighted on the Duc de Guise, my other brother-in-law, who held a view that rabid Catholicism was the only way to unify France. Guise and my husband continued to circle warily around one another, but Catherine and I could not predict how long their uneasy truce would last. Or when Protestant would attack Catholic.

Still, I refused to concede any point to Anjou. Snapping my fan open, I waved it wildly, moving his flowing golden brown hair out of place. "I take it you agree with your mother that moderation in both faiths is the best way for all Frenchmen."

"Aye, I do." He said it with such a soft voice I could not help but look at him. His expression was contrite and gentle. His bravado from a moment earlier dissipated. I immediately felt guilty myself for being so harsh with him.

THE DUC D'ANJOU WAS DETERMINED NOT TO LEAVE HIS PERCH beside me, although he took pains to appear as if the reason was that he was loath to leave the king's pregnant wife without a male champion to take care of her. He kept her plied with wine and sweetmeats, feeding her from his own plate. From all appearances, we were simply seeing to the queen's needs and her comfort.

The more time I spent with Anjou, the more I grew to enjoy his company. He was solicitous and kind to both of us, seeing to our every need as if he were a suitor. Despite my earlier reservation, I laughed at his quick jokes. Perhaps it was the mulled wine that went to my head, but in his presence I relaxed more than I had in the previous months. Unlike my husband, the Prince of Condé, Anjou was a lively and quick-witted man, one more than capable of flattering a young girl looking for attention and appreciation. The longer we sat together, the more I resented my husband in his treatment of me. I had brought prestige to our marriage and unlike Condé, my family was well connected at court. My position as a lady-in-waiting to the queen furthered our position at court. If my husband were unwilling to appreciate me, perhaps other members of the court would do so.

"Heavy thoughts, Madame?" Anjou cut into my reverie and I blushed at the thoughts that had been going through my head.

"No, I was thinking about how difficult it would be to make it to her majesty's chambers early tomorrow morning after tonight's festivities." I smiled at him despite myself and heard a laugh from the queen.

"I dismiss you until tomorrow afternoon, Marie. I could not ask for a more attentive servant tonight."

"And what am I? A decoration?" Anjou's mock offense caused both of us to laugh and the queen rolled her eyes at him in mock disgust.

"Well, you did get us some refreshments, so I believe that you have been somewhat useful. But not as useful as my ladies."

"Perhaps I should visit your rooms more often, Sister, to learn how to serve you better. It appears you have the best attendants in France." The meaning of his words was clear, and I felt a sharp sense of foreboding. I would do nothing to encourage the king's brother to visit me on such a pretense, but once again, I was trapped and had no means of extricating myself from the situation.

We spent the rest of the evening in easy companionship, as I tried desperately to downplay Anjou's obvious ardor. Finally, at two in the morning, the musicians played their last dance, and we were all instructed to remove our masks. The moment was anticlimactic for me and I used the end of the festivities as an excuse to find my wayward husband.

I found him once again scowling, but this time deep in conversation with the King of Navarre. While my cousin took pains to greet me, my husband barely spared a glance at me. "Well, I see this bit of frivolity is finally over."

"I am glad—attending the queen in her condition is challenging. She was kind enough to allow me to join her later in the afternoon." I motioned for my husband to place my cloak on my shoulders and as he spun around, he caught the eye of Anjou.

Anjou inclined his head as if the gesture were for my husband, but

I knew he intended it for me. I balled my hands and drove my finger-nails into my palms as I waited for his Condé's ire. "I wonder what Anjou is up to now." His comment, made so casually, made me realize that he had not noticed the hours we spent in each other's company. For now, at least, I was safe.

"I have no idea," I tried to appear as disinterested as possible.

"We'll find out soon enough; I'm sure of it."

Despite the extra hours of sleep, I struggled to make my way from the Hotel Nevers to the Louvre Palace in time to begin my service to the Queen. Upon entering her rooms, I found that she looked even more exhausted than I felt. I felt a bit of relief in that fact; if the Queen did not feel up to attending any more events, then perhaps I could avoid running into Anjou altogether.

The Queen and I spent an hour together as she and her Catholic ladies embroidered altar cloths for the churches of Paris. As a courtesy to my Protestant faith, I was excused from working on the altar cloths, although my skills with a needle were quite good. I was tasked instead to read from the Psalms as the rest of the Queen's suite continued their work. While the Queen took great pains to keep me from feeling like an outsider, activities like these still caused me to feel isolated from the rest of her household.

A few hours into our work, the Duc d'Anjou swept into the Queen's inner rooms, just as he had promised to do the night before. As was just my luck, there was an empty stool beside me and the Duc quickly settled upon it. "Ladies, I believe that I would like to begin my education on the proper attention to be paid to a Queen this very day."

Elisabeth's slight eyebrows shot up, "Would that have anything to do with your election to the throne of Poland?" Faced with an unstable government, the Poles had made overtures to Anjou to take the throne and strengthen the ties between the two countries. Once upon the throne, he would need to marry and secure a Queen of his own. His departure from the court would be a welcome occasion for my husband and the other leaders of the Protestant faith.

"Ah, the negotiations are going very slow, I'm afraid. My mother fears I will never find a throne upon which to sit. Besides," he shot a knowing look in my direction, "the process of finding a suitable bride is not the easiest of tasks."

"And what would your highness be looking for in a bride?" The words tumbled out of my mouth before I could stop them. I don't know if jealousy or stupidity motivated them, but there they were, hanging in the air for all to hear.

He stretched his legs out in front of him and crossed them at the ankles. Appearing to be deep in thought, he scratched his chin. "Well, I would prefer a well-bred French bride to all others, of course. .Alas, I would have to be of one religion and the Poles are Catholics like us. If I were to order her from Heaven, I would wish for a small woman with dark hair, a fair complexion. If it pleases God, I would like a well-educated wife who has no trouble with gaiety. I would need her to preside over our court, of course."

One of the teenage demoiselles let out a peal of laughter. "Good heavens, Monsieur, that sounds like our Marie!" A furious blush covered my entire face and I could have slapped the stupid creature.. I stood up to avoid looking at her or anyone else in the room.

Sensing the tension in the room, the Queen quickly put in, "Yes, but alas the Princess of Condé is married. Brother, you will have to find another ideal woman to be your Queen."

She turned to the ignorant girl and waved her hand to the ones sitting near her, "Girls, would you do me a favor and pick some roses out in the palace garden? I would love to smell them this afternoon." The girls rose and quickly filed out of the room. My gratitude to the Queen for relieving me of the presence of those quacking geese was immeasurable.

Anjou broke the silence moments later, "Madame, I hope you won't think me too forward, but your piety and grace is a standard that any great lady would be wise to emulate." As he spoke, he took olives from a tray and popped them one by one into his mouth.

How did he have the ability to put me completely ill at ease, then follow with a compliment that threw me off balance? The combination was maddening, but I would be lying if I claimed that I did not enjoy his presence. Sensing he had the advantage, he pressed further. "Tell me, Princess, how do you enjoy being at court?"

The subject was a safe one, and I was thankful for it. "I have been lucky to win the Queen's friendship. France is lucky to have such a generous and humble lady." Elisabeth turned to smile at me, embarrassed a little by the compliment.

"Marie has the opportunity to get to know her older sisters. She grew up under Jeanne of Navarre's loving care," both she and Anjou crossed themselves at the mention of my late aunt. "Now she has time to get to know her family."

"And you are living with your sister, are you not?" I was surprised to hear that he knew so much about my living situation, but I suppose the court's penchant for gossip meant that no topic was off limits.

"Yes, my husband and I have happily moved to the Hotel de Nevers during the wedding celebrations so that we can relieve the strained accommodations in the palace." The Duc's grandfather, Francis I had decided to turn the former fortress of the Louvre into a palace and his son and grandsons worked constantly to bring the structure up to royal standards. That work meant continuous construction and half-filled rooms that could only accommodate a typical sized court. The amount of wedding guests in Paris that August had spilled out of the city's walls and into the surrounding countryside.

"I do so enjoy spending time with both Louis and Henriette. In fact, I don't think that I spend enough time with them." I held in a breath—was he once again making plans to rendezvous with me for less than honorable purposes? I prayed not. When my husband caught wind of Anjou's plans, he would be furious.

"I'm afraid that their home is bursting with people right now. You

43

would be lost in the crowd. My husband is entertaining members of our faith and some of our other relations."

"Yes, space is at a premium in Paris these days." His comment seemed so offhand that I barely took any notice of it. It took most of my resolve to keep the blush that crept up my face from spreading to my hairline and betraying my discomfort. The fair complexion that he had praised earlier worked to my disadvantage.

WHEN I RETURNED TO MY SISTER'S HOME THAT EVENING, MY husband met me at the door of our bedchamber. He paced the room, and I prepared for a lecture. Did my husband know I had spent the day with Anjou? To my surprise, his agitation was not directed towards Anjou or me. "Marie, I insist that you stay home for the next few days."

"Whatever for?"

"We have heard rumors today that there is a credible threat towards Protestants. We don't know who they will target or when they will strike. For your safety, you must remain in the house at all times."

I wanted to protest that he was becoming more and more paranoid, but my relief in his failing to discover the time that I spent with Anjou led me to agree to his absurd demand. I could not control whether Anjou pursued me at the palace, but perhaps he would not make good on his plan to visit me at my sister's home. A few days apart might cool his ardor and I would no longer have to worry about his attentions towards me.

"Fine," for once, I decided that there was no need to argue.

DESPITE THE EXTRA HOURS OF SLEEP, I STRUGGLED TO MAKE MY WAY from the Hotel Nevers to the Louvre Palace in time to begin my service to the queen. Upon entering her rooms, I found that she looked even more exhausted than I felt. I felt relief in that fact; if the queen did not feel up to attending any more events, then perhaps I could avoid running into Anjou altogether.

The queen and I spent an hour together as she and her Catholic ladies embroidered altar cloths for the churches of Paris. As a courtesy to my Protestant faith, the queen excused me from working on the altar cloths, although my skills with a needle were good. As a compromise, I read from the Psalms as the rest of the queen's suite continued their work. While the queen took great pains to keep me from feeling like an outsider, activities like these still caused me to feel isolated from the rest of her household.

A few hours into our work, the Duc d'Anjou swept into the queen's inner rooms, just as he had promised to do the night before. As was just my luck, there was an empty stool beside me and the Duc quickly settled upon it. "Ladies, I believe that I would like to begin my education on the proper attention I must pay to a queen."

Elisabeth's slight eyebrows shot up, "Would that have anything to do with your election to the throne of Poland?" Faced with an unstable government, the Poles had made overtures to Anjou to take the throne and strengthen the ties between the two countries. Once upon the throne, he would need to marry and secure a queen of his own. His departure from the court would be a welcome occasion for my husband and the other leaders of the Protestant faith.

"Ah, the negotiations are going very slow, I'm afraid. My mother fears I will never find a throne upon which to sit. Besides," he shot a knowing look in my direction, "the process of finding a suitable bride is not the easiest of tasks."

"And what would your highness be looking for in a bride?" The words tumbled out of my mouth before I could stop them. I don't know if jealousy or stupidity motivated them, but there they were, hanging in the air for all to hear.

He stretched his legs out in front of him and crossed them at the ankles. Appearing to be deep in thought, he scratched his chin. "Well, I would prefer a well-bred French bride to all others. Alas, I would have to be of one religion and the Poles are Catholics like us. If I were to order her from Heaven, I would wish for a small woman with dark hair, a fair complexion. If it pleases God, I would like a well-educated wife who has no trouble with gaiety. I would need her to preside over our court."

One of the teenage demoiselles let out a peal of laughter. "Good heavens, Monsieur, that sounds like our Marie!" A furious blush covered my entire face and I could have slapped the stupid creature.. I stood up to avoid looking at her or anyone else in the room.

Sensing the tension in the room, the queen quickly put in, "Yes, but alas the Princess of Condé is married. Brother, you will have to find another ideal woman to be your queen."

She turned to the ignorant girl and waved her hand to the ones sitting near her, "Girls, would you do me a favor and pick some roses out in the palace garden? I would love to smell them this afternoon." The girls rose and quickly filed out of the room. My gratitude to the queen for relieving me of the presence of those quacking geese was immeasurable.

Anjou broke the silence moments later, "Madame, I hope you won't think me too forward, but your piety and grace is a standard that any great lady would be wise to emulate." As he spoke, he took olives from a tray and popped them one by one into his mouth.

How could he put me completely ill at ease, then follow with a compliment that threw me off balance? The combination was maddening, but I would be lying if I claimed that I did not enjoy his presence. Sensing he had the advantage, he pressed further. "Tell me, Princess, how do you enjoy being at court?"

The subject was a safe one, and I was thankful for it. "I have been lucky to win the queen's friendship. France is lucky to have such a generous and humble lady." Elisabeth turned to smile at me, embarrassed a little by the compliment.

"Marie also gets to know her older sisters. She grew up under Jeanne of Navarre's loving care," both she and Anjou crossed themselves at the mention of my late aunt. "Now she has time to get to know her family."

"And you are living with your sister, are you not?" It surprised me to hear that he knew so much about my living situation, but I suppose the court's penchant for gossip meant that no topic was off limits.

"Yes, my husband and I have happily moved to the Hotel de Nevers during the wedding celebrations so we can relieve the strained accommodations in the palace." The Duc's grandfather, Francis I had turned the former fortress of the Louvre into a palace and his son and grandsons worked constantly to bring the structure up to royal standards. That work meant continuous construction and half-filled rooms that could only accommodate a typical-sized court. The amount of wedding guests in Paris that August had spilled out of the city's walls and into the surrounding countryside.

"I do so enjoy spending time with both Louis and Henriette. In fact, I don't think I spend enough time with them." I held in a breath —was he once again making plans to rendezvous with me for less than honorable purposes? I prayed not. When my husband caught wind of Anjou's plans, he would be furious.

"I'm afraid that their home is bursting with people right now. You would be lost in the crowd. My husband is entertaining members of our faith and some of our other relations."

"Yes, space is at a premium in Paris these days." His comment seemed so offhand that I barely took any notice. It took most of my resolve to keep the blush that crept up my face from spreading to my hairline and betraying my discomfort. The fair complexion he had praised earlier worked to my disadvantage.

⚜

WHEN I RETURNED TO MY SISTER'S HOME THAT EVENING, MY husband met me at the door of our bedchamber. He paced the room, and I prepared for a lecture. Did my husband know I had spent the day with Anjou? To my surprise, his agitation was not directed towards Anjou or me. "Marie, I insist that you stay home for the next few days."

"Whatever for?"

"We have heard rumors today that there is a credible threat towards Protestants. We don't know who they will target or when they will strike. For your safety, you must remain in the house at all times."

I wanted to protest that he was becoming more and more paranoid, but my relief in his failure to discover the time I spent with

Anjou led me to agree to his absurd demand. I could not control whether Anjou pursued me at the palace, but perhaps he would not make good on his plan to visit me at my sister's home. A few days apart might cool his ardor and I would no longer have to worry about his attentions towards me.

"Fine," for once, I decided that there was no need to argue.

6

To my horror, my husband's prediction turned out to be correct. Only two days later, the following Friday, an attack on a leading Protestant did occur on the open streets of Paris. As the elderly Admiral Coligny walked from a worship service to his lodgings, a shot rang out. The bullet grazed him, but fearing for another attempt on his life, his men dragged him inside and to safety.

No one knew for certain who fired the shot, or in whose interest the assailant acted, but most placed blame at the feet of my brother-in-law, the Duc de Guise, and his mother, Anna. The Guise blamed the Admiral for the death of the previous Duc de Guise and Anna had many times been overhead threatening to take her revenge on Coligny. Whether the Guise had a hand in the assassination attempt or not, this put our family in a delicate situation that we had been dreading for months. While my husband considered Coligny a close mentor, my sister firmly stood in defense of her husband and his family. Henriette and her husband fell in the middle, with both sides eying each another with distrust.

As soon as he heard of the attack, my husband went with Navarre to check on the admiral, staying throughout the night. I would learn later that the leading Protestants formulated a plan to go directly to

the King and ask that the guilty party be punished for wounding
Coligny. It was short work to discover that the signor De Maurevert,
who Coligny had learned months earlier was working undercover for
Guise, was the man who fired the shot. The fact that the shot came
directly from a window of Guise's mother, implicated him further. As
soon as Henriette and my brother-in-law heard of this, they insisted
that I remain in their home and admit no guests whatsoever. As I
planned to avoid Anjou for the sake of propriety, I readily agreed.

The next morning, the twenty-third of August, Henriette received
a message from my husband that Coligny's wounds did not seem to be
life-threatening and after a quick amputation of parts of his fingers he
should make a quick recovery. Condé added that he and Navarre were
meeting in Navarre's chambers to discuss what they would say to the
King and not to expect him. By that afternoon, I felt terrible, and I
went to bed, caring very little what went on around me. My lungs felt
heavy and congested, a problem tha had plagued me since I was a
child. Usually, this condition occurred during colder months, but the
excitement, stress and lack of sleep lead me to feel weak. I was asleep
before the sun set on that day, oblivious to what was transpiring at the
nearby Louvre palace.

How can I describe the horror that took place the next
morning, that Sunday, as the people of Paris were supposedly going to
church? In truth, I can tell you nothing about it firsthand. I witnessed
none of it, shut up in my sickbed as I was, but later I would hear the
gory details from both Protestants and Catholics alike. I think that
both exaggerated, but from what I can reason out, the King that we
had put our trust in to offer us safe passage and hospitality turned on
the Protestants and ordered the mass killings of those of our faith.

Why did he allow it to happen? His mother and her allies were
later blamed; the guilt having passed from Guise alone to the woman
who wore her son down with the threat that the Protestants would
quickly kill His Majesty in retribution for the attack on Coligny. There
were many whispers that Catherine and even Anjou were behind the

plot against Coligny; and to Save Catherine, Coligny and his followers were slaughtered. Whatever the truth of that day, when I heard of the Protestants cut down without regard to their age or sex, I wept and my condition worsened by the day. I may not have been the most ardent follower of the Reformed religion, but no man or woman deserved to be slaughtered on the feast day dedicated to St. Bartholomew.

My first concern upon hearing of the slaughter, was to enquire about the condition of my husband. Henriette came to my bed and wiped my brow. After turning to give me a sip of water, she held my hand. "Condé and Navarre are safe; in fact, they are both in the King's bedroom for their protection."

Relief washed over me. "Thank God." I sank back in the pillows.

"Dearest, they aren't completely out of danger."

That caused me to worry anew. I struggled to sit up. "What do you mean?"

"The King has offered them a choice: they can convert to Catholicism, or they will be executed."

My blood ran cold. "The last thing that I expect Condé to do is to convert to Catholicism. Do you think Navarre will?"

She shook her head, "I have no idea. Guise and my husband argued for both of their lives and hopefully, in gratitude, they will agree to take the King's offer."

"Gratitude? You think that denying their beliefs is a show of gratitude? What about their souls? Are they to sacrifice them to the wishes of a King who betrayed them?"

Her expression darkened, "Careful, Marie—there are countless bodies of Protestants lying in the streets of Paris. Even some Catholic nobles have been cut down. Now is not the time to speak against the King."

Too weak to argue with her, I instead asked her when I would be allowed to see my husband. No matter how strained our marriage might be, I desperately wanted to speak with him, to hear from his lips of the unimaginable choice that he faced.

"Officially, they are under house arrest and are not allowed to speak with anyone, especially a Protestant. You will most likely not be allowed to see him until either he or you convert."

There it was—I was also to be offered the Devil's bargain. Would I take it, or would I remain steadfast in my professed faith? Would my husband stand firm or would he Save his life at the expense of his soul? Worse still, what if one of us took the offer while the other refused? The hangman's noose might not part us, but we might never meet in Eternity.

To my horror, my husband's prediction turned out to be correct. Only two days later, the following Friday, an attack on a leading Protestant occurred on the open streets of Paris. As the elderly Admiral Coligny walked from a worship service to his lodgings, a shot rang out. The bullet grazed him, but fearing for another attempt on his life, his men dragged him inside and to safety.

No one knew for certain who fired the shot, or in whose interest the assailant acted, but most placed blame at the feet of my brother-in-law, the Duc de Guise, and his mother, Anna. The Guise blamed the Admiral for the death of the previous Duc de Guise and Anna had many times been overhead threatening to take her revenge on Coligny. Whether the Guise had a hand in the assassination attempt or not, this put our family in a delicate situation we had been dreading for months. While my husband considered Coligny a close mentor, my sister firmly stood in defense of her husband and his family. Henriette and her husband fell in the middle, with both sides eying each another with distrust.

As soon as he heard of the attack, my husband went with Navarre to check on the admiral, staying throughout the night. I would learn later that the leading Protestants planned to go directly to the king and ask that the guilty party be punished for wounding Coligny. It was short work to discover that the signor De Maurevert, who Coligny had learned months earlier was working undercover for Guise, was the man who fired the shot. That the shot came directly from a window of Guise's mother, implicated him further. As soon as Henriette and my brother-in-law heard of this, they insisted that I remain in their home and admit no guests. As I planned to avoid Anjou for the sake of propriety, I readily agreed.

The next morning, the twenty-third of August, Henriette received a message from my husband that Coligny's wounds did not seem to be life threatening and after a quick amputation of parts of his fingers he should make a quick recovery. Condé added that he and Navarre were meeting in Navarre's chambers to discuss what they would say to the king and not to expect him. By that afternoon, I felt terrible, and I went to bed, caring little what went on around me. My lungs felt heavy and congested, a problem that had plagued me since I was a child. Usually, this condition occurred during colder months, but the excitement, stress and lack of sleep lead me to feel weak. I was asleep before the sun set on that day, oblivious to what was transpiring at the nearby Louvre palace

HOW CAN I DESCRIBE THE HORROR THAT TOOK PLACE THE NEXT morning, that Sunday, as the people of Paris walked to church? I can tell you nothing about it firsthand. I witnessed none of it, shut up in my sickbed as I was, but later I would hear the gory details from both Protestants and Catholics alike. I think both exaggerated, but from what I can reason out, the king that we had put our trust in to offer us safe passage and hospitality turned on the Protestants and ordered the mass killings of those of our faith.

Why did he allow it to happen? Most blamed the Queen Mother and her allies; guilt having passed from Guise alone to the woman who wore her son down with the threat that the Protestants would quickly kill His Majesty in retribution for the attack on Coligny. There were many whispers that Catherine and even Anjou were behind the plot against Coligny; and to Save Catherine, they slaughtered Coligny and his followers. Whatever the truth of that day, when I heard of the Protestants cut down without regard to their age or sex, I wept and my condition worsened by the day. I may not have been the most ardent follower of the Reformed religion, but no man or woman deserved slaughter on the feast day dedicated to St. Bartholomew.

My first concern upon hearing of the slaughter, was to enquire about the condition of my husband. Henriette came to my bed and wiped my brow. After turning to give me a sip of water, she held my hand. "Condé and Navarre are safe; in fact, they are both in the king's bedroom for their protection."

Relief washed over me. "Thank God." I sank back in the pillows.

"Dearest, they aren't completely out of danger."

That caused me to worry anew. I struggled to sit up. "What do you mean?"

"The king has offered them a choice: they can convert to Catholicism, or they will be executed."

My blood ran cold. "The last thing I expect Condé to do is to convert to Catholicism. Do you think Navarre will?"

She shook her head, "I don't know Guise and my husband argued for both of their lives and hopefully, in gratitude, they will agree to take the king's offer."

"Gratitude? You think denying their beliefs is a show of gratitude? What about their souls? Are they to sacrifice them to the wishes of a king who betrayed them?"

Her expression darkened, "Careful, Marie—there are countless bodies of Protestants lying in the streets of Paris. Even some Catholic nobles are dead in those streets. Now is not the time to speak against the king."

Too weak to argue with her, I instead asked her when I could see my husband. No matter how strained our marriage might be, I desperately wanted to speak with him, to hear from his lips of the unimaginable choice he faced.

"Officially, they are under house arrest and may not speak with anyone, especially a Protestant. You will most likely not be allowed to see him until either he or you convert."

There it was—I was also to be offered the Devil's bargain. Would I take it, or would I remain steadfast in my professed faith? Would my husband stand firm or would he save his life at the expense of his soul? Worse still what if one of us took the offer while the other refused? The hangman's noose might not part us, but we might never meet in Eternity.

❧ 7 ❧

I spent the next few days begging ill health as I awaited news from my husband. Before, I had chafed at the idea of him ordering me about, but after the massacre in the streets of Paris, I wished for nothing other than to ask his advice. I could not stand the idea of us being parted at such a time.

My days in my sickbed were not without incident—I was treated to the unexpected visit of my sisters' confessor, an Italian priest who made every effort to sit with me and spend part of the day discussing issues of faith. At any other time in my life, I might have welcomed the opportunity to satisfy my curiosity about the Catholic faith, but separated from my husband and worried as I was about his safety, I deeply resented the intrusion. I was not a stupid woman, and I knew that his "visits" were initial efforts to convert me.

August turned into September and I finally received word that my husband and the Navarre were safe, but both were stubbornly refusing to abjure their faith. The word came by my sister Catherine, who unlike Henriette decided not to mince her words with any hesitation. "Marie, the King, is growing angrier each day—and if they do not give into his demands, they may both be killed."

"But I thought your husband and Henriette's both argued that they should be Saved."

"Yes, Saved so that they be given the chance to convert. This was the only reason the King agreed." I knew that there was more to it. The King's reasoning couldn't have been so simple; he and his mother wanted to keep the senior members of the Bourbon family alive to balance the growing power of the Guise family.

"If he does not convert, am I never to see my husband again? Surely the King could not be that cruel."

She hesitated as if unsure of her next words. "Perhaps the Queen could appeal to the King to allow you to see him. We could argue that you could talk some sense into him and Navarre."

"But how could I get word to Elisabeth?" Stuck in the bed as I was, I was in no shape to attend upon the Queen.

"I will have Henriette speak with Queen Margot. They are close enough that Margot will get the message to her."

THE QUEEN RECEIVED THE MESSAGE THE NEXT DAY AND BY THE TIME we sent it, Catherine and I had a solid plan. I would receive instruction in the Catholic faith and would do my best to encourage my husband and cousin to do the same. The King and Queen were relieved that I was willing to convert and sensing that I could influence my fellow Protestants to do the same, I was allowed to speak with my husband in private at the Louvre.

When I found Condé, he looked haggard as if he hadn't slept in days. Likely, this was the case as I had heard that both Bourbon cousins had been harassed to convert almost continually. He sat in a chair, his body deflated.

"Are you hurt?" I kneeled at his side and studied his face. The same face that had annoyed me in the past two months was now a welcomed sight. He gave me a rare smile which reassured me somewhat.

"You know what they are threatening to do to us? Recant or die— as if we were simply some cult of pagans." He banged his fist on the arm of the chair as he spoke.

I took his head in my hands and tried to soothe him. Once I had his ear close to my lips, I whispered to him. There was a guard at the door and I was sure that he was there to hear our every word. "I have agreed to go through with the instruction in the Catholic faith. I have no desire to lose my life or yours. I suggest that you do the same until you can find a way out of this nightmare."

He jerked his head away from me, "You would willingly betray all that our Aunt has taught us? With so little provocation?"

I lost my temper, "Little? Do you know how many of our faith are lying dead right now? Do you not realize that had I not agreed to listen to the catechism, we would continue to be separated? Come to your senses, for God's sake."

"I cannot stand to speak to you. You have broken my heart and if Jeanne of Navarre were here, you would have broken hers as well." He placed his head in his hands and began to sob.

I stood, once again exasperated at my husband's shortsightedness. In a loud voice, I proclaimed, "I am being realistic. You may choose to remain a prisoner, or you can agree to reconcile yourself to the King. It would serve you well to look at your present circumstances before you make your decision." With that, I nodded to the guard and swept from the room. I had no doubt that the guards would make all haste to report my words to the King. God willing, I would be allowed further opportunities to "convince" my husband to convert. Our very lives depended on my ability to do so.

ONCE WORD SPREAD THAT I WAS AMIABLE TO CONVERSION, I HAD several additional visitors to my sister's home. The confessor assigned to me came on a daily basis and despite myself, I enjoyed learning from him. The longer we spoke, the more I identified with the beliefs and practices of the Roman church. I had never been given the opportunity to question my faith before. I found the relative freedom I had to examine my true beliefs for the first time in my life refreshing.

Other visitors to the house caused me more distress, in particular, the Queen Mother and the Duc d'Anjou. Rumors spread that these two Valois were the real architects of the bloody events on St. Bartholomew's Day, but I had little way of knowing if the rumors were true or not. Regardless of their truth, I felt uncomfortable with Anjou's numerous visits. It was not that I felt his presence distasteful; on the contrary, I very much enjoyed his company. I questioned the propriety of his visits to me and the fact that he offered to be a sponsor when I was received into the Catholic Church. I politely refused and asked Louis and Henriette to stand for me.

On the ninth day of September, the King became so enraged by Navarre and my husband's refusal to convert that he dictated a decree for their death. Once again, the Queen heard of his plans and inter-vened, despite her advanced pregnancy. I knew that I had to act and do so in a decisive manner. Five days later, I was received into the Catholic Church, a penitent and a true believer. My decision had an almost immediate effect of lifting the suspicion of me. I was allowed to return to the Queen's service, which I did as soon as possible. Her child was due in October and I had no desire to miss being there for the woman who had supported me on so many occasions.

Returning to the Queen's service also restored my life to some semblance of normalcy. While the court generally broke into camps of victorious Catholic radicals, moderate Catholics and Protestants, in the Queen's presence, I had a kind of buffer. After my conversion, I spent more time with her as I was allowed to attend daily Mass at her side and to stitch the altar cloths with the rest of the ladies in her retinue. We became closer friends, if that were possible, and during our long hours of conversations, I confessed to her my fear for my husband.

"I cannot thank you and the King enough for your compassion, but I am afraid that my husband is digging his heels in on remaining a Protestant."

She nodded, as always saying little, but understanding everything. "I believe that he must come to the point that his heart sees the way to the church. Perhaps it is a longer road for him, nein?" She had reverted to her native German and her voice broke with genuine emotion.

"I hope to continue my visits to him and to aid in the instruction of the church. It is my fondest wish that we are united together in

Paradise." I had initially resented my conversion, yet the more time I spent with the Catholic faith, the more I drew comfort from it. My words were not merely to assure the Queen that I was no threat to the King's reign. On the contrary, I thought that I could cause Condé to see reason more than a priest ever could.

I SPENT THE NEXT FEW DAYS BEGGING ILL HEALTH AS I AWAITED news from my husband. Before, I had chafed at the idea of him ordering me about, but after the massacre in the streets of Paris, I wished for nothing other than to ask his advice. I could not stand being parted at such a time.

My days in my sickbed were not without incident—they treated me to the unexpected visit of my sisters' confessor, an Italian priest who tried to sit with me and spend part of the day discussing issues of faith. At any other time in my life, I might have welcomed the opportunity to satisfy my curiosity about the Catholic faith, but separated from my husband and worried as I was about his safety, I deeply resented the intrusion. I was not a stupid woman, and I knew that his "visits" were initial efforts to convert me.

August turned into September and I finally received word that my husband and the Navarre were safe, but both were stubbornly refusing to abjure their faith. The word came by my sister Catherine, who unlike Henriette decided not to mince her words with any hesitation. "Marie, the king, is growing angrier each day—and if they do not give into his demands, they may both be killed."

"But I thought your husband and Henriette's both argued that they should be saved."

"Yes, saved to give them the chance to convert. This was the only reason the ling agreed." I knew that there was more to it. The king's reasoning couldn't have been so simple; he and his mother wanted to keep the senior members of the Bourbon family alive to balance the growing power of the Guise family.

"If he does not convert, am I never to see my husband again? Surely the king could not be that cruel."

She hesitated as if unsure of her next words. "Perhaps the queen could appeal to the king to allow you to see him. We could argue that you could talk some sense into him and Navarre."

"But how could I get word to Elisabeth?" Stuck in the bed as I was, I was in no shape to attend upon the queen.

"I will have Henriette speak with Queen Margot. They are close enough that Margot will get the message to her."

THE QUEEN RECEIVED THE MESSAGE THE NEXT DAY AND BY THE TIME we sent it, Catherine and I had a solid plan. I would receive instruction in the Catholic faith and would do my best to encourage my husband and cousin to do the same. It relieved the king and queen that I would convert and sensing I could influence my fellow Protestants to do the same; the king allowed me to speak with my husband in private at the Louvre.

When I found Condé, he looked haggard as if he hadn't slept in days. Likely, this was the case as I had heard that they had harassed both Bourbon cousins to convert almost continually. He sat in a chair, his body deflated.

"Are you hurt?" I kneeled at his side and studied his face. The same face that had annoyed me in the past two months was now a welcomed sight. He gave me a rare smile which reassured me somewhat.

"You know what they are threatening to do to us? Recant or die—as if we were nothing more than some cult of pagans." He banged his fist on the arm of the chair as he spoke.

I took his head in my hands and tried to soothe him. Once I had his ear close to my lips, I whispered to him. There was a guard at the door and I was sure that he was there to hear our every word. "I have agreed to go through with the instruction in the Catholic faith. I have no desire to lose my life or yours. I suggest that you do the same until you can find a way out of this nightmare."

He jerked his head away from me, "You would willingly betray all that our Aunt has taught us? With so little provocation?"

I lost my temper, "Little? Do you know how many of our faith are lying dead right now? Do you not realize that had I not agreed to listen to the catechism, we would continue to be separated? Come to your senses, for God's sake."

"I cannot stand to speak to you. You have broken my heart and if Jeanne of Navarre were here, you would have broken hers, too." He placed his head in his hands and sobbed.

I stood, once again exasperated at my husband's shortsightedness. In a loud voice, I proclaimed, "I am being realistic. You may choose to remain a prisoner, or you can agree to reconcile yourself to the king. It would serve you well to look at your present circumstances before you make your decision." With that, I nodded to the guard and swept from the room. I knew that the guards would make all haste to report my words to the king. God willing, his Majesty would allow me further opportunities to "convince" my husband to convert. Our very lives depended on my ability to do so.

۝

ONCE WORD SPREAD I WAS AMIABLE TO CONVERSION, I HAD SEVERAL additional visitors to my sister's home. The confessor assigned came on a daily basis and despite myself; I enjoyed learning from him. The longer we spoke, the more I identified with the beliefs and practices of the Roman church. I had never had the opportunity to question my faith before. I found the relative freedom I had to examine my true beliefs for the first time in my life refreshing.

Other visitors to the house caused me more distress, in particular, the Queen Mother and the Duc d'Anjou. Rumors spread that these two Valois were the real architects of the bloody events on St. Bartholomew's Day, but I had little way of knowing if the rumors were true or not. Regardless of their truth, I felt uncomfortable with Anjou's many visits. Not that I felt his presence distasteful; I very much enjoyed his company. I questioned the propriety of his visits and the fact he offered to be a sponsor when I was received into the Catholic Church. I politely refused and asked Louis and Henriette to stand for me.

On the ninth day of September, the king became so enraged by Navarre and my husband's refusal to convert that he dictated a decree for their death. Once again, the Queen heard of his plans and inter-vened, despite her advanced pregnancy. I knew that I had to act and do so hastily. Five days later, I was received into the Catholic Church, a penitent and a true believer. My decision had an almost immediate effect of lifting the suspicion of me. They allowed me to return to the Queen's service, which I did as soon as possible. Her child was due in October and I had no desire to miss being there for the woman who had supported me on so many occasions.

Returning to the queen's service also restored my life to normalcy. While the court broke into camps of victorious Catholic radicals, moderate Catholics and Protestants, in the queen's presence, I had a kind of buffer. After my conversion, I spent more time with her. I attended daily Mass at her side and stitched the altar cloths with the rest of the ladies in her retinue. We became closer friends, if that were possible, and during our long hours of conversations, I confessed to her my fear for my husband.

"I cannot thank you and the king enough for your compassion, but I am afraid that my husband is digging his heels in on remaining a Protestant."

She nodded, as always saying little, but understanding everything. "I believe that he must come to the point that his heart sees the way to the church. Perhaps it is a longer road for him, nein?" She had reverted to her native German and her voice broke with genuine emotion.

"I hope to continue my visits to him and to aid in the church's instruction. It is my fondest wish to be united in Paradise." I had initially resented my conversion, yet the more time I spent with the Catholic faith, the more I drew comfort from it. My words were not merely to assure the queen that I was no threat to the king's reign. I thought I could cause Condé to see reason more than a priest ever could.

8

My belief that I could convince my husband to convert proved to be a naïve one. Condé remained as intransigent as ever, mocking my conversion as a ruse to stay at court. "How am I to aid the King of Navarre in leading our people if you have gone over to Papistry under my very nose? What kind of resolve does that show, wife? What kind of faithfulness? You spend a few months at court and your head can be turned by fripperies and baubles?"

My face hot, I shot to my feet. "As always, I offer you an opportunity to Save your life. It is no fault of mine if you are too pigheaded to see the truth. The King has kept his resolve for so long; I'm sure that he will be willing to keep you here." Both he and Navarre were still being held under close watch a month after they were given the choice of death or conversion. The longer they held out, the more I feared that even my powerful brothers-in-law could not protect him.

Standing before the door, I turned to face him. His face was as resolute as ever. "Do you want me to become a widow? It's less than a year since your father passed. You do not even have an heir to which to pass your title. What would become of me?'

He released a heavy sigh. "I'm sure that you will manage without me." He said no more, but I waited for a few minutes. Fed up with his sullen behavior, I knocked on the door and marched out the door. He would not see the tears that welled in my eyes.

☙❧

THE TRUTH WAS, I COULD DO VERY WELL WITHOUT HIM. A wealthy, titled Catholic widow was a much sought-after commodity at court. Like Navarre and my husband, I was a Bourbon and Catherine was determined to keep at least some of us alive to check the Guise power. During the last King's reign, the Guise had run roughshod over Catherine and her eldest son, virtually ruling the country and she never forgot them for their coup. Before Admiral Coligny's fall and death, the Coligny family had provided a Protestant counterweight to the Guise, and we Bourbons were the only family left that could compete with them for power and influence at court.

If I was a cynic, I would assume that this was the reason why the Duc d'Anjou was determined to spend so much time with me. My sister, Catherine had been previously married to a major Protestant Lord, widowed young, then snatched up by an influential Catholic. Why would Anjou not assume that I was just as ripe for the taking? As, I am not that hard-hearted, I assumed that the feelings Anjou displayed towards me were as sincere as those that I was developing for him.

Within the quiet walls of Elisabeth's apartments, we sat, the Duc as solicitous towards his sister-in-law as he had been the night of the banquet. Perhaps motivated by so base a feeling as jealousy, I decided one day to probe the Duc's plans for his marriage.

"I am told, Monsieur, that you have in the past courted the Queen of England, is it not so?"

He nodded, a wistful look in his eye. "It's true—Elizabeth, and I were very close to becoming man and wife."

"So," I plucked a stray thread from the altar cloth the Queen and I were working on, "why did you not go ahead with the ceremony?"

He raised his eyebrows dismissively, "Well, for one, she is not of our faith. I cannot be united with a heretic."

"But your sister was."

"She is not in line to the French throne, as I am. Until the birth of the King's son," he swept to his feet and gave the Queen a very courtly bow, "I am heir to the throne. France must be secured and cannot be ruled in any way by a woman."

"And it was Elizabeth's religion and her status as the Queen that barred you from marrying her?" My voice sounded high and tight, even to my ears. I cursed my inability to keep the jealousy out of my words.

"There are too many women in France who are her superior, many of them found under my very nose." He gave me a look that promised more than mere friendship and I knew at once his intentions were more than flirting.

"And will you search France for a bride now?"

He threw up his hands. "I would prefer a French wife, how could I not? But as my dear sister knows, for a prince, it is not the easy to pick a wife."

"True, I knew as a girl that I could be shipped off to the furthermost corners of Christianity and I could say nothing about it." The Queen tried to keep the wistfulness out of her voice, but in her condition, her moods would suddenly swing. To break the dark turn the conversation had taken, I rose to get her a drink. After assuring that she was fine, I returned to my seat.

"If my mother would simply see that it is best for me to choose my wife, she would make my life much easier." He tapped on his knee with his finger, the motion almost hypnotic.

"Ah, is there another marriage in the works?"

"Yes." he spat out, suddenly petulant. I did not like this side of him. He seemed less of a man and more of a toddler at this sudden change of mood. "She is determined to make inquiries of the Swedish court. The entire country is a frozen block of ice and I have heard that the women are barely more than simple farmers." He shuddered at the thought.

I thought back to the day I saw him standing beside Margot, the splendor of his outfit almost outshining the bride. A simple-minded wife would drive the Duc d'Anjou to the point of madness. Despite myself, a giggle escaped my lips. He turned to me, outraged.

"Forgive me, Sir—it's just the idea of you being shut up with a

woman wearing coarsely spun wool seemed perfectly ludicrous to me."
I held out a hand to him in an attempt to sooth him. "I would never
wish an unhappy marriage upon anyone, even my enemies."

He looked at me, the sparkle returning to his eyes. He was up to
some mischief, but I could not tell exactly what. "Indeed, well, at least
I can count on your support, Princess."

๑๕๛

THE DUC'S VISITS CONTINUED WITH REGULARITY AND THE QUEEN
prepared for the birth of her child. October opened with only a faint
break from the oppressive summer heat, although we all welcomed a
respite from the suffocating humidity that had hung over Paris since
that bloody August.

I moved my lodgings from my sister's home to a suite of rooms
adjacent to the Queen's at the Louvre. We knew that at any moment,
her labor could begin and she was determined that she would have
Madame de Sauve and myself near her when the time came. I had no
further contact with my husband, although the confessors the Queen
mother sent to him gave me regular updates of their attempts to
convert him and Navarre to the Catholic church. The death threats
from the King changed into a waiting game. Either the King would
relent and allow Navarre and Condé to be released, or they would be
permanent residents of the royal prisons.

Luckily, my status as the wife of a political and religious prisoner of
the King did not prove to be a handicap in court, thanks to the influence of my sisters and the Duc de Anjou. I was received with every
courtesy and even the notorious gossips of the French court refrained
for the time being from making me into a scandal.

In mid—October, the Queen's labor pains began. As she requested,
Madame de Suave and I were present along with the midwife and the
Queen's chambermaids. After an exhausting labor, the Queen delivered
her first child. Despite our hopes, the first child of Charles IX and
Elisabeth of Austria was not to be the heir for which France had
prayed. The tiny baby was a girl, and the Duc d'Anjou remained his
brother's heir and the first gentleman of the court.

After the Queen recovered from the birth and was churched, I returned to my sister's home at the Hotel de Nevers. We had not made any plans about my lodgings after the wedding of Margot and Navarre and without a husband by my side, I had little option other than return to my sister's home. Thankfully, both Henriette and Louis were more than willing to take me on as a houseguest.

I had assumed that by staying at Henriette's home, it would make it difficult for Anjou to make regular visits to me. On the contrary, he made daily visits to me, stopping for the flimsiest and most obvious reasons. At first, he claimed to be interested in my progress as a new Catholic, but I knew exactly where his true interests lay. Louis considered the Duc a protégé and began advising him in governance if the Poles decided to make him their new sovereign. The more time I spent with Anjou, the more I realized what we shared in common. In place of my dour and plain husband, the Duc chose to dress in the most fashionable clothing of the day. He carried an air of elegance and authority that Condé never could. Anjou looked like a prince. Despite myself, I fell in love with him during those days. In my loneliness, my tongue loosened around him and Anjou became my confidant during those long weeks that I worried over my husband's fate.

"I have lost my ability to influence my husband. We are not married a year and I would have more luck speaking to a stone wall." Anjou kept pace with me as I marched through the gardens of the Hotel de Nevers. I enjoyed his boundless energy during our walks together.

"Perhaps it is for the best. Perhaps fate has intervened to send you towards a greater destiny?"

His words caught my attention, "What greater destiny?"

"If it is Condé's wish that he end his days mired in heresy, it is best for his soul that he be delivered to his Lord. You would be free to make a more suitable match with a loyal Catholic Lord."

I shook my head, "No, I made my vows between God."

"But that was in a Protestant ceremony. In the eyes of God and the Church, the two of you are living in sin. I beg you, sweet Marie, have a care for your soul and ask His Holiness for an annulment. Given the circumstances, you are in; he will not deny you a release."

Guilt pricked at my conscience. "But what about Condé?

Anjou took my hand, encircling it with is larger, warmer ones. His touch sent a thrill up my spine. "Condé will have to answer to God for his sins. If he chooses to die as a heretic, he has no right to drag you to the depths of hell with him."

Was he right? Would my husband drag my soul to hell? Or by giving up on him, was I the one Condémning him to hell?

MY BELIEF THAT I COULD CONVINCE MY HUSBAND TO CONVERT proved to be a naïve one. Condé remained as intransigent as ever, mocking my conversion as a ruse to stay at court. "How am I to aid the King of Navarre in leading our people if you have gone over to Papistry under my nose? What kind of resolve does that show, wife? What kind of faithfulness? You spend a few months at court and fripperies and baubles turn your head?"

My face hot, I shot to my feet. "As always, I offer you an opportunity to save your life. It is no fault of mine if you are too pigheaded to see the truth. The king has kept his resolve for so long; I'm sure he will agree to keep you here." Both he and Navarre were still being held under close watch a month after they had the choice of death or conversion. The longer they held out, the more I feared that even my powerful brothers-in-law could not protect him.

Standing before the door, I turned to face him. His face was as resolute as ever. "Do you want me to become a widow? It's less than a year since your father passed. You do not even have an heir to which to pass your title. What would become of me?"

He released a heavy sigh. "I'm sure you will manage without me." He said no more, but I waited for a few minutes. Fed up with his sullen behavior, I knocked on the door and marched out the door. He would not see the tears that welled in my eyes.

THE TRUTH WAS, I COULD DO WELL WITHOUT HIM. A WEALTHY, titled Catholic widow was a much sought-after commodity at court. Like Navarre and my husband, I was a Bourbon and the Queen Mother wanted to keep at least some of us alive to check the Guise power. During the last king's reign, the Guise had run roughshod over Catherine and her eldest son, virtually ruling the country and she never forgot them for their coup. Before Admiral Coligny's fall and death, the Coligny family had provided a Protestant counterweight to the Guise, and we Bourbons were the only family left that could compete with them for power and influence at court.

If I was a cynic, I would assume that this was the reason why the Duc d'Anjou continued to spend so much time with me. They had previously married Catherine to a major Protestant Lord. After fate made my sister a widow, she was snatched up by an influential Catholic. Why would Anjou not assume that I was just as ripe for the taking? As, I am not that hard-hearted; I assumed that the feelings Anjou displayed towards me were as sincere as those that I was developing for him.

Within the quiet walls of Elisabeth's apartments, we sat, the Duc as solicitous towards his sister-in-law as he had been the night of the banquet. Perhaps motivated by so base a feeling as jealousy, I decided one day to probe the Duc's plans for his marriage.

"I am told, Monsieur, that you have in the past courted the Queen of England, is it not so?"

He nodded, a wistful look in his eye. "It's true—Elizabeth, and I were close to becoming man and wife."

"So," I plucked a stray thread from the altar cloth the queen and I were working on, "why did you not go ahead with the ceremony?"

He raised his eyebrows dismissively, "Well, for one, she is not of our faith. I cannot marry a heretic."

"But your sister married a heretic."

"She is not in line to the French throne, as I am. Until the birth of the king's son," he swept to his feet and gave the queen a very courtly bow, "I am heir to the throne. France cannot be ruled by a woman."

"And it was Elizabeth's religion and her status as the queen that barred you from marrying her?" My voice sounded high and tight, even to my ears. I cursed my inability to keep the jealousy out of my words.

"There are too many women in France who are her superior, many of them found under my nose." He gave me a look that promised more than mere friendship and I knew at once his intentions were more than flirting.

"And will you search France for a bride now?"

He threw up his hands. "I would prefer a French wife, how could I not? But as my dear sister knows, for a prince, it is not the easy to pick a wife."

"True, I knew as a girl they could ship me off to the furthermost corners of Christianity and I could say nothing about it." The queen tried to keep the wistfulness out of her voice, but in her condition, her moods would suddenly swing. To break the dark turn the conversation had taken, I rose to get her a drink. After assuring that she was fine, I returned to my seat.

"If my mother would agree that it is best for me to choose my wife, she would make my life much easier." He tapped on his knee with his finger, the motion almost hypnotic.

"Ah, is there another marriage in the works?"

"Yes." he spat out, suddenly petulant. I did not like this side of him. He seemed less of a man and more of a toddler at this sudden change of mood. "She is determined to make inquiries of the Swedish court. The entire country is a frozen block of ice and I have heard that the women are barely more than simple farmers." He shuddered at the thought.

I thought back to the day I saw him standing beside Margot, the splendor of his outfit almost outshining the bride. A simple-minded wife would drive the Duc d'Anjou to the point of madness. Despite myself, a giggle escaped my lips. He turned outraged.

"Forgive me, Sir—it's just the idea of you being shut up with a woman wearing coarsely spun wool seemed perfectly ludicrous to me." I held out a hand to him in an attempt to sooth him. "I would never wish an unhappy marriage upon anyone, even my enemies."

He looked at me; the sparkle returning to his eyes. He was up to some mischief, but I could not tell exactly what. "Indeed. Well, at least I can count on your support, Princess."

THE DUC'S VISITS CONTINUED WITH REGULARITY AND THE QUEEN prepared for the birth of her child. October opened with only a faint break from the oppressive summer heat, although we all welcomed a respite from the suffocating humidity that had hung over Paris since that bloody August.

I moved my lodgings from my sister's home to a suite of rooms adjacent to the queen's at the Louvre. We knew that at any moment, her labor could begin and insisted that she would have Madame de Sauve and myself near her when the time came. I had no further contact with my husband, although the confessors the Queen Mother sent to him gave me regular updates of their attempts to convert him and Navarre to the Catholic church. The death threats from the king changed into a waiting game. Either the king would relent and allow Navarre and Condé's release, or they would be permanent residents of the royal prisons.

Luckily, my status as the wife of a political and religious prisoner of the king did not prove to be a handicap in court, thanks to the influence of my sisters and the Duc de Anjou. The court received me with every courtesy and even the notorious gossips of the French court refrained for the time being from making me into a scandal.

In mid—October, the queen's labor pains began. As she requested, Madame de Suave and I were present along with the midwife and the queen's chambermaids. After an exhausting labor, the queen delivered her first child. Despite our hopes, the first child of Charles IX and Elisabeth of Austria was not to be the heir for which France had prayed. The tiny baby was a girl, and the Duc d'Anjou remained his brother's heir and the first gentleman of the court.

AFTER THE QUEEN RECOVERED FROM THE BIRTH AND WAS CHURCHED,

I returned to my sister's home at the Hotel de Nevers. We had made no plans about my lodgings after the wedding of Margot and Navarre and without a husband by my side; I had little option other than return to my sister's home. Thankfully, both Henriette and Louis were more than willing to take me on as a houseguest.

I had assumed that by staying at Henriette's home, it would make it difficult for Anjou to continue his regular visits to me. On the contrary, he made daily visits to me, stopping for the flimsiest and most obvious reasons. At first, he claimed an interest in my progress as a new Catholic, but I knew exactly where his true interests lay. Louis considered the Duc a protégé and advised him in governance if the Poles made him their new sovereign. The more time I spent with Anjou, the more I realized what we shared in common. In place of my dour and plain husband, the Duc dressed in the most fashionable clothing of the day. He carried an air of elegance and authority that Condé never could. Anjou looked like a prince. Despite myself, I fell in love with him during those days. In my loneliness, my tongue loosened around him and Anjou became my confidant during those long weeks as I worried over my husband's fate.

"I have lost my ability to influence my husband. Married less than a year, and I would have more luck speaking to a stone wall." Anjou kept pace with me as I marched through the gardens of the Hotel de Nevers. I enjoyed his boundless energy during our walks together.

"Perhaps it is for the best. Perhaps fate has intervened to send you towards a greater destiny?"

His words caught my attention, "What greater destiny?"

"If it is Condé's wish that he end his days mired in heresy, it is best for his soul that he be delivered to his Lord. You would be free to make a more suitable match with a loyal Catholic Lord."

I shook my head, "No, I made my vows between God."

"But that was in a Protestant ceremony. In the eyes of God and the Church, the two of you are living in sin. I beg you, sweet Marie, have a care for your soul and ask His Holiness for an annulment. Given the circumstances, you are in; he will not deny you a release."

Guilt pricked at my conscience. "But what about Condé?"

Anjou took my hand, encircling it with is larger, warmer ones. His touch sent a thrill up my spine. "Condé will have to answer to God for his sins. If he chooses to die as a heretic, he has no right to drag you to the depths of hell with him."

Was he right? Would my husband drag my soul to hell? Or by giving up on him, was I the one Condémning him to hell?

❧ 9 ❧

Scarcely a week after my interview with Anjou, as October slid into November, a messenger arrived at the Hotel de Nevers bearing a message for me. Expecting a letter from the Queen or perhaps a note from my husband, I shut the door to my bedchamber and opened the missive. What I discovered caused me to pause. I beheld a poem, written by Phillip Desportes, a noted poet and a favorite of the Queen Mother. The poem told the tale of Eurylas and Olympus and carried the title of "A First Adventure." I could not fail to notice that the two characters in the story were meant to represent Anjou and I, and despite myself, I felt a pride in knowing that someone had put our relationship into verse.

While the poem carried all the characteristics of Deportes, there was no doubt that Anjou himself had commissioned the work as a veiled way to declare his feelings for me. This must be what a genuine courtship felt like. I was not unaware that both my sisters had lovers, but I confess that before that day, I could hardly understand why they did so. I felt giddy and a warm glow spread throughout my body. It was like standing in a sunbeam, but the warmth of the sun was contained within my body. This, happy feeling, then, must be what being in love with someone must feel like.

Did I feel guilt in those early days? I must confess that I did not. Anjou's warning that Condé and I both faced the wrath of hell for our illegal marriage caused me to fear for my soul. My husband may not have worried about the fate of his soul, but I was terribly concerned for mine.

A royal prince felt love for me. Dare I hope that I could begin another life with him? What would life be like with a man who cherished me, adored me and gave all outward signs that he wished to spend his time with me? Such a marriage would be so unlike the one I had with Condé. I began to resent the fact that the marriage with Condé had been forced upon me by my aunt and with no more consideration for our compatibility than our shared religion. Now that singular reason was no longer valid, and I had the opportunity to grasp happiness for myself.

It was this promise of future happiness that caused me to indulge the Duc d'Anjou wholeheartedly in his pursuit of me. Did I consider the scandal that my behavior would cause? My husband had lingered in a royal jail since the end of August, holding my status at French court in limbo. Also, if Anjou was correct, and the church did not recognize my marriage to Condé, I was guilty of no transgressions against a man to whom I was not lawfully wed.

My husband was by no means ignorant of the goings on outside of his prison within his apartments in the Louvre. The Queen Mother herself took joy in telling him of my happiness in converting and I have no doubt that either she or another mentioned of the time I spent with Anjou. By the beginning of November, Condé started to fade from my mind as if he never existed. Anjou and I began to see one another in more public places, chatting at the tennis court or walking alongside one another as we exited Mass. Buoyed by his suggestion of an annulment, I began to picture a life with him more clearly. As our recklessness grew, however, so did the resentment of the rest of the court. Our affair came to a head one crisp day in early November.

The Duchess of Montpensier, only sister of the Duc de Guise, became the unlikely catalyst for the open scandal of exposing our relationship. Although the entire court knew of Anjou's visits, none dared to speak of it openly until she dared to do so. Linking her arm in

Catherine's she called out in a singsong voice. "Ah, the sweet honeyed lips of my love, which doth rain kisses down my neck. Like the warmth of your arms, encircling me in my bower."

I stopped cold; I had heard those words, but there was only one place that I could have heard them from—the poems composed by Desportes. When I read them, they seemed poetic and romantic, but their words were very much divorced from reality as neither of us had made an attempt to make our attraction physical. They were the words of an admirer to his lady. Coming from Montpensier, they sounded lewd.

Turning, I faced my sister and the foul woman beside her. The only way that she could have heard those words would be if my room had been entered and my private papers rifled and stolen. My immediate suspicion fell upon Catherine, but once I looked at her face, I realized she was just as horrified as I was.

My sister pulled her arm from Montpensier and clapped her hand over my shoulder. "Come, dearest, don't' make a scene."

"It already is a scene," my face hot with embarrassment and anger. I had been betrayed. The assembled group in the garden fell deathly quiet as if none of us knew what to do next. Montpensier, however, took the opportunity to continue.

"I wonder what Eurylas' poor lord and husband would say about Olympus sneaking into her chambers every night while he lingered away, chained up in the King's, that is, the gods' prison. One might say that Eurylas delighted in the opportunity to cuckold him."

Before I could say a word, Catherine stalked towards her sister-in-law, "Silence, you snake! I'll have you whipped and sent off to the countryside before you can say another word." To her credit, Montpensier blanched, but while the exchange diverted attention away from me, I felt it moments later returning to me. Still, in my horror, I had lost the ability to speak and Catherine pulled me away, out of the garden.

Catherine acted immediately, calling in her husband. In her bedchambers, she railed against Guise's foolish younger sister. "It is one thing to humiliate my sister, but is she ignorant enough to alienate the Duc d'Anjou in public? Is our marriage not enough to Save the

Guise family from the hangman's noose? Must your sister put your entire family back in line for execution at every turn?"

Guise exhaled a long sigh. "My sister is not the smartest woman at court. I'll grant you that. I will speak to her."

"That is the least I expect you to do, as you are the head of her family. I told her I would have her whipped and I think that in this case the action is warranted."

He threw up his hands, "So what would you have me do?"

"Tell your insipid sister to stop provoking Anjou and to stop doing it by humiliating my sister."

"She's only following my lead; the spoiled boy has heaped humiliation upon me for years."

My sister's face turned a shade of red I had never seen before. Whirling to face her past few months husband, Catherine spat, "And that 'humiliation' includes having to marry me to Save face when you were barred from marrying Margot, no?"

That last jab hit Guise in a most tender place. We all knew that Guise would be Margot's husband had the Queen Mother not checked his power play in attempting to marry into the Valois family two years earlier. Despite the separation of the former lovers, my sister still harbored a suspicion that Margot and Guise remained lovers.

"We all do what we have to, to survive at court, my dear," he gave a sarcastic bow to his wife, whose face still looked murderous.

"I believe that my family has done more than enough to Save the Guise from destroying yourselves. I won't have my sister drawn into your feud with the Valois."

"And what are we to do about Anjou?" His question hung in the air, one that I had not found the answer to during the heady past weeks of our infatuation.

Catherine exhaled a long sigh, "I doubt that there is much we can do."

SCARCELY A WEEK AFTER MY INTERVIEW WITH ANJOU, AS OCTOBER slid into November, a messenger arrived at the Hotel de Nevers bearing a message for me. Expecting a letter from the queen or perhaps a note from my husband, I shut the door to my bedchamber and opened the missive. What I discovered caused me to pause. I beheld a poem, written by Phillip Desportes, a noted poet and a favorite of the Queen Mother. The poem told the tale of Eurylas and Olympus and carried the title of "A First Adventure." I could not fail to notice that the two characters in the story represented Anjou and I, and despite myself, I felt a pride in knowing that someone had put our relationship into verse.

While the poem carried all the characteristics of Desportes, it was obvious Anjou himself had commissioned the work as a veiled way to declare his feelings for me. This must be what a genuine courtship felt like. I was not unaware that both my sisters had lovers, but I confess that before that day, I could hardly understand why they did so. I felt giddy and a warm glow spread throughout my body. It was like standing in a sunbeam, but I contained the warmth of the sun within my body. This, happy feeling must be what being in love with someone must feel like.

Did I feel guilt in those early days? I must confess that I did not. Anjou's warning that Condé and I both faced the wrath of hell for our illegal marriage caused me to fear for my soul. My husband may not have worried about the fate of his soul, but I worried over mine.

A royal prince felt love for me. Dare I hope that I could begin another life with him? What would life be like with a man who cherished me, adored me and gave all outward signs he wished to spend his time with me? Such a marriage would be so unlike the one I had with Condé. I resented that my aunt had forced the marriage with Condé upon me by my aunt and with no more consideration for our compatibility than our shared religion. Now that singular reason was no longer valid, and I wanted happiness for myself.

It was this promise of future happiness that caused me to indulge the Duc d'Anjou wholeheartedly in his pursuit of me. Did I consider the scandal that my behavior would cause? My husband had lingered in a royal jail since the end of August, holding my status at French court in limbo. Also, if Anjou was correct, and the church did not recognize my marriage to Condé, I was guilty of no transgressions against a man to whom I was not lawfully wed.

My husband was not ignorant of the goings on outside of his prison within his apartments in the Louvre. The Queen Mother herself took joy in telling him of my happiness in converting and either she or another mentioned the time I spent with Anjou. By the beginning of November, Condé faded from my mind as if he never existed. Anjou and I saw one another in more public places, chatting at the tennis court or walking alongside one another as we exited Mass. Buoyed by his suggestion of an annulment, I began to picture a life with him more clearly. As our recklessness grew, however, so did the resentment of the rest of the court. Our affair came to a head one crisp day in early November.

The Duchesse of Montpensier, only sister of the Duc de Guise, became the unlikely catalyst for the open scandal of exposing our relationship. Although the entire court knew of Anjou's visits, none dared to speak of it openly until she dared to do so. Linking her arm in Catherine's she called out in a singsong voice. "Ah, the sweet honeyed lips of my love, which doth rain kisses down my neck. Like the warmth of your arms, encircling me in my bower."

I stopped cold; I had heard those words, but there was only one place that I could have heard them from—the poems composed by Desportes. When I read them, they seemed poetic and romantic, but their words were very much divorced from reality as neither of us had attempted to make our attraction physical. They were the words of an admirer to his lady. Coming from Montpensier, they sounded lewd.

Turning, I faced my sister and the foul woman beside her. The only way she could have heard those words would be if someone entered my chamber and my private papers stolen. My immediate suspicion fell upon Catherine, but once I looked at her face, I realized she was just as horrified as I was.

My sister pulled her arm from Montpensier and clapped her hand over my shoulder. "Come, dearest, don't' make a scene."

"It already is a scene," my face hot with embarrassment and anger. Someone had betrayed me. The assembled group in the garden fell deathly quiet as if none of us knew what to do next. Montpensier, however, continued.

"I wonder what Eurylas' poor lord and husband would say about

Olympus sneaking into her chambers every night while he lingered away, chained up in the king's, that is, the gods' prison. One might say that Eurylas delighted in the opportunity to cuckold him."

Before I could say a word, Catherine stalked towards her sister-in-law, "Silence, you snake! I'll have you whipped and sent off to the countryside before you can say another word." To her credit, Montpensier blanched, but while the exchange diverted attention away from me, I felt it moments later returning. Still, in my horror, I had lost the ability to speak and Catherine pulled me away, out of the garden.

Catherine acted immediately, calling in her husband. In her bedchambers, she railed against Guise's foolish younger sister. "It is one thing to humiliate my sister, but is she ignorant enough to alienate the Duc d'Anjou in public? Is our marriage not enough to save the Guise family from the hangman's noose? Must your sister put your entire family back in line for execution at every turn?"

Guise exhaled a long sigh. "My sister is not the smartest woman at court. I'll grant you that. I will speak to her."

"That is the least I expect you to do, as you are the head of her family. I told her I would have her whipped and I think in this case it warrants the action."

He threw up his hands, "So what would you have me do?"

"Tell your insipid sister to stop provoking Anjou and to stop doing it by humiliating my sister."

"She's only following my lead; the spoiled boy has heaped humiliation upon me for years."

My sister's face turned a shade of red I had never seen before. Whirling to face her past few months husband, Catherine spat, "And that 'humiliation' includes having to marry me to Save face when they barred you from marrying Margot, no?"

That last jab hit Guise in a most tender place. We all knew that Guise would be Margot's husband had the Queen Mother not checked his power play in attempting to marry into the Valois family two years earlier. Despite the separation of the former lovers, my sister still harbored a suspicion that Margot and Guise remained lovers.

"We all do what we have to, to survive at court, my dear," he gave a sarcastic bow to his wife, whose face still looked murderous.

"I believe that my family has done more than enough to Save the Guise from destroying yourselves. I won't have my sister drawn into your feud with the Valois."

"And what are we to do about Anjou?" His question hung in the air, one I had not found the answer to during the heady past weeks of our infatuation.

Catherine exhaled a long sigh, "I doubt that there is much we can do."

❦ 10 ❦

The next day, The Duchess of Montpensier departed for the Guise lands to the east and I exhaled a sigh of relief for her absence. Catherine and I had assumed that our silencing of Montpensier would be the end of the scandal, but instead, it pushed it further underground. When I entered rooms, I noticed the gossip stopped, and as I waited on the Queen, I noticed prying eyes upon me. I was no longer an object of pity; I was a topic of scandal.

The unfairness of it all infuriated me, I had made no moves to start an affair, and the verses were at his urging, yet the court viewed me as a harlot. For his part, Anjou seemed unmoved by the court's behavior, and he continued to visit me on an almost daily basis. For my protection, I insisted on having either of my sisters beside me at all times, hoping that the fact that Anjou and I were never alone would silence the wagging tongues of Paris.

As Catherine and I walked one early morning from Mass, I looked down to see that our pace was in rhythm, something that young girls would do at play. "No matter what the gossips may do to me, I am relieved to have an excuse to spend so much time together."

"Was it so bad in Navarre with all of those Protestants scolding you?" Regret at the fact that we had not had the opportunity to grow up together washed over me.

"Actually, no. Aunt Jeanne was incredibly loving towards me. It was hard to tell that I wasn't her daughter."

"Given her penchant for sermonizing, I'm surprised she didn't take every opportunity to tell you how grateful you should be for her taking you in." As soon as she said it, she winced. Before she could apologize, I stopped her.

"Protestantism may not have been for me, but I never lacked for a mother in my life. Now, a beautiful older sister, yes. Cousin Catherine was a wonderful younger sister, but to find someone to boss me around, I had to come to France."

She threw her head back, laughing. "Henriette is that good at ordering you around? I shall have to tell her that." I squeezed her hand, and we fell into a companionable silence.

"Your Highness!" One of my pages called to me. Turning, I saw the boy running at full speed.

"Whatever is it?" Visions of my husband marched to his execution flashed in my head and I felt momentary guilt for our levity a moment earlier.

He handed me a message, and I hurried to unfold it and read its contents. It was a letter written by my sister's confessor. Of his volition, my husband had decided to convert to the Catholic faith. I stared at the message, rereading it several times.

"What is it?" Catherine's face was grave, her concern showing in her eyes.

"He's going to become a Catholic." I was unable to keep the disbelief out of my voice.

Catherine tried to force cheerfulness, "So, I guess he will be returning to you, then."

"Yes, returning to me..." But, did I want him?

◈

MY HUSBAND AND NAVARRE HAD HAD A CHANGE OF HEART, AND both had decided to embrace the Catholic faith. Like me, they received instruction in the catechism and in late November, both were received into the church as repentant sinners. I have no doubt that my Aunt Jeanne's heart broke at the sound of both of them renouncing their affiliation to Protestantism since unlike me, their devotion to Protestantism seemed to be genuine.

I attended the service in a daze, worrying how Condé's reappearance in my life would affect me and what I would do about Anjou's attentiveness. For that matter, what was my relationship to Condé, since we had married as Protestants and not as Catholics in good standing? Were we to remain man and wife? Did I have the freedom to choose another marriage? Could Anjou and I be together? My heart leapt at the thought.

After the celebratory Mass, I hurried to speak with Anjou, to tell him of my thoughts. I found him standing next to Condé. As I approached, I could not make out their words, but once I was within earshot, my heart sank.

"Ah, now that you are a part of the True Church, nothing is barring your way to serve the King in his fight against the Heretics."

My blood froze, was Anjou suggesting that a Bourbon make war against his own people, his own family?

My husband turned his face away from me, his voice tight. "I would never give His Majesty reason to doubt my loyalty or my sincerity."

"Loyalty? My brother will be pleased to hear that you value loyalty so highly." Anjou's voice became a sneer and I could feel the hatred between the two men. Neither of them turned to acknowledge me.

"Yes, without loyalty to one's vows, what are we? No better than a crude animal rutting in the pasture?" His meaning was clear, and I began to seek a way to escape the two of them.

"You might find your dedication misplaced, My Lord, given the events happening in Paris these days."

"Doubt it not; I plan to hold on to everything that is mine and defend it against anyone who would dare take it."

I caught the Queen's eye and hastened to her side. So, Anjou's flirtation with me had been nothing more than a way to get at my husband. I had been making a fool of myself, daydreaming that his feelings for me were genuine. Tears stung at my eyes.

"Marie, isn't it wonderful?" Mistaking my tears for those of happiness, the Queen embraced me.

"Yes, it truly is."

"I am so relieved that your troubles are over. Our prayers have been answered, yours and mine."

THAT EVENING, I SAT IN OUR BEDCHAMBER AT MY SISTER'S HOME, attempting to garner some heat from the fire. A click alerted me that my husband was entering the room, and wordlessly, I rose to greet him.

"As part of my bargain with the King, I have written Rome on both our behalf to seek the Pope's forgiveness for marrying outside of a Catholic rite."

"Does that mean that I am still your wife?" I could not tell if the idea comforted me or not.

"We are to marry in two weeks according to Catholic rites. The King has given his permission, and I see no reason to do so with any delay."

"Are you to depart with Anjou's army, then?" I wrung my hands, desperate for any change of topic.

"We leave in January. For La Rochelle."

"Henry, you cannot be a part of a violent assault on your own people!"

"You forget, Madame, that we are both Catholics. Is it not our duty to exterminate Heretics?" He lingered over me, his voice growing higher with every word.

"If you had no desire to recant, then why become a Catholic?"

He snorted. "It was my only option. My wife was here, playing the whore with the Duc d'Anjou. I figured I might as well get out of prison before she gave him a bastard."

Had he slapped me, he would have wounded me less. I turned my face towards the fire so that he would not see my tears. "I have played the whore with no one. You can ask my sisters. I remained faithful to you, even when you left me vulnerable while you stayed imprisoned by your own stubbornness."

He pounded the table with his fist, "And now I am out of one prison and into another one. Perhaps I Saved my life, or perhaps not. I doubt not that I failed to Save my own soul."

THE NEXT DAY, THE DUCHESSE OF MONTPENSIER DEPARTED FOR THE Guise lands to the east and I exhaled a sigh of relief for her absence. Catherine and I had assumed that our silencing of Montpensier would be the end of the scandal, but it pushed it further underground. When I entered rooms, I noticed the gossip stopped, and as I waited on the queen, I noticed prying eyes upon me. I was no longer an object of pity; I was a topic of scandal.

The unfairness of it all infuriated me, I had made no moves to start an affair, and the verses were at his urging, yet the court viewed me as a harlot. Anjou seemed unmoved by the court's behavior, and he continued to visit me on an almost daily basis. For my protection, I insisted on having either of my sisters beside me at all times, hoping that the fact that Anjou and I were never alone would silence the wagging tongues of Paris.

As Catherine and I walked one early morning from Mass, I looked down to see that our pace was in rhythm, something that young girls would do at play. "No matter what the gossips may say I am relieved to have an excuse to spend so much time together."

"Was it so bad in Navarre with all of those Protestants scolding you?" Regret at the fact we were denied the opportunity to grow up together washed over me.

"Actually, no. Aunt Jeanne was very loving towards me. It was hard to tell that I wasn't her daughter."

"Given her penchant for sermonizing, I'm surprised she didn't take every opportunity to tell you how grateful you should be for her taking you in." As soon as she said it, she winced. Before she could apologize, I stopped her.

"Protestantism may not have been for me, but I never lacked for a mother in my life. Now, a beautiful older sister, yes. Cousin Catherine was a wonderful younger sister, but to find someone to boss me around, I had to come to France."

She threw her head back, laughing. "Henriette is that good at ordering you around? I shall have to tell her that." I squeezed her hand, and we fell into a companionable silence.

"Your Highness!" One of my pages called to me. Turning, I saw the boy running at full speed.

"Whatever is it?" Visions of my husband marched to his execution flashed in my head and I felt momentary guilt for our levity a moment earlier.

He handed me a message, and I hurried to unfold it and read its contents. It was a letter written by my sister's confessor. Of his volition, my husband had converted to the Catholic faith. I stared at the message, rereading it several times.

"What is it?" Catherine's face was grave, her concern showing in her eyes.

"He will become a Catholic." I could not keep the disbelief out of my voice.

Catherine tried to force cheerfulness, "So, I guess he will be returning to you, then."

"Yes, returning to me..." But, did I want him?

❧

MY HUSBAND AND NAVARRE HAD RECONSIDERED, AND BOTH HAD embraced the Catholic faith. Like me, they received instruction in the catechism and in late November, both were received into the church as repentant sinners. I have no doubt that my Aunt Jeanne's heart broke at the sound of both of them renouncing their affiliation to Protestantism since unlike me, their devotion to Protestantism seemed to be genuine.

I attended the service in a daze, worrying how Condé's reappearance in my life would affect me and what I would do about Anjou's attentiveness. For that matter, what was my relationship to Condé, since we had married as Protestants and not as Catholics in good standing? Were we to remain man and wife? Did I have the freedom to choose another marriage? Could Anjou and I be together? My heart leapt at the thought.

After the celebratory Mass, I hurried to speak with Anjou, to tell him of my thoughts. I found him standing next to Condé. As I approached, I could not make out their words, but once I was within earshot, my heart sank.

"Ah, now that you are a part of the True Church, nothing is barring your way to serve the king in his fight against the Heretics."

My blood froze, was Anjou suggesting that a Bourbon make war against his own people, his own family?

My husband turned his face away from me, his voice tight. "I would never give His Majesty reason to doubt my loyalty or my sincerity."

"Loyalty? My brother will be pleased to hear that you value loyalty so highly." Anjou's voice became a sneer and I could feel the hatred between the two men. Neither of them turned to acknowledge me.

"Yes, without loyalty to one's vows, what are we? No better than a crude animal rutting in the pasture?" His meaning was clear, and I sought a way to escape the conversation.

"You might find your dedication misplaced, My Lord, given the events happening in Paris these days."

"Doubt it not; I plan to hold on to everything that is mine and defend it against anyone who would dare take it."

I caught the queen's eye and hastened to her side. So, Anjou's flirtation with me had been nothing more than a way to get at my husband. I had been making a fool of myself, daydreaming that his feelings for me were genuine. Tears stung at my eyes.

"Marie, isn't it wonderful?" Mistaking my tears for those of happiness, the queen embraced me.

"Yes, it truly is."

"I am so relieved that your troubles are over. It has answered our prayers, yours and mine."

THAT EVENING, I SAT IN OUR BEDCHAMBER AT MY SISTER'S HOME, attempting to garner heat from the fire. A click alerted me that my husband was entering the room, and wordlessly, I rose to greet him.

"As part of my bargain with the king, I have written Rome on both our behalf to seek the Pope's forgiveness for marrying outside of a Catholic rite."

"Does that mean that I am still your wife?" I could not tell if the idea comforted me or not.

"We are to marry in two weeks according to Catholic rites. The king has given his permission, and I see no reason to do so with any delay."

"Are you to depart with Anjou's army, then?" I wrung my hands, desperate for any change of the topic.

"We leave in January. For La Rochelle."

"Henry, you cannot be a part of a violent assault on your own people!"

"You forget, Madame, that we are both Catholics. Is it not our duty to exterminate Heretics?" He lingered over me, his voice growing higher with every word.

"If you had no desire to recant, then why become a Catholic?"

He snorted. "It was my only option. My wife was here, playing the whore with the Duc d'Anjou. I figured I might as well get out of prison before she gave him a bastard."

Had he slapped me, he would have wounded me less. I turned my face towards the fire so he would not see my tears. "I have played the whore with no one. You can ask my sisters. I remained faithful to you, even when you left me vulnerable while you stayed imprisoned by your own stubbornness."

He pounded the table with his fist, "And now I am out of one prison and into another one. Perhaps I saved my life, or perhaps not. I doubt not that I failed to save my own soul."

❧ II ❧

Word spread immediately through the court that we were to remarry and in the intervening time, my waking hours were spent with Condé close by my side. Determined to show to the world that I was his, he accompanied me to every ball and event, not once allowing me to leave his side. I appealed to the Queen that I was failing in my duties to her, but mistaking my pleas for the false protestations of a bride in love, she only told me "Marie, you deserve to spend time with your husband. After your separation, it will do you good to get to know one another again."

I had worried that Anjou would take the opportunity to stroke Condé's jealousy by openly flirting with me or by a few well-placed poems, but I heard nothing from the prince. Perhaps I was right and his attention towards me was merely a ruse to stir up mischief against Condé and the Bourbons. Anjou's time was devoted to planning the New Year's siege of La Rochelle and I scarcely even saw him in the days before my second wedding.

The day of the ceremony dawned, cold and black as if Heaven itself voiced its objection to our second union. The Pope had readily sent his blessing for the ceremony and the Cardinal de Bourbon, our kinsman, was to perform the ceremony. Unlike our day in Blandy, there were a few of our lifelong friends in attendance and I carried none of my naïve hopefulness as I walked down the aisle. Looking back on that day, I believe that my husband's motivation for our remarriage was from a desire to exact his revenge upon Anjou, who was responsible for the death of my father-in-law and who had seized the title of Lieutenant General from the Condés.

A confident part of me stood at the altar, wishing that Anjou would appear suddenly to object to the ceremony. If he would not do it out of love for me, at least he would do it for spite. Anjou would twist the knife in the ultimate revenge upon both Princes of Condé. I convinced myself that if he did love me, Anjou would Save me from this fate. His silence would indicate that he did not love me, after all. I realize later what a ridiculous bargain I made with destiny and with God as I stood there, but I clung to any hope that I could back out of our marriage.

To my disappointment, however, no one voiced an objection to our vows, not even my sisters. I knew well what they both thought of Condé, but they sat behind me, silent as statues. When I heard only silence, I resolved to go ahead with the ceremony. Voicing my assent, more so than Navarre had at his ceremony to Margot, I, once again, became the wife of the Prince of Condé. If Anjou tried to catch my eye after the ceremony or during the banquet that evening, I pointedly ignored him. I realized that I had been holding my breath the past weeks, waiting for a declaration of love from him, yet he had artfully given no concrete demonstration of his feelings towards me. His words were simply hollow and meant to perfume the air between us. Not only was I twice-wed to a man I did not love, but I had also foolishly thought myself in love and during the ceremony I had the proof that my feelings were not reciprocated. At least I had my husband's wealth and title to comfort me. As we were now Catholics, he could not be barred from any further favors from the King. As a close friend and lady-in-waiting to the Queen, I would work with him to strengthen our position at court. If we could not be lovers, we would be partners.

We had little time to celebrate our renewed marriage, as

the King commenced a siege of La Rochelle in the bitter cold of December. If the King wished to strengthen his ties to the newly Catholic Bourbon princes, his decision to send them to wage war against their friends and allies was a curious way to do so. I would have thought that forcing them to attack the city would be the perfect excuse for both my husband and Navarre to defect, but apparently, the King was determined to force them to prove that their conversion was genuine. Denied the opportunity to spend time with my husband, I was also unable to move into the Hotel de Bourbon, which was my due as Princess de Condé. I remained at my sister's home as the guest of Henriette and her husband.

"Cheer up, Marie—at least you won't have the pressure of being a new bride on top of running a new household." Henriette's breath puffed in the stark light of the afternoon. Despite the cold, I was determined to walk outdoors and nothing that my older sister said could dissuade me. I was determined to be as obstinate as the rest of the court.

"How am I supposed to begin life, living on my family's charity and sitting in Paris, all but abandoned?" I could hear the self-pity in my voice, but I set my teeth in defiance. Hadn't I been through enough in the past few months?

"Think about it another way: with Henry gone, you have the opportunity to bend the King's ear without Condé's blunt manner souring things." My sister did have a point—my husband purposefully spoke in the most undiplomatic way possible.

"You're suggesting that I use my friendship with the Queen to our advantage?'

"Of course," her brown eyes sparked, "everyone does and you have an opportunity most wives would kill for—the ability to speak without a clumsy husband undoing your efforts."

I considered her words for a moment. My sister had spent more time at court than I and unlike me, she was not bogged down with the moralizing of the Navarrese court. At the thought, I instantly felt guilty. My aunt had taught me the best she knew, in line with her own principles. But here at the French court, I would need to use different tactics.

Before I could respond, a servant approached with a letter. He handed to the Henriette, who broke the seal open. Her eyes widened as she read. A few seconds later, she blushed. "Ah, this is for you, Marie. I suggest that you read it in private." She quickly folded the letter back into its envelope and slid it under my forearm, looking for all the world like a naughty school girl caught snooping.

"Fine, I'll read it later." I had no idea what kind of missive my husband has sent me, or what he planned to complain about, but I had no desire to read it immediately. Lost in my feelings of self-pity, a coughing fit overcame me and I was unable to stop it from shaking my body.

Henriette shot a look of disapproval. "See, I told you that going out in this cold, dry air was bad for your lungs."

I waved away her concern with my hand. "If I stay inside all day, I'll go mad. Do you want that—a madwoman sharing your home?'

She shrugged, "In this court, it would be a novelty."

WORD SPREAD IMMEDIATELY THROUGH THE COURT THAT CONDÉ AND I we were to remarry and in the intervening time, I spent my waking hours with Condé close by my side. Determined to show to the world I was his, he accompanied me to every ball and event, not once allowing me to leave his side. I appealed to the queen that I was failing in my duties to her, but mistaking my pleas for the false protestations of a bride in love, she only told me "Marie, you deserve to spend time with your husband. After your separation, it will do you good to get to know one another again."

I had worried that Anjou would take the opportunity to stroke Condé's jealousy by openly flirting with me or by a few well-placed poems, but I heard nothing from the prince. Perhaps I was right and his attention towards me was merely a ruse to stir up mischief against Condé and the Bourbons. Anjou devoted his time to planning the New Year's siege of La Rochelle and I scarcely even saw him in the days before my second wedding.

The day of the ceremony dawned, cold and black as if Heaven itself voiced its objection to our second union. The Pope had readily sent his blessing for the ceremony and the Cardinal de Bourbon, our kinsman, was to perform the ceremony. Unlike our day in Blandy, there were a few of our lifelong friends in attendance and I carried none of my naïve hopefulness as I walked down the aisle. Looking back on that day, I believe that my husband's motivation for our remarriage was from a desire to exact his revenge upon Anjou, who was responsible for the death of my father-in-law and who had seized the title of Lieutenant General from the Condés.

A confident part of me stood at the altar, wishing that Anjou would appear suddenly to object to the ceremony. If he would not do it out of love for me, at least he would do it for spite. Anjou would twist the knife in the ultimate revenge upon both Princes of Condé. I convinced myself that if he loved me, Anjou would save me from this fate. His silence would show that he did not love me, after all. I realize later what a ridiculous bargain I made with destiny and with God as I stood there, but I clung to any hope that I could back out of our marriage.

To my disappointment, however, no one voiced an objection to our vows, not even my sisters. I knew well what they both thought of Condé, but they sat behind me, silent as statues. When I heard only silence, I resolved to go ahead with the ceremony. Voicing my assent, more so than Navarre had at his ceremony to Margot, I, once again, became the wife of the Prince of Condé. If Anjou tried to catch my eye after the ceremony or during the banquet that evening, I pointedly ignored him. I realized that I had been holding my breath the past weeks, waiting for a declaration of love from him, yet he had artfully given no concrete demonstration of his feelings towards me. His words were hollow and meant to perfume the air between us. Not only was I twice-wed to a man I did not love, but I had also foolishly thought myself in love and during the ceremony I had the proof he did not reciprocate my feelings. At least I had my husband's wealth and title to comfort me. As we were now Catholics, he could not be barred from any further favors from the king. As a close friend and lady-in-waiting to the queen, I would work with him to strengthen our position at court. If we could not be lovers, we would be partners.

WE HAD LITTLE TIME TO CELEBRATE OUR RENEWED MARRIAGE ONCE the king started the siege of La Rochelle in the bitter cold of December. If the king wished to strengthen his ties to the newly Catholic Bourbon princes, his decision to send them to wage war against their friends and allies was a curious way to do so. I would have thought forcing them to attack the city would be the perfect excuse for both my husband and Navarre to defect, but apparently, the king wanted to force them to prove that their conversion was genuine. Denied the opportunity to spend time with my husband, I also could not move into the Hotel de Bourbon, which was my due as Princess de Condé. I remained at my sister's home as the guest of Henriette and her husband.

"Cheer up, Marie—at least you won't have the pressure of being a new bride on top of running a new household." Henriette's breath puffed in the stark light of the afternoon. Despite the cold, I wanted to walk outdoors and nothing that my older sister said could dissuade me. I could to be as obstinate as the rest of the court.

"How am I supposed to begin life, living on my family's charity and sitting in Paris, all but abandoned?" I could hear the self-pity in my voice, but I set my teeth in defiance. Hadn't I been through enough in the past few months?

"Think about it another way: with Henry gone, you have the opportunity to bend the king's ear without Condé's blunt manner souring things." My sister had a point—my husband purposefully spoke in the most undiplomatic way possible.

"You're suggesting that I use my friendship with the queen to our advantage?"

"Of course." Her brown eyes sparked, "Everyone does and you have an opportunity most wives would kill for—the ability to speak without a clumsy husband undoing your efforts."

I considered her words for a moment. My sister had spent more time at court than I and unlike me, she was not bogged down with the moralizing of the Navarrese court. At the thought, I instantly felt guilty. My aunt had taught me the best she knew, in line with her own principles. But here at the French court, I would need to use different tactics.

Before I could respond, a servant approached with a letter. He handed to the Henriette, who broke the seal open. Her eyes widened as she read. A few seconds later, she blushed. "Ah, this is for you, Marie. I suggest that you read it in private." She quickly folded the letter back into its envelope and slid it under my forearm, looking for all the world like a naughty schoolgirl caught snooping.

"Fine, I'll read it later." I could not imagine what kind of missive my husband has sent me, or what he planned to complain about, but I had no desire to read it immediately. Lost in my feelings of self-pity, a coughing fit overcame me and I could not stop it from shaking my body.

Henriette shot a look of disapproval. "See, I told you that going out in this cold, dry air was bad for your lungs."

I waved away her concern with my hand. "If I stay inside all day, I'll go mad. Do you want that—a madwoman sharing your home?"

She shrugged, "In this court, it would be a novelty."

❧ 12 ❧

The letter from La Rochelle sat on the table where I had thrown it earlier in the afternoon. It was not until I readied for bed that I remembered to look at it. The only thing worse than being cursed with an absent, quarrelsome husband was being cursed with a letter from that absent, quarrelsome husband. Suddenly, I longed for the moments when he seemed much further away from me. My shoulders sagged, and I allowed a long sigh to escape my lips as I opened the letter to read its contents.

The letter was not from my husband, after all. It was instead a love letter from the Duc d' Anjou. Anger burned within me as I read the letter which was filled with professions of his love for me and apologizing for his inability to stop my remarriage to Condé. He feared that I did not return his love, he wrote in the letter, and his feared his mother's wrath if he did try to break up my marriage.

Despite his fear, he continued, during the season of Advent, he could not stop himself from professing his true feelings for me. After reading the last line, I stood and crumpled the letter in my hand. A hearty fire blazed in my bedchamber and in my anger, I threw the letter into the fire. As the parchment blackened and crumpled, I felt a sense of self-satisfaction. Anjou had squandered his opportunity and I would not be tormented with declarations of love that came too late.

Determined to remove all thoughts of Anjou from my mind, I decided to take Henriette's advice and use my position at court to advance our own fortunes. In this, Henriette's proved to be a capable role model. Upon becoming my father's heir, she had inherited a large amount of our family's debt and through her shrewdness, had changed it into a substantial fortune. My title of Marquess d'Isles, given me at birth, came with it some property, but my father had done a poor job of managing it. With the Queen's intercession, I secured the King's help in collecting the rents due to me. By the time the New Year came, I was on my way to becoming a wealthy woman in my own right.

The week before Christmas, I received a letter from my husband, filled with his characteristic complaints and criticisms. The siege was going terribly, a fact that Anjou had tried desperately to hide from his brother, the King. Condé related with pride the ability of the populace of La Rochelle to withstand the bombardment from the Catholic army. I was glad to hear of their bravery, yet at the same time, I did not like his recklessness in sending such blunt reports to me. Beneath the pages of my husband's complaints, I noticed another page, written in a familiar hand. I held my breath as I read, but I laughed when I recognized my cousin Navarre's handwriting, thanking me profusely for the pairs of woolen hose I had packed for the both of them.

The winter raged on, bitterly cold and loath as I am to admit it, during those cold nights, I even missed my cold husband. The King granted an increase of my pay as a lady-in-waiting and the Queen and I visited the little Princess Elisabeth as often as possible. As the girl was not the heir to the French throne, there were few restrictions over her upbringing. Despite her reputation for stringently supervising her children's households, Catherine de Medici allowed her daughter-in-law to manage the princesses' household.

In February, the Queen and I sat, playing with the Princess, whose easygoing manner even managed to attract Queen Margot, who willingly played the part of a doting aunt. "Marie, have you heard from your husband?" Margot braced as her niece made a play for her diamond brooch.

"In his last letter, he stated that the siege would likely go on for months."

Margot sighed, "I guess then we will be forced to endure Paris on our own for much longer." Her joy in being left to her own devices was obvious. For my part, I was anxious to begin my marriage, no matter how ill-considered it had been. "I wish I could enjoy my freedom as much as you do, Madame. I think too much time in the Navarrese countryside made me needy for company."

Margot shuddered, "I don't know that I would long for the countryside of Navarre. After the French court, I likely would find it boring. Still," she glanced at Elisabeth, "it would be nice to spend some time as Queen for once."

"I would hate to see you go," a sigh escaped Elisabeth. "I'll still have Marie here for company, though."

Margot nodded, "It's likely, Sister, that we will be forced to enjoy Paris for many more months."

❧

THROUGH THOSE COLD MONTHS, I CARRIED A SECRET. I HAD BEGUN corresponding with Anjou, despite my initial anger in his letter at Christmastide. Loneliness finally wore at me and I gave into a girlish infatuation with the romantic Duc as he sent me love letters and poems that made my heart soar. Some letters came to me from La Rochelle, while others were apparently composed at court, featuring the same romantic imagery of Desportes. Unable to resist the flattery, I began responding to the Duc, once again, finding in him a confidant and ally.

Finally, in late April, as I returned from Mass, my sister Catherine met me and bowing her blonde head, whispered in my ear.

"Is it true that the Duc d'Anjou, and you have begun a friendship?" My furious blushing gave her all the response she needed.

"How did you know?"

She slowed our pace as we walked out of earshot of the rest of the court. "My husband told me that the Duc recently bragged that he planned to make you his lover. Have you given him any promises?"

I shook my head, "No, we only exchange letters." Deep, passionate letters that made my day when they arrived each morning.

"That is wise—while an affair is nothing at court, I would not advise you to stroke the anger of the Protestants. Their views of 'morality' are, shall we say, extreme?"

I rolled my eyes, "You needn't tell me that."

"Does Condé know about the Duc's letters?"

"If he does, he has not mentioned in his own letters. They are full of petty complaints as usual."

Catherine nodded, understanding my frustration with the dour Condé. "if the Duc returns soon, do you plan to do something to deepen your relationship?"

That was what ate at me. While part of me wanted to explore the passion the Duc offered, still I worried what the decision to enter into an affair would cost me. "What do you advise?"

She smiled, "Henriette and I can give you pointers of managing a jealous husband and a passionate lover. And in your case, your lover will one day become King of France. You could not reach higher. I suggest that you continue to encourage the Duc in his affections." True, my sisters had grown up in the French court, while I was still trying to make my way within it. With my husband constantly enumerating his complaints, it would be wise for us to cultivate a friend within the Valois family. Besides, my heart fluttered at the idea of starting a relationship with the dashing and romantic prince.

Henriette, in particular, proved to be willing to help me in my long distance relationship with Anjou. In those early days of our friendship, I had not made up my mind how far I was willing to allow our interactions to go and I convinced myself that by sheer will, I could resist his physical advances. I suppose it was arrogance, but part of me thought myself morally superior to those who had grown up in the Valois court. I suppose it was an echo of my Aunt Jeanne's teachings. Still, watching several other women fall prey to their attractions to men to whom they were not wed made it easy for me to do the same thing.

Anjou and I fell into an easy pattern, his letters arriving alongside those of my husband's. Convincing myself that I was being somewhat loyal to Condé, I read his dour letters first and after enduring them, I cheered myself up with those from Anjou. At Henriette's suggestion, Anjou addressed his letters to her, the official explanation being Anjou's constant need for loans from my wealthy sister. While Henriette was more than willing to keep Anjou in her debt, even an impoverished Valois prince would not possibly need the amounts that would require the volume of letters that came to the Hotel de Nevers. Eventually, even with Henriette's help, the court learned of our relationship.

❦

I CONSTANTLY READIED MYSELF TO DEFEND MY FLIRTATION WITH Anjou. We had exchanged mere words, after all, and the court could only accuse us of a passing infatuation. My words to Anjou were measured, hardly the proof of adultery. Even I was appalled, however, at how casually the court looked at our relationship. If anything, it seemed as if most of the nobles supported it. For one thing, Anjou was the Dauphin, likely to inherit the throne as Queen Elisabeth continued to fail in producing an heir. Her misery could be to my advantage and it was only the idea of giving her heartache that caused me to feel guilt in my relationship with Anjou. No one wished to deny the next King of France what he wanted, particularly a King who held Catherine's de Medici in his youthful palm.

Perhaps it was simply that we slipped into the morass of illicit behavior around us. Each week there was a new scandalous relationship and most of them were more illicit than ours. We could not provide the court with jealous screaming as we were stationed on opposite corners of the kingdom. Any angry or jealous words would have to wait until the siege of La Rochelle was over.

In mid-March, Catherine called me to her private apartment, where I dreaded the dressing down I would receive for my conduct with her favorite son. As I curtsied low, memories of the accusations of witchcraft and debauchery Aunt Jeanne had hurled at this formidable woman swirled in my head.

"I am told, Madame Condé, that you enjoy a close friendship with my son, Henri. Is that so?"

My mouth felt thick; many had walked unwarily into the spider web that Catherine wove. My next words would likely determine the rest of my short life.

"His Highness has been kind to me since my conversion to the Catholic church. I am grateful to his and your kindness this past few months." With any luck, throwing myself at her mercy would soften whatever punishment she had in mind for me.

She paced the room, as if lost in thought. "I must say, your sincerity is a model for your husband. It is sad that Condé seems to treasure his soul so lightly."

"His sincerity was to the Reformed faith; it would seem." What was the point in lying to the Queen Mother of France? She knew more than most that my husband came to his conversion virtually at the point of a sword.

"My son writes to me daily," the Queen deftly turned the topic of conversation. Although I was grateful that I would not have to defend my husband further, I knew that the time for a lecture and warning had finally arrived. I held my breath as she continued.

"He tells me that the rigors of war are wearing on his soul. Quite the soldier, my Edouard Alexandre," her voice took on a dreamy quality. "Yet he says that your letters buoy his spirits on a daily basis." At his compliment, I smiled and quickly tried to hide it.

"I see you enjoy speaking with my son, is that not so?"

"Other than my sisters and the Queen, I have few friends here at court. Any friendly face is a comfort to me." I would continue to be honest with her. Too many unwary men and women had fallen into the spider's trap, weaving their way to their death before they were aware that they were in trouble. I would be smarter than that.

"I must say, I am not thrilled at the idea of my son conversing with a married woman. As you know, I deplore immorality in my court."

Her last statement stretched credulity. Catherine de Medici was well known for demanding an outer facade of morality while employing members of her Flying Squadron to seduce any man Catherine deemed a threat to her. My father-in-law had fallen prey to her ladies, yet Catherine would happily deny that she employed a spy network at all. This fluid morality was the duplicity of the French court at work. Was I seconds away from walking into a trap?

"Madame, The Duc and I have a friendship that is as chaste as the one I enjoy with the Queen. Neither of us is guilty of infidelity or any other kind of immorality. When compared with other members of the court, The Duc and I are practically as innocent as babes. I was under the impression that Renee de Rioux was His Highnesses' paramour, not I."

At the mention of the woman who had openly and wantonly thrown herself at her favorite son, the Queen Mother bristled. "The woman's lack of discretion led to her decision to return to the country."

"I would also add, Madame, that the Duc has initiated all of our meetings, not I. I can assure you that I am not a huntress out to snag a royal prey. As with my service to your daughter-in-law, I am ever willing to render my respect to the Valois family."

Had I gone too far? Would Catherine think that my last words were impertinent? I had no idea why I said them, other than weariness from the months of accusations from the members of the court. Defensiveness made me bold, I suppose. On the other hand, I had spoken the truth when I said that neither of us had committed any sin against my wedding vows. Still, given the Queen Mother's reputation, I stood quietly until she decided to respond.

Several minutes passed. Catherine rubbed her chin, ruminating over everything that I had said. Suddenly, she shot to her feet, and I rose to mine in deference to her station. "My son has assured me that his feelings for you are pure and that you are the most chaste of women in France. It is his wish that I keep an eye out for you while you are at court. With your mother and your beloved aunt gone," she crossed herself twice, and I hastened to do likewise," the court can be a dangerous place."

The suspicious woman was gone, replaced by one who more closely resembled a maiden aunt. I had passed a test with Catherine de Medici, but what that test might be, escaped me.

Eschewing a coach, I walked back from the Tuileries to the Hotel Nevers, turning over what had just happened before my eyes. That the Queen Mother had given her blessing for me to continue my correspondence was shocking enough. What was almost beyond my belief was the fact that I had stood my ground before the most powerful woman in France. Apparently, the months alone and without my husband had done some good for me.

Before I realized it, I was standing in the courtyard of my sister's massive home, a stone bench before me. Taking a seat on the bench, I began to formulate a plan. With Condé halfway across the kingdom, he was hardly in a position to stop me. I knew my sisters well enough to know that they would support me. As Catherine had told me months ago, I was in a unique position to further the Cleves and Condé fortunes.

Lost in my thoughts, I barely heard the shouting behind me. "What on earth are you doing out here in the cold? You'll harm your lungs, you silly creature!" Henriette rushed towards me, a gray cloak in her hands. I blinked up at her, an apparition complete with curly blonde hair waving in the Spring wind as she ran. Henriette rarely ran; she mostly glided from ballroom to ballroom. I started to giggle at her, thinking that perhaps my sister was right and I was mad.

She threw the cloak across my shoulders and began tucking it in as if swaddling one of her children. Clucking her disapproval, she tried to pull me inside.

"I need your help," I murmured.

"Yes, you do, you ignorant girl!" She pulled me to my feet and began dragging me inside. Had I spent more time with an older sister, I probably would have rebelled, resentful at being bossed around. Instead, I found it touching. She continued to chide and lecture me as she pulled me into my antechamber. Once she had me inside, she began rubbing my hands and arms as if to warm me.

"Thank God—you aren't as cold as I'd thought. Did you walk all the way from the Tuileries?" As she spoke, she shook her blonde curls even further askew, and I was unable to keep from laughing at her comical appearance.

"Yes, I did. And it's not that cold out, even for April. I've just come from meeting with the Queen Mother."

She expelled a long sigh and took a seat before me. "And what did Catherine say?"

"She gave me her permission to continue corresponding with Anjou."

Her eyebrows shot up. I really must find a way to keep laughing at my eldest sister, but she was making things difficult for me. "Really? Margot told me that she was hard at work getting a Swedish princess for him. I would think that she would be determined to wipe away any trace of scandal."

"Maybe what I told her convinced her that I was not a disgrace." I stood and began to pace the room. Henriette's took my shoulders and shoved me down to a sitting position, determined to make me sit down.

"I would think that Anjou has Catherine in quite a bind. She can never say no to him, no matter how outrageous his behavior. It's more likely that he told her in no uncertain terms that he will have you as his mistress and there is nothing that she can do to stand in his way."

"She would agree to that?"

"He is the Dauphin. He is also the only child that she has been unable to rule. Even Margot is afraid to defy her sometimes. If Catherine alienates her favorite, and he becomes King, she will lose her position as the power behind the throne. So what will you do?"

That was easy, now that I had made my decision. "Since I have spent so many months having to bear the ill effects of gossip that I am the Duc's mistress, I think that I will start to reap the rewards of being his lover."

She cocked her head to the side, "Are you the kind of woman to spend her evenings in another man's bed?"

"I don't know." It was true; I had never considered going through with it. But with Anjou also halfway across France, there was no bed into which to hop. "I could just encourage his feelings and when we see one another, there may not be any feelings. Then our relationship will be as chaste as ever."

Henriette broke into a laugh, "Good God, sister—you're even more devious than I am. I hadn't thought of that."

"The court has forced me to this, branding me a courtesan when I've done nothing. As the Dauphin's mistress, I would be able to control who has access to him and who gets the favors given to the nobility. If he were to become King," I choked at the idea, realizing that if he were to ascend to the throne, Elisabeth would lose her station. She would most likely return to Austria, perhaps to a second marriage.

She grabbed my hand, "Charles has been sickly since birth. His lungs aren't strong, and if he dies without an heir, that is entirely out of your hands. Elisabeth knows this and I doubt that she'll resent you for taking her place. She would hardly begrudge you for taking Marie Touchet's place."

I rolled my eyes to heaven at the name of the King's mistress. At any moment, the woman would give birth to the King's second child and if it were a boy, it would give Elisabeth more heartbreak than my affair with Anjou would. Still, I had no desire to add to her misery.

"You said you needed my help, Dearest. What do you need from me?" The big sister was back, and she searched my face.

"I would love it if you would hold some salons here at the Hotel. Be sure to invite as many members of the court as possible."

Henriette burst into laughter. "I'll speak to Margot and the Duchess de Retz. We'll throw the most dazzling salons that Paris has ever seen."

THE LETTER FROM LA ROCHELLE SAT ON THE TABLE WHERE I HAD thrown it earlier in the afternoon. It was not until I readied for bed I remembered to look at it. The only thing worse than being cursed with an absent, quarrelsome husband was being cursed with a letter from that absent, quarrelsome husband. Suddenly, I longed for the moments when he seemed much further away from me. My shoulders sagged, and I allowed a long sigh to escape my lips as I opened the letter to read its contents.

The letter was not from my husband. It was instead a love letter from the Duc d' Anjou. Anger burned within me as I read the letter filled with professions of his love for me and apologizing for his inability to stop my remarriage to Condé. He feared that I did not return his love; he wrote in the letter, and his feared his mother's wrath if he tried to break up my marriage.

Despite his fear, he continued, during the season of Advent, he could not stop himself from professing his true feelings for me. After reading the last line, I stood and crumpled the letter in my hand. A hearty fire blazed in my bedchamber and in my anger, I threw the letter into the fire. As the parchment blackened and crumpled, I felt a sense of self-satisfaction. Anjou had squandered his opportunity and he would not torment me with declarations of love that came too late.

Determined to remove all thoughts of Anjou from my mind, I took Henriette's advice and use my position at court to advance our own fortunes. In this, Henriette's proved to be a capable role model. Upon becoming my father's heir, she had inherited a large amount of our family's debt and through her shrewdness, had changed it into a substantial fortune. My title of Marquess d'Isles, given me at birth, came with it some property, but my father had done a poor job of managing it. With the Queen's intercession, I secured the king's help in collecting the rents due to me. By the time the New Year came, I was on my way to becoming a wealthy woman in my own right.

The week before Christmas, I received a letter from my husband, filled with his characteristic complaints and criticisms. The siege was going terribly, a fact that Anjou had tried desperately to hide from his brother, the king. Condé related with pride the ability of the populace of La Rochelle to withstand the bombardment from the Catholic army. I was glad to hear of their bravery, yet I did not like his recklessness in sending such blunt reports. Beneath the pages of my husband's complaints, I noticed another page, written in a familiar hand. I held my breath as I read, but I laughed when I recognized my cousin Navarre's handwriting, thanking me profusely for the pairs of woolen hose I had packed for the both of them.

The winter raged on, bitterly cold and loath as I am to admit it, during those cold nights, I even missed my cold husband. The king granted an increase of my pay as a lady-in-waiting and the queen and I visited the little Princess Elisabeth as often as possible. As the girl was not the heir to the French throne, there were few restrictions over her upbringing. Despite her reputation for stringently supervising her children's households, Catherine de Medici allowed her daughter-in-law to manage the princesses' household.

In February, the queen and I sat, playing with the baby Princess, whose easygoing manner even attracted Queen Margot, who willingly played the part of a doting aunt. "Marie, have you heard from your husband?" Margot braced as her niece made a play for her diamond brooch.

"In his last letter, he stated that the siege would likely go on for months."

Margot sighed, "I guess then we will have to endure Paris on our own for much longer." Her joy in being left to her own devices was obvious. I was eager to begin my marriage, no matter how ill-considered it had been. "I wish I could enjoy my freedom as much as you do, Madame. I think too much time in the Navarrese countryside made me needy for company."

Margot shuddered, "I don't know that I would long for the countryside of Navarre. After the French court, I likely would find it boring. Still," she glanced at Elisabeth, "it would be nice to spend time as queen for once."

"I would hate to see you go," a sigh escaped Elisabeth. "I'll still have Marie here for company, though."

Margot nodded, "It's likely, Sister, that it will force us to enjoy Paris for many more months."

THROUGH THOSE COLD MONTHS, I CARRIED A SECRET. I corresponded with Anjou, despite my initial anger in his letter at Christmastide. Loneliness finally wore at me and I gave into a girlish infatuation with the romantic Duc as he sent me love letters and poems that made my heart soar. Some letters came from La Rochelle, while others were composed at court, featuring the same romantic imagery of Desportes. Unable to resist the flattery, I responded to the Duc, once again, finding in him a confidant and ally.

Finally, in late April, as I returned from Mass, my sister Catherine met me and bowing her blonde head, whispered in my ear.

"Is it true that the Duc d'Anjou, and you have begun a friendship?" My furious blushing gave her all the response she needed.

"How did you know?"

She slowed our pace as we walked out of earshot of the rest of the court. "My husband told me that the Duc recently bragged that he planned to make you his lover. Have you given him any promises?"

I shook my head, "No, we only exchange letters." Deep, passionate letters that made my day when they arrived each morning.

"That is wise—while an affair is nothing at court, I would not advise you to stroke the anger of the Protestants. Their views of 'morality' are, shall we say, extreme?"

I rolled my eyes, "You needn't tell me that."

"Does Condé know about the Duc's letters?"

"If he does, he has not mentioned in his own letters. They are full of petty complaints as usual."

Catherine nodded, understanding my frustration with the dour Condé. "if the Duc returns soon, do you plan to do something to deepen your relationship?"

That was what ate at me. While part of me wanted to explore the passion the Duc offered, still I worried what the decision to enter into an affair would cost me. "What do you advise?"

She smiled, "Henriette and I can give you pointers of managing a jealous husband and a passionate lover. And in your case, your lover will one day become King of France. You could not reach higher. I suggest that you continue to encourage the Duc in his affections." True, my sisters had grown up in the French court, while I was still trying to make my way within it. With my husband constantly enumerating his complaints, it would be wise for us to cultivate a friend within the Valois family. Besides, my heart fluttered at starting a relationship with the dashing and romantic prince.

Henriette, in particular, helped me in my long distance relationship with Anjou. In those early days of our friendship, I had not decided how far I was willing to allow our interactions to go and I convinced myself that by sheer will, I could resist his physical advances. I suppose it was arrogance, but part of me thought myself morally superior to those who had grown up in the Valois court. I suppose it was an echo of my Aunt Jeanne's teachings. Still, watching several other women fall prey to their attractions to men to whom they were not wed made it easy for me to do the same thing.

Anjou and I fell into an easy pattern, his letters arriving alongside those of my husband's. Convincing myself that I was being loyal to Condé, I read his dour letters first and after enduring them; I cheered myself up with those from Anjou. At Henriette's suggestion, Anjou addressed his letters to her, the official explanation being Anjou's constant need for loans from my wealthy sister. While Henriette was more than willing to keep Anjou in her debt, even an impoverished Valois prince would not possibly need the amounts that would require the volume of letters that came to the Hotel de Nevers. Eventually, even with Henriette's help, the court learned of our relationship.

I CONSTANTLY READIED MYSELF TO DEFEND MY FLIRTATION WITH Anjou. We had exchanged mere words, and the court could only accuse us of a passing infatuation. I measured my words, hardly the proof of adultery. Even I was appalled, however, at how casually the court looked at our relationship. It seemed as if most of the nobles supported it. Anjou was the Dauphin, likely to inherit the throne as Queen Elisabeth continued to fail in producing an heir. Her misery could be to my advantage and it was only the thought of causing her heartache that caused me to feel guilt in my relationship with Anjou. No one wished to deny the next King of France what he wanted, particularly a king who held Catherine's de Medici in his youthful palm.

Perhaps it was simply that we slipped into the morass of illicit behavior around us. Each week there was a new scandalous relationship and most of them were more illicit than ours. We could not provide the court with delicious scenes of jealous screaming. They stationed us on opposite corners of the kingdom. Any angry or jealous words would have to wait until the siege of La Rochelle was over.

In mid-March, Catherine called me to her private apartment, where I dreaded the dressing down I would receive for my conduct with her favorite son. As I curtsied low, memories of the accusations of witchcraft and debauchery Aunt Jeanne had hurled at this formidable woman swirled in my head.

"I am told, Madame Condé, that you enjoy a close friendship with my son, Henri. Is that so?"

My mouth felt thick; many had walked unwarily into the spider web that Catherine wove. My next words would likely determine the rest of my short life.

"His Highness has been kind since my conversion to the Catholic church. I am grateful to his and your kindness this past few months." With any luck, throwing myself at her mercy would soften whatever punishment she had in mind for me.

She paced the room, as if lost in thought. "Your sincerity is a model for your husband. It is sad that Condé seems to treasure his soul so lightly."

"His sincerity was to the Reformed faith; it would seem." What was the point in lying to the Queen Mother of France? She knew more than most that my husband came to his conversion virtually at the point of a sword.

"My son writes me daily," the queen deftly turned conversation. Although I was grateful that I would not have to defend my husband further, I knew that the time for a lecture and warning had finally arrived. I held my breath as she continued.

"He tells me that the rigors of war are wearing on his soul. Quite the soldier, my Edouard Alexandre," her voice took on a dreamy quality. "Yet he says your letters buoy his spirits every day." At his compliment, I smiled and quickly tried to hide it.

"I see you enjoy speaking with my son, is that not so?"

"Other than my sisters and the queen, I have few friends here at court. Any friendly face is a comfort to me." I would continue to be honest with her. Too many unwary men and women had fallen into the spider's trap, weaving their way to their death before they knew that they were in trouble. I would be smarter than that.

"I must say, I am not thrilled at the idea of my son conversing with a married woman. As you know, I deplore immorality in my court."

Her last statement stretched credulity. Catherine de Medici was famous for demanding an outer facade of morality while using members of her Flying Squadron to seduce any man Catherine deemed a threat to her. My father-in-law had fallen prey to her ladies, yet Catherine would happily deny that she used a spy network at all. This fluid morality was the duplicity of the French court at work. Was I seconds away from walking into a trap?

"Madame, The Duc and I have a friendship that is as chaste as the one I enjoy with the queen. Neither of us is guilty of infidelity or any other kind of immorality. When compared with other members of the court, The Duc and I are practically as innocent as babes. I thought Renee de Rioux was His Highnesses' paramour, not I."

At the mention of the woman who had openly and wantonly thrown herself at her favorite son, the Queen Mother bristled. "The woman's lack of discretion led to her decision to return to the country."

"I would also add, Madame, that the Duc has started all of our meetings, not I. I am not a huntress out to snag a royal prey. As with my service to your daughter-in-law, I am ever willing to render my respect to the Valois family."

Had I gone too far? Would Catherine think my last words were impertinent? I did not understand why I said them, other than weariness from the months of accusations from the members of the court. Defensiveness made me bold, I suppose. On the other hand, I had spoken the truth when I said neither of us had committed any sin against my wedding vows. Still, given the Queen Mother's reputation, I stood quietly until she responded.

Several minutes passed. Catherine rubbed her chin, ruminating over everything I had said. Suddenly, she shot to her feet, and I rose to mine in deference to her station. "My son has assured me that his feelings for you are pure and that you are the most chaste of women in France. He hopes that I keep an eye out for you while you are at court. With your mother and your beloved aunt gone," she crossed herself twice, and I hastened to do likewise," the court can be a dangerous place."

The suspicious woman disappeared, replaced by one who more closely resembled a maiden aunt. I had passed a test with Catherine de Medici, but what that test might involve escaped me.

Eschewing a coach, I walked back from the Tuileries to the Hotel Nevers, turning over what had just happened before my eyes. That the Queen Mother had given her blessing for me to continue my correspondence was shocking enough. What was almost beyond my belief was the knowledge I had stood my ground before the most powerful woman in France. Apparently, the months alone and without my husband had done some good for me.

Before I realized it, I was standing in the courtyard of my sister's massive home, a stone bench before me. Taking a seat on the bench, I formulated a plan. With Condé halfway across the kingdom, he was hardly in a position to stop me. I knew my sisters well enough to know that they would support me. As Catherine had told me months ago, I was in a unique position to further the Cleves and Condé fortunes.

Lost in my thoughts, I barely heard the shouting behind me. "What on earth are you doing out here in the cold? You'll harm your lungs, you silly creature!" Henriette rushed towards me, a gray cloak in her hands. I blinked up at her, an apparition complete with curly blonde hair waving in the Spring wind as she ran. Henriette rarely ran; she mostly glided from ballroom to ballroom. I giggled at her, thinking perhaps my sister was right and I was mad.

She threw the cloak across my shoulders and tucked it in as if swaddling one of her children. Clucking her disapproval, she tried to pull me inside.

"I need your help," I murmured.

"Yes, you do, you ignorant girl!" She pulled me to my feet and dragged me inside. Had I spent more time with an older sister, I probably would have rebelled, resentful at being bossed around. Instead, I found it touching. She continued to chide and lecture me as she pulled me into my antechamber. Once she had me inside, she rubbed my hands and arms as if to warm me.

"Thank God—you aren't as cold as I'd thought. Did you walk all the way from the Tuileries?" As she spoke, she shook her blonde curls even further askew, and I could not keep from laughing at her comical appearance.

"Yes, I did. And it's not that cold out, even for April. I've just come from a meeting with the Queen Mother."

She expelled a long sigh and took a seat before me. "And what did Catherine say?"

"She gave me her permission to continue corresponding with Anjou."

Her eyebrows shot up. I really must find a way to keep laughing at my eldest sister, but she was making things difficult for me. "Really? Margot told me she was hard at work getting a Swedish princess for him. I would think she wanted to wipe away any trace of scandal."

"Maybe what I told her convinced her I was not a disgrace." I stood and paced the room. Henriette's took my shoulders and shoved me down to a sitting position, determined to make me sit down.

"I would think Anjou has Catherine in quite a bind. She can never say no to him, no matter how outrageous his behavior. It's more likely that he told her in no uncertain terms he will have you as his mistress and there is nothing she can do to stand in his way."

"She would agree to that?"

"He is the Dauphin. He is also the only child she could not rule. Even Margot is afraid to defy her sometimes. If Catherine alienates her favorite, and he becomes king, she will lose her position as the power behind the throne. So what will you do?"

That was easy, now I had made my decision. "Since I have spent so many months having to bear the ill effects of gossip I am the Duc's mistress, I think I will reap the rewards of being his lover."

She cocked her head to the side, "Are you the kind of woman who spends her evenings in another man's bed?"

"I don't know." It was true; I had never considered going through with it. But with Anjou also halfway across France, there was no bed into which to hop. "I could just encourage his feelings and when we see one another, there may not be any feelings. Then our relationship will be as chaste as ever."

Henriette broke into a laugh, "Good God, sister—you're even more devious than I am. I hadn't thought of that."

"The court has forced me to this, branding me a courtesan when I've done nothing. As the Dauphin's mistress, I could control who has access to him and who gets the favors given to the nobility. If he were to become king," I choked at the idea, realizing that if he were to ascend to the throne, Elisabeth would lose her station. She would most likely return to Austria, perhaps to a second marriage.

She grabbed my hand, "Charles has been sickly since birth. His lungs aren't strong, and if he dies without an heir, that is entirely out of your hands. Elisabeth knows this and I doubt that she'll resent you for taking her place. She would hardly begrudge you for taking Marie Touchet's place."

I rolled my eyes to heaven at the name of the king's mistress. At any moment, the woman would give birth to the king's second child and if it were a boy, it would give Elisabeth more heartbreak than my affair with Anjou would. Still, I had no desire to add to her misery.

"You said you needed my help, Dearest. What do you need from me?" The big sister was back, and she searched my face.

"I would love it if you would hold salons here at the Hotel. Be sure to invite as many members of the court as possible."

Henriette burst into laughter. "I'll speak to Margot and the Duchesse de Retz. We'll throw the most dazzling salons that Paris has ever seen."

❧ 13 ❧

As I had assumed, the gossips were more than willing to attend yet another salon thrown by Margot and the Duchess de Nevers. Unlike me, Henriette's husband, Louis was more than prepared to allow the court to roam the halls of his home. A consummate politician and a pragmatist, Louis knew that a well-connected and popular wife meant advancement that constant warfare could hardly bring to their family. Unlike warfare, most of the combatants in the salons survived until the next morning.

The Queen Mother's tacit approval of my relationship with Anjou led to an immediate rise in my status. I quickly gained new "friends" at court and with their dubious friendship came more influence at court. Although the King rallied in late Spring, the court followed the fickle winds of power. The Dauphin was in the ascendency and to curry his favor, one must go through me.

One evening, at a banquet given for the Polish envoys, Catherine clucked over me as if I were one of her children. Henriette took my elbow and led me to an alcove. "She is worried about losing his love and since you have it, keeping you happy is the key to keeping him in her hands."

"She has to be scared of you as well." Catherine gave Henriette a glass of wine. "They've started calling Marie "Reinette.'" *The Little Queen*, now the court looked to me as the leader of the French court. They had called Mary of Scots that when she and Francis II came to the throne. A throne that the Guise family controlled. Was it a sly reference to my sister, the Duchess of Guise? Was I said to be in the employ of the Duc de Guise?

❦

THREE DAYS LATER, I SAT AT THE SIDE OF THE QUEEN MOTHER. THE three matrons accompanying us made us the picture of domesticity, a young girl and her three aunts. As the days passed, Catherine took to treating me more and more like her child. I had no shame in basking in her attention. I was starting to enjoy the power and the immunity that came from her favor. It was a pleasant surprise to find that far from the fire-breathing dragon I had imagined from my aunt that the Queen Mother was instead inclined to be a maternal figure. I started to think of myself as her surrogate child. Perhaps it was easy to do so because I had been the same to my Aunt Jeanne years earlier.

A page appeared at the doorway. "Forgive me, Majesty. An important message from the Polish court." Startled at the news, Catherine dropped the embroidery in her hands. She opened the letter and read quickly. "Get my secretary at once!"

Alarmed, I looked at her face, afraid that something had happened in La Rochelle. Instead of fear, her face beamed. As Catherine's private secretary scurried in with a paper in hand, she clasped her hands together. "It has happened! Nostradamus' prediction has come true! Three crowns for the house of Valois!"

I understood her immediately; the Duc d'Anjou was the new King of Poland.

❦

MY HEART THRUMMED IN MY CHEST AS I STOOD IN THE COURTYARD of the Chateau de Blois. The heat of early July beat down on the lords and ladies assembled that morning, but I cared little about the heat. The Queen Mother stood in front of the group, clasping her hands and craning her neck in the most un-royal fashion. She cared little for decorum; her beloved son, the Duc d' Anjou was finally coming home from La Rochelle to take his place on the throne of Poland. The King had bowed to his mother's wishes and hastily signed a peace accord with the Protestant armies to bring his brother home that much sooner. As the drums and trumpets sounded, we knew that Catherine's work had finally come to fruition.

"Thank God! Thank God and the Holy Virgin, he is home!" I half expected her to jump and clap her hands in glee, but she curbed her enthusiastic behavior before doing so. The gates flew open, and Anjou, at the head of a large and weather-beaten army, rode into the courtyard on a white horse.

"He never does anything halfway, does he?" The King shifted, impatient to get the ceremony over with a soon as possible. The haste with which he arranged the peace was not due completely to his desire to please the Queen Mother. The rivalry between the King and his flamboyant younger brother would resume with Anjou's return to court. The sooner the King delivered the King of Poland to the Poles and out of France's, the happier he would be. Before he could do that, however, he would have to endure his brother's triumphant return.

Drawing his mount directly in front of his mother, Anjou leaped off of his saddle and raced towards his mother. The two embraced, Catherine kissing her son's hands. She cooed loving words to him, oblivious to the rest of the court standing nearby. As the two continued with their private reunion made awkwardly public, the rest of us began to shuffle our feet awkwardly as the King had done moments before.

"Brother, I assume you will want to begin preparations for your trip to Poland?" I heard a barely concealed snort behind me. The King was more anxious to rid himself of his brother than we had thought.

Anjou turned from his emotional mother to face his older brother. Waving his hand, he chuckled, "I still have the dirt of the road on me. And the army," he gestured to the exhausted men behind him, "will need to be taken care of before I go." Striding past the King, whose face had started to redden, he pulled his mother to the side of the assembled crowd.

With Anjou greeted, attention turned to the rest of the men who had entered the courtyard. The awkwardness of the royal brothers was palatable, so it was a relief when Navarre stepped forward and bowed to the King. "It's nice to see the beauty of the Loire again." He bowed to Margot, who barely acknowledged him. Then he turned to wink at me, "there is much to be missed at the French court."

I blushed so furiously that I could hardly meet my cousin's eye. I knew that he was merely teasing me, yet his flirtatious remark made me uncomfortable. Against my will, I began to search for my husband. I found him inspecting a horseshoe with his long-time page. Determined to rid myself of the feelings of embarrassment, I threaded my way past the men.

"Henry, are you all right?" Our meeting would be awkward, no matter how it occurred. I would take the initiative and break the ice between us.

"As well as can be expected." He glowered at Anjou, whose back was turned to us as he accepted the congratulations of the court.

"I can't imagine what it was like, having to go back there; and as the aggressor."

"It was part of the devil's bargain that we made, remember? The one you suggested that I make?" I bit my tongue, determined to avoid getting into an argument with him in front of the entire court. I had hoped that we could reunite and display some level of civility towards one another, but my husband was just as intransigent as always.

I glanced over at my sister, Catherine, who was deep in conversation with her husband, the Duc de Guise. Their marriage was just as strained as ours was, but I was jealous of their ability to put their animosity aside to discuss business. The Guise stuck together as a united front, something that we Bourbons had yet to learn.

Catherine caught my eye and shot me a sympathetic look. I felt an overwhelming desire to grab my older sister and hide under her skirts. Had I been years younger, I would have done so. I was a grown woman, however, and a wife and I did not have the option of hiding from my problems.

A long sigh escaped me and at the sound, Condé turned to look at me with a puzzled look. "You look unhappy, wife. I can't imagine why, since your dear friend, Anjou has been returned to you."

"My husband has been returned to me as well." I hissed in his ear, unwilling to let anyone hear our conversation. How my husband could manage to get my anger up so quickly was beyond me. "Now I would like to return home and begin our lives together."

Condé shot another angry look at Anjou, who was still oblivious to him. "Our household may be a little crowded. Is there even room for me?"

There was no chance that I could keep my cool had I remained standing next to him. I stalked off from him and headed towards Queen Elisabeth. "Madame, if you'll excuse me, I need to return to my apartments."

Perceptive as always, Elisabeth squeezed my hand and looked me directly in the eye. "Marie, I think that heat has gotten to you. I order you to lie down until you feel better." With her permission, I walked into the chateau, willing myself to walk as slowly as possible so that no one could detect my anger. I would have to deal with my husband's childish taunts later when I managed to regain my senses. We were off to a terrible start, indeed.

As I HAD ASSUMED, THE GOSSIPS WERE MORE THAN WILLING TO attend yet another salon thrown by Margot and the Duchesse de Nevers. Unlike me, Henriette's husband, Louis was more than prepared to allow the court to roam the halls of his home. A consummate politician and a pragmatist, Louis knew that a well-connected and popular wife meant advancement that constant warfare could hardly bring to their family. Unlike warfare, most of the combatants in the salons survived until the next morning.

The Queen Mother's tacit approval of my relationship with Anjou led to an immediate rise in my status. I quickly gained new "friends" at court and with their dubious friendship came more influence at court. Although the king rallied in late Spring, the court followed the fickle winds of power. The Dauphin was in the ascendency and to curry his favor, one must go through me.

One evening, at a banquet given for the Polish envoys, Catherine clucked over me as if I were one of her children. Henriette took my elbow and led me to an alcove. "She is worried about losing his love and since you have it, keeping you happy is the key to keeping him in her hands."

"She has to fear you." Catherine gave Henriette a glass of wine. "They've started calling Marie 'Reinette.'" *The Little Queen*, now the court looked to me as the leader of the French court. They had called Mary of Scots that when she and Francis II came to the throne. A throne that the Guise family controlled. Was it a sly reference to my sister, the Duchesse of Guise? Was I said to be in the employ of the Duc de Guise?

◎◇◎

THREE DAYS LATER, I SAT AT THE SIDE OF THE QUEEN MOTHER. THE three matrons accompanying us made us the picture of domesticity, a young girl and her three aunts. As the days passed, Catherine treated me more and more like her child. I had no shame in basking in her attention. I was enjoying the power and the immunity that came from her favor. It was a pleasant surprise to find that far from the fire-breathing dragon I had imagined from my aunt that the Queen Mother was a maternal figure. As time passed, I started to think of myself as her surrogate child. Perhaps it was easy to do so because I had been the same to my Aunt Jeanne years earlier.

A page appeared at the doorway. "Forgive me, Majesty. An important message from the Polish court." Startled at the news, Catherine dropped the embroidery in her hands. She opened the letter and read quickly. "Get my secretary at once!"

Alarmed, I looked at her face, afraid that something had happened in La Rochelle. Instead of fear, her face beamed. As Catherine's private secretary scurried in with a paper in hand, she clasped her hands together. "It has happened! Nostradamus' prediction has come true! Three crowns for the house of Valois!"

I understood her immediately; the Duc d'Anjou was the new King of Poland.

❦

My heart thrummed in my chest as I stood in the courtyard of the Chateau de Blois. The heat of early July beat down on the lords and ladies assembled that morning, but I cared little about the heat. The Queen Mother stood in front of the group, clasping her hands and craning her neck in the most un-royal fashion. She cared little for decorum; her beloved son, the Duc d' Anjou was finally coming home from La Rochelle to take his place on the throne of Poland. The king had bowed to his mother's wishes and hastily signed a peace accord with the Protestant armies to bring his brother home that much sooner. As the drums and trumpets sounded, we knew that Catherine's work had finally come to fruition.

"Thank God! Thank God and the Holy Virgin, he is home!" I half expected her to jump and clap her hands in glee, but she curbed her enthusiastic behavior before doing so. The gates flew open, and Anjou, at the head of a large and weather-beaten army, rode into the courtyard on a white horse.

"He does nothing halfway, does he?" The king shifted, impatient to get the ceremony over with a soon as possible. The haste with which he arranged the peace was not due completely to his desire to please the Queen Mother. The rivalry between the king and his flamboyant younger brother would resume with Anjou's return to court. The sooner the king delivered the King of Poland to the Poles and out of France's, the happier he would be. Before he could do that, however, he would have to endure his brother's triumphant return.

Drawing his mount directly in front of his mother, Anjou leaped off of his saddle and raced towards his mother. The two embraced, Catherine kissing her son's hands. She cooed loving words to him, oblivious to the rest of the court standing nearby. As the two continued with their private reunion made awkwardly public, the rest of us shuffled our feet awkwardly as the king had done moments before.

"Brother, I assume you will want to begin preparations for your trip to Poland?" I heard a barely concealed snort behind me. The king was more eager to rid himself of his brother than we had thought.

Anjou turned from his emotional mother to face his older brother. Waving his hand, he chuckled, "I still have the dirt of the road on me. And the army," he gestured to the exhausted men behind him, "should be taken care of before I go." Striding past the king, whose face had reddened, he pulled his mother to the side of the assembled crowd.

With Anjou greeted, attention turned to the rest of the men who had entered the courtyard. The awkwardness of the royal brothers was palatable, so it was a relief when Navarre stepped forward and bowed to the king. "It's nice to see the beauty of the Loire again." He bowed to Margot, who barely acknowledged him. Then he turned to wink at me, "there is much to be missed at the French court."

I blushed so furiously that I could hardly meet my cousin's eye. I knew that he was merely teasing me, yet his flirtatious remark made me uncomfortable. Against my will, I searched for my husband. I found him inspecting a horseshoe with his long-time page. Determined to rid myself of the feelings of embarrassment, I threaded my way past the men.

"Henry, are you all right?" Our meeting would be awkward, no matter how it occurred. I would take the initiative and break the ice between us.

"As well as can be expected." He glowered at Anjou, whose back was turned to us as he accepted the congratulations of the court.

"I can't imagine what it was like, having to go back there; and as the aggressor."

"It was part of the devil's bargain we made, remember? The one you suggested that I make?" I bit my tongue, determined to avoid getting into an argument with him in front of the entire court. I had hoped that we could reunite and display some level of civility towards one another, but my husband was just as intransigent as always.

I glanced over at my sister, Catherine, who was deep in conversation with her husband, the Duc de Guise. Their marriage was just as strained as ours was, but I was jealous of their ability to put their animosity aside to discuss business. The Guise stuck together as a united front, something that we Bourbons had yet to learn.

Catherine caught my eye and shot me a sympathetic look. I felt an overwhelming desire to grab my older sister and hide under her skirts. Had I been years younger, I would have done so. I was a grown woman, however, and a wife and I did not have the option of hiding from my problems.

A long sigh escaped me and at the sound, Condé turned to look at me with a puzzled look. "You look unhappy, wife. I can't imagine why, since your dear friend, Anjou has been returned to you."

"My husband has been returned to me as well." I hissed in his ear, unwilling to let anyone hear our conversation. How my husband could manage to get my anger up so quickly was beyond me. "Now I would like to return home and begin our lives together."

Condé shot another angry look at Anjou, who was still oblivious to him. "Our household may be a little crowded. Is there even room for me?"

There was no chance I could keep my cool had I remained standing next to him. I stalked off from him and headed towards Queen Elisabeth. "Madame, if you'll excuse me, I need to return to my apartments."

Perceptive as always, Elisabeth squeezed my hand and looked me directly in the eye. "Marie, I think the heat has gotten to you. I order you to lie down until you feel better." With her permission, I walked into the chateau, willing myself to walk as slowly as possible so that no one could detect my anger. I would have to deal with my husband's childish taunts later when I regained my senses. We were off to a terrible start indeed.

❧ 14 ❦

The reunited court took a while to get used to one another once again. When the Protestant princes, the Duc de Guise and Anjou were gone, most of the tension between the factions of the court were gone. With them returned, the court returned to a boiling point, as if it was moments away from spilling over into violence. As always, there was scheming and illicit behavior, yet we had enjoyed a brief season of quiet while the Siege of La Rochelle raged on halfway across the country.

As childish as it was, I endeavored to avoid my husband as much as possible. Pleading sickness or headaches, I retired to my bedchamber before my husband finished his daily activities. During the day, I regularly stayed at the Queen or Queen Mother's side to discourage my husband from isolating me and picking a quarrel. He could not legitimately accuse me of spending an inappropriate amount of time with Anjou. On the day of his return, I was careful not to be seen with the Duc. In the days after the army's return to Blois, Anjou spent his days behind closed doors, meeting with the Polish envoys. Overwhelmed with his new duties, he scarcely had time to write me any letters, chaste or otherwise.

Early on a July morning, Condé marched into my bedchamber, startling me. "What do I owe the pleasure of your visit?" I laid my hands in my lap and tried to wait patiently for him to begin.

"I have been appointed the new governor of Picardy. I am to leave for Amiens immediately."

"The King gave you a governorship? That's marvelous!" I meant what I said; the income and influence that came with a royal governorship were something of which to be proud. My work to raise our status at court those past months had paid off handsomely.

"You won't be going with me," he added bluntly. "Apparently, the King is concerned that I will use the position to raise an army against him. You are to stay here as a hostage of the sort." He grimaced at the word. I was not sure if he was angrier at the idea of his wife being used as a hostage or to the idea of my staying behind at court.

"It's probably best that I do stay. Catherine's child will come soon." My sister was again pregnant, but given her penchant for taking lovers, I was not sure if the child was her husband's. I wondered if Condé had heard the rumors of the child's parentage. Perhaps he had not, given how quickly the Protestants rose a cry at the loose morals of the French court.

৩৯৫৩

ON A SWELTERING JULY AFTERNOON, I BID GOODBYE TO MY husband in the courtyard of the Chateau St. Germain as he prepared to leave for Picardy. Although the court usually fled the heat of Paris during the Summer for the Loire Valley, the King had returned to Paris. Given the rivalry between the King and his younger brother, it was likely due to the King's determination to remind Anjou of who ruled France and who would soon be packed off to the cold hinterlands of Poland.

Determined to speak to my husband before he left, I took his arm and led him to a quiet spot behind a balustrade. "Henry, I know that you believe that I am your enemy, but I do have both of our interests at heart." I had always tried to be honest with my husband and this was no exception.

To his credit, he did look shamefaced for a moment. Taking the advantage, I pressed further. "I've done my best to keep us in the King's favor these past months and I will do the same while you are in the countryside."

He glanced at Anjou and drew me closer. To an outside observer, we were a loving couple enjoying a few last stolen moments together. "Navarre and I are convinced that I'm being sent there to check the power of the Guise."

That came as a surprise. I knew that Picardy bordered land owned by the Guise. "Is the King softening his stance against the Protestants, then?"

He snorted, "Hardly. He's determined to balance the power of both religious camps and keep the Guise in check."

If that were so, it would make things awkward between my sister Catherine and myself. We Cleves were distant cousins of the Guise, as were the Bourbons. This was the French court, however, and family ties could quickly be disregarded in the quest for power.

"No matter where I worship, my loyalty will always be to my friends and relatives. I hope you realize that."

He turned to me, shocked. "Are you volunteering to act as a go-between?'

I nodded, "Yes. If you would trust me, I can be of value to you. I have the Queen and the Queen Mother's ears."

My husband could hardly doubt the truth of my words. "Very well, I could use a spy in the French court. I'll write to you when it's safe."

His men signaled that it was time to leave and with the briefest touch of my arm, he walked away from me. Perhaps I had managed to get through to him finally. My victory could only help our faltering union. For the first time in almost a year, it looked as if my husband and I had come to an understanding and were finally on the way to becoming true partners.

۞

THE MORNING AFTER MY HUSBAND'S DEPARTURE FOR PICARDY, I entered my brother-in-law's study to discover that he had a visitor. It was the Duc d'Anjou, and the two were deep in conversation. Not wanting to disturb them, I turned and started to leave the room. Seeing me, he and Anjou rose to their feet and gave me a brief nod. "Marie, you're a welcome distraction," Louis winked at me and Anjou gave me a hungry look.

"Monsieur, I had no idea you were here." I gave him a brief curtsey. I had gone into the study to borrow a book, but finding Anjou there made a little uncomfortable. Mindful of my offer to work with my husband, I had no desire to give him the impression that I would cuckold him the moment he left my side.

Anjou's white hands absentmindedly traced the papers he held in his hand. I tried my best not to notice them, but I failed. Seeing the direction of my glance, he gave me a broad smile. "Louis is advising me on my new role as sovereign of Poland. Living in a foreign court can be challenging, as Louis well knows. His advice has been very helpful to me."

"France's loss will be Poland's gain." I tried to keep my voice neutral, but the tremble gave me away. The more I tried to adopt a formal tone towards Anjou, the more I failed in my attempts. I was giving myself away despite myself. I had missed him those long months, and it was evident to all of us.

"The process of setting up my rule has taken longer than I had hoped so that I will need Louis' advice."

"Then don't let me interrupt your meeting. I only came to borrow a book." I turned to leave the room and Anjou hastened to follow me to the door.

"We've finished our business for the day. I can't monopolize Louis' time any longer today." Anjou gave him an elegant bow and Louis responded with a nod of his own. Placing his hand on my forearm, Anjou started to lead me out of the door.

"Highness, I don't want to give you the idea--"

"Idea, Madame de Condé? Whatever idea are you referring to?"

"I don't want to become another man's mistress. My husband and I are completely mismatched, but as a twice—wedded wife, I do plan to honor my marriage vows."

He took my hands in his larger ones. Staring directly into my eyes, he was silent for a moment. "Marie, I have no desire to turn you into a harlot. My feelings for you are honorable. You can rest easy that am not planning to lure you into my bed. There is no need to be afraid of me. Your virtue is too important to me."

I felt at that moment that he was sincere and I relaxed in his presence. The fire between us still burned, but perhaps he was right. We could simply remain as chaste friends and I would do nothing to betray my marriage vows.

"I enjoy being around you and in this court, it's hard to find a woman who does not use her body to advance her prospects at court. The fact that you are different is what drew me to you. It is one of the reasons why I value your friendship."

"I would be honored to count your Highness as my friend, as long as that is all that we will be."

THE REUNITED COURT TOOK A WHILE TO GET USED TO ONE ANOTHER once again. With the Protestant princes, the Duc de Guise and Anjou absent, most of the tension between the factions of the court faded. With them returned, the court returned to a boiling point, as if it was moments away from spilling over into violence. As always, there was scheming and illicit behavior, yet we had enjoyed a brief season of quiet while the Siege of La Rochelle raged on halfway across the country.

As childish as it was, I endeavored to avoid my husband as much as possible. Pleading sickness or headaches, I retired to my bedchamber before my husband finished his daily activities. During the day, I regularly stayed at the queen or Queen Mother's side to discourage my husband from isolating me and picking a quarrel. He could not legitimately accuse me of spending an inappropriate amount of time with Anjou. On the day of his return, I was careful not to be seen with the Duc. In the days after the army's return to Blois, Anjou spent his days behind closed doors, meeting with the Polish envoys. Overwhelmed with his new duties, he scarcely had time to write me any letters, chaste or otherwise.

Early on a July morning, Condé marched into my bedchamber, startling me. "What do I owe the pleasure of your visit?" I laid my hands in my lap and tried to wait patiently for him to begin.

"The king appointed me the new governor of Picardy. I am to leave for Amiens immediately."

"The king gave you a governorship? That's marvelous!" I meant what I said; the income and influence that came with a royal governorship were a reason to be proud. My work to raise our status at court those past months had paid off handsomely.

"You won't be going with me," he added bluntly. "Apparently, the king is concerned that I will use the position to raise an army against him. You are to stay here as a hostage of the sort." He grimaced at the word. I was not sure if he was angrier at the idea of his wife a hostage or to the idea of my staying behind at court.

"It's probably best I stay. Catherine's child will come soon." My sister was again pregnant, but given her penchant for taking lovers, I was not sure if the child was her husband's. I wondered if Condé had heard the rumors of the child's parentage. Perhaps he had not, given how quickly the Protestants rose a cry at the loose morals of the French court.

⊗⋙

ON A SWELTERING JULY AFTERNOON, I BID GOODBYE TO MY husband in the courtyard of the Chateau St. Germain as he prepared to leave for Picardy. Although the court usually fled the heat of Paris during the Summer for the Loire Valley, the king had returned to Paris. Given the rivalry between the king and his younger brother, it was likely because of the king's determination to remind Anjou of who ruled France and who would soon be packed off to the cold hinterlands of Poland.

Determined to speak to my husband before he left, I took his arm and led him to a quiet spot behind a balustrade. "Henry, I know that you believe that I am your enemy, but I have both of our interests at heart." I had always tried to be honest with my husband and this was no exception.

To his credit, he looked shamefaced for a moment. Taking the advantage, I pressed further. "I've done my best to keep us in the king's favor these past months and I will do the same while you are in the countryside."

He glanced at Anjou and drew me closer. To an outside observer, we were a loving couple enjoying a few last stolen moments together. "Navarre and I are convinced that I'm being sent there to check the power of the Guise."

That came as a surprise. I knew that Picardy bordered land owned by the Guise. "Is the king softening his stance against the Protestants, then?"

He snorted, "Hardly. He's determined to balance the power of both religious camps and keep the Guise in check."

If that were so, it would make things awkward between my sister Catherine and myself. We Cleves were distant cousins of the Guise, as were the Bourbons. This was the French court, however, and family ties could quickly be disregarded in the quest for power.

"No matter where I worship, my loyalty will always be to my friends and relatives. I hope you realize that."

He turned to me, shocked. "Are you volunteering to act as a go-between?"

I nodded, "Yes. If you would trust me, I can be of value to you. I have the queen and the Queen Mother's ears."

My husband could hardly doubt the truth of my words. "Very well, I could use a spy in the French court. I'll write to you when it's safe."

His men signaled that it was time to leave and with the briefest touch of my arm, he walked away from me. Perhaps I had managed to get through to him finally. My victory could only help our faltering union. For the first time in almost a year, it looked as if my husband and I had come to an understanding and were finally on the way to becoming true partners.

❦

THE MORNING AFTER MY HUSBAND'S DEPARTURE FOR PICARDY, I entered my brother-in-law's study to discover that he had a visitor. It was the Duc d'Anjou, and the two were deep in conversation. Not wanting to disturb them, I turned and started to leave the room. Seeing me, he and Anjou rose to their feet and gave me a brief nod. "Marie, you're a welcome distraction," Louis winked at me and Anjou gave me a hungry look.

"Monsieur, I did not realize you were here." I gave him a brief curt-sey. I had gone into the study to borrow a book, but finding Anjou there made a little uncomfortable. Mindful of my offer to work with my husband, I had no desire to give him the impression I would cuckold him the moment he left my side.

Anjou's white hands absentmindedly traced the papers he held in his hand. I tried my best not to notice them, but I failed. Seeing the direction of my glance, he gave me a broad smile. "Louis is advising me on my new role as sovereign of Poland. Living in a foreign court can be challenging, as Louis well knows. His advice has been very helpful."

"France's loss will be Poland's gain." I tried to keep my voice neutral, but the tremble gave me away. The more I tried to adopt a formal tone towards Anjou, the more I failed in my attempts. I was giving myself away despite myself. I had missed him those long months, and it was clear to all of us.

"Setting up my rule has taken longer than I had hoped, so I will need Louis' advice."

"Then don't let me interrupt your meeting. I only came to borrow a book." I turned to leave the room and Anjou hastened to follow me to the door.

"We've finished our business for the day. I can't monopolize Louis' time any longer today." Anjou gave him an elegant bow and Louis responded with a nod of his own. Placing his hand on my forearm, Anjou motioned to lead me out of the door.

"Highness, I don't want to give you the idea--"

"Idea, Madame de Condé? Whatever idea are you referring to?"

"I don't want to become another man's mistress. My husband and I are completely mismatched, but as a twice—wedded wife, I plan to honor my marriage vows."

He took my hands in his larger ones. Staring directly into my eyes, he was silent for a moment. "Marie, I have no desire to turn you into a harlot. My feelings for you are honorable. You can rest easy that am not planning to lure you into my bed. There is no need to be afraid of me. Your virtue is too important to me."

I felt at that moment he was sincere and I relaxed in his presence. The fire between us still burned, but perhaps he was right. We could remain as chaste friends and I would do nothing to betray my marriage vows.

"I enjoy being around you and in this court, it's hard to find a woman who does not use her body to advance her prospects at court. The fact that you are different is what drew me to you. It is one reason I value your friendship."

"I would be honored to count your Highness as my friend, as long as that is all that we will be."

✺ 15 ✺

Satisfied that Anjou would do nothing to blemish my reputation, I continued to relax in his presence. With his return to court, I remembered how easy it was to talk to him and to share my thoughts. The Queen Mother continued to treat me as a beloved daughter and in her presence, the Duc was the powerful portrait of decorum.

Mindful of his upcoming coronation, the court remained in Paris to aid Anjou as he prepared to leave to rule Poland. The King continued to be impatient with his brother's lackadaisical attitude towards leaving France and gossip began to spread that I was the reason for Anjou's reluctance to leave for his new kingdom.

I paid little attention to the gossip, confident that Anjou would do nothing to damage my reputation purposefully. I began to dread the day that Anjou would leave and I would feel more alone than ever. With my husband halfway across the kingdom, our relationship began to thaw, and he sent me a cipher to use during our correspondence. Taking advantage of my position as the unofficial second lady of the court, the Protestant-leaning courtiers and the Anti-Guise factions began coming to me to ask for my husband's support.

As I had feared, Condé's presence in Picardy created a rift between my sister, Catherine and I. While we were always outwardly cordial towards one another, we rarely shared any confidences.. The relationship between both of my older sisters began to disintegrate, as Henriette and Catherine began to argue over our inheritance of our late father's estate. Since I continued to live with Henriette and Louis, Catherine began to assume that I was firmly on our eldest sister's side when it came to their conflict. Alienated from my family, I began to spend more time confiding in Anjou about my troubles.

As we walked back from morning mass late that July, he turned to look at me. "There are storm clouds in your face, Marie. Can I relieve some of them for you?"

"I don't think that I am used to having siblings. Are they always that much trouble?"

He burst into hysterical laughter. I glanced at him, shocked at the uncharacteristic show of emotion. He was usually calm and calculating in his behavior.

"I'm sorry, you are asking a Valois if having a family is trouble? We are experts in causing trouble for one another." He wiped the tears from his eyes and continued to struggle to contain himself.

"Then, how do you suggest I deal with the arguing?"

He pursed his lips and blew a long burst of air out of them. "Move to Poland? I'm sorry, that was in bad taste. If my years at court have taught me anything, it is that your best and only ally is yourself. Others may swear to have your best interests at heart, but no one can watch out for you better than you can for yourself."

"In the end, we are all out of our self-interest?" I tried to sound more innocent than I felt. After all, I had volunteered to be a go-between for my husband and the Protestants left at court. Anjou could never learn that fact and certainly not from me.

He nodded, "Granted, no one schemes more than my family, yet the court is a dangerous place for the innocent and unwary. One grows up quickly here."

My shoulders slumped. Anjou took my hand in his and patted it. "I think that is why I enjoy your company so much. You are not as jaded as the women who have grown up in the French court."

I smiled; perhaps more of my character was due to my Aunt

Jeanne's teaching than I had realized. My husband would laugh to hear that my Protestant upbringing had affected me more than he had initially suspected. Even now, as a devoted Catholic, I could not turn my back on my childhood. Wherever Jeanne was, I was sure she was smiling down on me.

I returned to my suite at the Hotel de Nevers to find a letter from my husband. The cipher he had devised was complicated, yet I was sure that once I had studied it, I could manage to use it successfully. To safeguard our secrets, he suggested that I hide the cipher and burn his letters upon reading them. Both of my sisters were married to powerful Catholic lords and Condé had no desire to risk someone discovering his plans. Given the tense situation between the three of us, I agreed that it was best that I hide my deepest secrets from my sisters.

I spent the rest of the morning practicing our code, frustrated at the beginning, but eventually I managed to compose a letter that would pass by undetected yet be legible once my husband received it. I was under no illusion that my status as a favorite of Anjou and the Queen Mother would place me above suspicion by the spies in the court. No matter how safe I might assume I was, I would have to be vigilant.

In the afternoon, my maid announced that I had a visitor. I frowned, knowing that I hadn't expected to receive anyone. "It's your cousin, My Lady," she bobbed a quick curtsey.

I looked up to see Navarre stride into my room. "This is a surprise!"

"Forgive me, Marie—all those months of war have caused me to forget my manners." His face broke into a wide grin, a boyish behavior that he frequently employed to keep himself out of trouble, or at least to keep himself from being blamed for the trouble he caused. His ruse worked with everyone, including me.

Embracing him fondly, I motioned for him to sit next to me at my desk. "I can help you regain your social graces unless you're beyond all hope."

Crossing his legs at the ankles, he drummed his fingers on the wooden table. For a moment, he was silent, as if considering his next words. "I have been told that you are in contact with Condé."

"Yes, we're communicating much better these days. I had hoped that our relationship would improve, and it looks as if my wish has come true."

He nodded, falling silent once again. "It is refreshing to know that some people at court are happy with their spouse." He was referring to his icy relationship with Margot, a relationship that had not thawed since his return from La Rochelle in June.

"Considering how hard I worked to Save his life, it would hardly do for me to give up on our marriage completely." I could tell that my cousin was working his way towards telling me something, but I did not yet know what that thing was. As children in Navarre, we had been friends, but we rarely shared confidences. I could no more read his expressions than I could a stone wall.

"Would it be unreasonable for me to think that you are corresponding with him during his time in Picardy?" He continued to test me and I decided to wait until he told me the actual reason for his visit.

"We discuss things that any spouses do, cousin." I lifted an eyebrow and looked him in the eye. Folding my hands in my lap, I continued to wait for him to confide in me.

He leaned forward, lowering his voice. Although we were completely alone, I could understand his caution. The very walls of the court had ears and in his position, he could never be too careful with his words. "Condé told me that you offered to send word from Paris to Picardy if need be."

We had at last arrived in the actual reason for his visit. "Yes, I told Condé before he left that I could be of use to him in Paris. Given my position here at court and especially under the Queen Mother's protection, I think that I am more valuable here at court."

"Have you spoken to my sister Catherine lately?" His abrupt change of topic drew my interest. I shook my head, feeling a momentary bit of guilt at the fact that I had been remiss in my correspondence with the Princess of Navarre.

"Catherine has always had my best interests at heart and I think that is something that you both have in common."

I gave him a smile, "Would you like me to write to Catherine?"

He nodded, "Yes, I am sure that my sister would love to hear from you. Princess Catherine must be quite lonely with all of us here in Paris. Sometimes, she does write to me, but I think that my letters are under too much close inspection."

I nodded, continuing to follow his reasoning. "As far as I know, my letters are not being read surreptitiously. If you would like, I could send word to your sister from time to time."

Noticing his expression, I added, "Or I could pass on a message from Navarre to Picardy. Would you like that?"

He brightened at that, "As a matter of fact, Marie, I would be in your debt if you would do so!"

SATISFIED THAT ANJOU WOULD DO NOTHING TO BLEMISH MY reputation, I continued to relax in his presence. With his return to court, I remembered how easy it was to talk to him and to share my thoughts. The Queen Mother continued to treat me as a beloved daughter and in her presence, the Duc was the powerful portrait of decorum.

Mindful of his upcoming coronation, the court remained in Paris to aid Anjou as he prepared to leave to rule Poland. The king continued to be impatient with his brother's lackadaisical attitude towards leaving France and the gossip spread that I was the reason for Anjou's reluctance to leave for his new kingdom.

I paid little attention to the gossip, confident that Anjou would do nothing to damage my reputation purposefully. I dreaded the day that Anjou would leave and I would feel more alone than ever. With my husband halfway across the kingdom, our relationship thawed, and he sent me a cipher to use during our correspondence. Taking advantage of my position as the unofficial second lady of the court, the Protestant-leaning courtiers and the Anti-Guise factions came to me to ask for my husband's support.

As I had feared, Condé's presence in Picardy created a rift between my sister, Catherine and I. While we were always outwardly cordial towards one another, we rarely shared any confidences.. The relationship between both of my older sisters disintegrated, as Henriette and Catherine argued over our inheritance of our late father's estate. Since I continued to live with Henriette and Louis, Catherine assumed that I was firmly on our eldest sister's side in their conflict. Alienated from my family, I filled my time confiding in Anjou about my troubles.

As we walked back from morning mass late that July, he turned to look at me. "There are storm clouds in your face, Marie. Can I relieve some of them for you?"

"I don't think I am used to having siblings. Are they always that much trouble?"

He burst into hysterical laughter. I glanced at him, shocked at the uncharacteristic show of emotion. He was usually calm and calculating in his behavior.

"I'm sorry, you are asking a Valois if having a family is troublesome? We are experts in causing trouble for one another." He wiped the tears from his eyes and continued to struggle to contain himself.

"Then, how do you suggest I deal with the arguing?"

He pursed his lips and blew a long burst of air out. "Move to Poland? I'm sorry, that was in bad taste. If my years at court have taught me anything, it is that your best and only ally is yourself. Others may swear to have your best interests at heart, but no one can watch out for you better than you can for yourself."

"In the end, we are all out of our self-interest?" I tried to sound more innocent than I felt. After all, I had volunteered to be a go-between for my husband and the Protestants left at court. Anjou could never learn that fact and certainly not from me.

He nodded, "Granted, no one schemes more than my family, yet the court is a dangerous place for the innocent and unwary. One grows up quickly here."

My shoulders slumped. Anjou took my hand in his and patted it. "I think that is why I enjoy your company so much. You are not as jaded as the women who have grown up in the French court."

I smiled; perhaps more of my character was a product of my Aunt Jeanne's teaching than I had realized. My husband would laugh to hear that my Protestant upbringing had affected me more than he had initially suspected. Even now, as a devoted Catholic, I could not turn my back on my childhood. Wherever Jeanne was, I was sure she was smiling down on me.

I returned to my suite at the Hotel de Nevers to find a letter from my husband. The cipher he had devised was complicated, yet I was sure that once I had studied it, I could use it successfully. To safeguard our secrets, he suggested that I hide the cipher and burn his letters upon reading them. Both of my sisters were married to powerful Catholic lords and Condé had no desire to risk someone discovering his plans. Given the tense situation between the three of us, I agreed that it was best I hide my deepest secrets from my sisters.

I spent the rest of the morning practicing our code, frustrated at the beginning, but eventually I composed a letter that would pass by undetected yet be legible once my husband received it. I was under no illusion that my status as a favorite of Anjou and the Queen Mother would place me above suspicion by the spies in the court. No matter how safe I might assume I was, I would have to be vigilant.

In the afternoon, my maid announced that I had a visitor. I frowned, knowing I hadn't expected to receive anyone. "It's your cousin, My Lady," she bobbed a quick curtsey.

I looked up to see Navarre stride into my room. "This is a surprise!"

"Forgive me, Marie—all those months of war have caused me to forget my manners." His face broke into a wide grin, a boyish behavior he frequently used to keep himself out of trouble, or at least to keep himself from being blamed for the trouble he caused. His ruse worked with everyone, including me.

Embracing him fondly, I motioned for him to sit next to me at my desk. "I can help you regain your social graces unless you're beyond all hope."

Crossing his legs at the ankles, he drummed his fingers on the wooden table. For a moment, he was silent, as if considering his next words. "Someone has told me you are in contact with Condé."

"Yes, we're communicating much better these days. I had hoped that our relationship would improve, and it looks as if my wish has come true."

He nodded, falling silent once again. "It is refreshing to know that some people at court are happy with their spouse." He was referring to his icy relationship with Margot, a relationship that had not thawed since his return from La Rochelle in June.

"Considering how hard I worked to save his life, it would hardly do for me to give up on our marriage completely." I could tell that my cousin was working his way towards telling me something, but I did not yet know what that thing was. As children in Navarre, we had been friends, but we rarely shared confidences. I could no more read his expressions than I could a stone wall.

"Would it be unreasonable for me to think you are corresponding with him during his time in Picardy?" He continued to test me and I decided to wait until he told me the actual reason for his visit.

"We discuss things that any spouses do, cousin." I lifted an eyebrow and looked him in the eye. Folding my hands in my lap, I continued to wait for him to confide in me.

He leaned forward, lowering his voice. Although we were alone, I could understand his caution. The walls of the court had ears and in his position, he could never be too careful with his words. "Condé told me you offered to send a word from Paris to Picardy if need be."

We had at last arrived in the actual reason for his visit. "Yes, I told Condé before he left that I could be of use to him in Paris. Given my position here at court and especially under the Queen Mother's protection, I think I am more valuable here at court."

"Have you spoken to my sister Catherine lately?" His abrupt change of topic drew my interest. I shook my head, feeling a momentary bit of guilt at the fact I had been remiss in my correspondence with the Princess of Navarre.

"My sister has always had my best interests at heart and I think that is something you both have in common."

I gave him a smile, "Would you like me to write to Catherine?"

He nodded, "Yes, I am sure that my sister would love to hear from you. Princess Catherine must be lonely with all of us here in Paris.

Sometimes, she writes me, but I think my letters are under too much close inspection."

I nodded, continuing to follow his reasoning. "As far as I know, my letters are not being read surreptitiously. If you would like, I could send word to your sister from time to time."

Noticing his expression, I added, "Or I could pass on a message from Navarre to Picardy. Would you like that?"

He brightened at that, "As a matter of fact, Marie, I would be in your debt if you would do so!"

❧ 16 ❧

While I worked to remain the secret go-between amongst the Protestants in Paris, Navarre and Picardy, not all of my time that sweltering, humid summer consisted of gathering and disseminating information. With Anjou returned to the court, I indulged in his company as often as possible. We both knew that his time in France was limited and we were determined to spend it in one another's company.

The seemingly endless rounds of balls, banquets and fetes held in honor of the upcoming Coronation, gave us the perfect excuse to enjoy our time together. I had feared that Anjou would press to make our relationship sexual, but unlike his contemporaries, he seduced with words and actions, not his body. To the amusement of the court, we continued a relationship of the mind in stark contrast with the clandestine couplings that others indulged in amongst the darkly lit corridors of the palaces of Paris.

As Anjou led me around the ballroom of the Louvre one humid August night, I noticed the Polish envoys standing awkwardly against a wall. "They look severe," I tried, but failed, to catch their eyes.

"They're more boring than the Protestants," he pulled his face into a scowl. His misery was palatable.

"Are you dreading your trip to Poland?'

"It tears me away from you, from my mother and France. How can I do anything other than resent it?'

His admission surprised me. Since hearing of his election to the throne, I had assumed he saw it as a stepping stone to power and the place that he and his mother had always hoped for him. Fate might not give him the throne of France, but it had delivered the kingdom of Poland.

"I hate to see you in such misery," I squeezed his hand, desperate to lighten his mood. "I hated leaving Navarre for Paris after I married Condé, so I can understand how much you will miss France."

He expelled a long sigh, never breaking in the steps of the intricate dance. "Oh, Marie—it is your compassion that I think I will miss the most." He looked deep into my eyes as if preparing to say more. At that moment, the dance ended, and he led me from the dance floor to the dais where the King and Queen Elisabeth sat. The King's face was hard as a stone and he gave his brother a stern look. For his part, Anjou acted as if he was oblivious to the King's anger.

"Back so soon, brother?" Although the comment was meant to refer to his return from the dance, we all knew that the King referred to Anjou's continued delay in leaving France for his kingdom.

"It is my duty to return the Princess de Condé to the Queen," he fixed a courtly bow to Elisabeth, who returned his gesture with a nod of her head.

"Ladies, would you like refreshment," opening his arms wide, he gestured to the Queen and me. His charm was, as always, irresistible. As the King scowled at his brother, the Queen gave him a warm smile.

"Brother, I believe that we have been here before. The only difference is that this time, I can see my feet." Elisabeth was right; it was almost exactly a year since the masquerade ball when Anjou sat attentively at our side. This time, however, I was not so determined to keep Anjou from me. I had grown to genuinely enjoy his company and the knowledge that he would leave me as my husband had been forced to do scarcely a month earlier, filled me with a sudden sadness. There would always be the endless rounds of balls, receptions and masques of the court, but the person who made them all worthwhile for me would soon be gone. I spent the rest of the evening trying to keep my expression cheerful, but I knew that nights like this would soon be a thing of the past. France's loss was my loss, and I resented the Poles for taking Anjou from me.

❧

SEPTEMBER BROUGHT THE CHILL OF AUTUMN AND THE REALIZATION that Anjou could delay his departure for the cold nation of Poland no longer. As the ceremony officially crowning him King grew closer; he became more and more melancholy. His meetings with my brother-in-law, Louis took on a more intense tone and by mid-September, I began to worry that he would work himself until a serious malady.

On the seventeenth of September in the Cathedral of Notre Dame, we stood as the Duc d'Anjou officially became an anointed King. The ceremony, while simple, was beautiful. Catherine de Medici wept throughout the ceremony and I used the event as an excuse to let the tears flow from my own eyes. I was not ready to let the man who had become my closest friend and confident leave me. I gave into my selfishness and my resentment of the uncultured Poles deepened into pure anger.

Dressed in cloth of gold, Henri I, the new King of Poland, looked resplendent. Adding to my misery, I suddenly realized that he would once again start to look for a wife and queen of his own. Unfortunately, I would not be that woman. I was doubly married and the Pope would never grant me a divorce from Condé now. As I stood in the packed cathedral, jealousy for a lady who did not yet exist boiled within me.

After the ceremony, the court celebrated with an additional round of banquets and balls. Adding to my misery, I began to notice that with his elevation to his throne, the new King became less of my friend and more of a divine being from whose presence I was barred. I started to panic, thinking that his new subjects saw me like a common whore, one not worthy of their new sovereign. Anxious to set up a new reign and return their country from the brink of chaos, the Polish delegation established the end of September for their departure from France.

Deep in my melancholy, my health began to deteriorate and my childhood problem with my lungs returned. As a result, I was not there when the former Duc d'Anjou left France for what could be the last time. Henriette stayed by my bedside, hovering over at all hours as if I were one of her children. Once again, I was grateful for her over-bearing nature and during the hours that she sat with me, we began to repair the awkwardness in our relationship.

"Are you and Catherine speaking to one another?" I fingered the embroidery on the sheets of my bed. Boredom had long since set in and while I knew that it was a sore subject, I keenly felt the need to have a substantive conversation with someone.

She shook her head and pursed her lips, "No. She returned from her estate in Eu yesterday, but I have not seen or heard from her." If my health improved in time, I would join her on her journey to Joinville. The opulent seat of the Guise family, sat uncomfortably close to Picardy and while I would be well-placed to pass information on to Condé, I was nervous about my part in the espionage against my sister's family. Before Henriette could say more, a knock sounded at the door. One of the maids came in, carrying a large wooden box in her hands.

"Delivery from the Chateau St. Germain, Your Highness." She sat the box next to me and bowed as she left the room. Lifting her eyebrows, Henriette looked at the box, then glanced at me.

"What is this?" Grateful for the distraction from our conversation about Catherine, she was more than willing to stick her nose into my business.

"I have no idea. Perhaps it's from the Queen Mother?'

Henriette snorted, "If that's so, then don't touch it and most certainly, don't drink it." I did not appreciate her levity. For years, many people accused Catherine de Medici of using poison indiscrimi-nately to rid herself of troublesome people. I had never been a bother to Catherine, but could she suddenly view me as a stumbling block to her son's new reign in Poland? I hoped not. I expelled a long sigh, suddenly tired. "Just put it on my desk, I'll look at it later."

But my sister would not be swayed, "Absolutely not! This is the most excitement that you've had in days. In fact," she leaned towards me, "it's the most excitement that *I've* had in days."

A cough bubbled up in my throat, taking me by surprise. "Henriette, I'm not really in the mood for mysteries and surprises. As a matter of fact, I would like to sleep now."

She sighed and rolled her eyes melodramatically. "Fine, have it your way. But I fully expect you to tell me the contents of that box as soon as you open it."

I spent the next two days in bed, partly due to exhaustion and partly due to my stubborn decision not to give Henriette the satisfaction of knowing what the box contained. Once I rose from bed, as my maid set my breakfast, I walked towards the table. As I lifted the cover of the box, my mouth formed an "O" as I saw what for myself what was inside.

It was an exquisite rosary, complete with seed pearls. Their milky iridescent colors danced in the light of the early autumn morning. The piece was a marvel of craftsmanship and I stood for several moments admiring its beauty.

Underneath the rosary was a handwritten note, in a hand that I well recognized. "Keep this close to your heart and always within your hands. As you have always done for me, I hope that it gives your peace and comfort. It pains me to know that I will not have your presence with me. Henri, King of Poland."

I beamed with happiness, a feeling that I had not felt in weeks. Anjou, the King of Poland, had not forgotten me. His thoughtful gift meant that my fears that he might forget me in Poland had been unfounded. Oh, how my heart would miss him, but I would hold his beautiful gift close to my heart until I could see him once again.

SEPTEMBER BROUGHT THE CHILL OF AUTUMN AND THE REALIZATION that Anjou could delay his departure for the cold nation of Poland no longer. As the ceremony officially crowning him king grew closer; he became more and more melancholy. His meetings with my brother-in-law, Louis took on a more intense tone and by mid-September, I worried that he would work himself until a serious malady.

On the seventeenth of September in the Cathedral of Notre Dame, we stood as the Duc d'Anjou officially became an anointed king. The ceremony, while simple, was beautiful. Catherine de Medici wept throughout the ceremony and I used the event as an excuse to let the tears flow from my own eyes. I was not ready to let the man who had become my closest friend and confident leave me. I gave into my selfishness and my resentment of the uncultured Poles deepened into pure anger.

Dressed in cloth of gold, Henri I, the new King of Poland, looked resplendent. Adding to my misery, I suddenly realized that he would once again look for a wife and queen of his own. Unfortunately, I would not be that woman. I was doubly married and the Pope would never grant me a divorce from Condé now. As I stood in the packed cathedral, jealousy for a lady who did not yet exist boiled within me.

After the ceremony, the court celebrated with an additional round of banquets and balls. Adding to my misery, I noticed that with his elevation to his throne, the new king became less of my friend and more of a divine being from whose presence I was barred. I started to panic, thinking his new subjects saw me like a common whore, one not worthy of their new sovereign. Eager to set up a new reign and return their country from the brink of chaos, the Polish delegation established the end of September for their departure from France.

Deep in my melancholy, my health deteriorated and my childhood problem with my lungs returned. As a result, I was not there when the former Duc d'Anjou left France for what could be the last time. Henriette stayed by my bedside, hovering over at all hours as if I were one of her children. Once again, I was grateful for her overbearing nature and during the hours she sat with me; we repaired the awkwardness in our relationship.

"Are you and Catherine speaking to one another?" I fingered the embroidery on the sheets of my bed. Boredom had long since set in and while I knew that it was a sore subject, I keenly felt the need to have a substantive conversation with someone.

She shook her head and pursed her lips, "No. She returned from her estate in Eu yesterday, but I have not seen or heard from her." If my health improved in time, I would join her on her journey to Joinville. The opulent seat of the Guise family, sat uncomfortably close to Picardy and while I would be well-placed to pass information on to Condé, I was nervous about my part in the espionage against my sister's family. Before Henriette could say more, a knock sounded at the door. One maid came in, carrying a large wooden box in her hands.

"Delivery from the Chateau St. Germain, Your Highness." She sat the box next to me and bowed as she left the room. Lifting her eyebrows, Henriette looked at the box, then glanced at me.

"What is this?" Grateful for the distraction from our conversation about Catherine, she was more than willing to stick her nose into my business.

"I don't know. Perhaps it's from the Queen Mother?"

Henriette snorted, "If that's so, then don't touch it and, don't drink it." I did not appreciate her levity. For years, many people accused Catherine de Medici of using poison indiscriminately to rid herself of troublesome people. I had never been a bother to Catherine, but could she suddenly view me as a stumbling block to her son's new reign in Poland? I hoped not. I expelled a long sigh, suddenly tired. "Just put it on my desk, I'll look at it later."

But it would not sway my sister, "Absolutely not! This is the most excitement you've had in days. In fact," she leaned towards me, "it's the most excitement *I've* had in days."

A cough bubbled up in my throat, taking me by surprise. "Henriette, I'm not really in the mood for mysteries and surprises. As a matter of fact, I would like to sleep now."

She sighed and rolled her eyes melodramatically. "Fine, have it your way. But I fully expect you to tell me the contents of that box as soon as you open it."

I spent the next two days in bed, partly because of exhaustion and partly because of my stubborn decision not to give Henriette the satisfaction of knowing what the box contained. Once I rose from bed, as my maid set my breakfast, I walked towards the table. As I lifted the cover of the box, my mouth formed an "O" as I saw what for myself what was inside.

It was an exquisite rosary, complete with seed pearls. Their milky iridescent colors danced in the light of the early autumn morning. The piece was a marvel of craftsmanship and I stood for several moments admiring its beauty.

Underneath the rosary was a handwritten note, in a hand that I well recognized. "Keep this close to your heart and always within your hands. As you have always done for me, I hope that it gives your peace and comfort. It pains me to know that I will not have your presence with me. Henri, King of Poland."

I beamed with happiness, a feeling that I had not felt in weeks. Anjou, the King of Poland, had not forgotten me. His thoughtful gift meant that my fears that he might forget me in Poland had been unfounded. Oh, how my heart would miss him, but I would hold his beautiful gift close to my heart until I could see him once again.

WHILE I WORKED TO REMAIN THE SECRET GO-BETWEEN AMONGST the Protestants in Paris, Navarre and Picardy, not all of my time that sweltering, humid summer comprised gathering and disseminating information. With Anjou returned to the court, I indulged in his company as often as possible. We both knew that his time in France was limited and we wanted to spend it in one another's company.

The seemingly endless rounds of balls, banquets and fetes held in honor of the upcoming Coronation, gave us the perfect excuse to enjoy our time together. I had feared that Anjou would press to make our relationship sexual, but unlike his contemporaries, he seduced with words and actions, not his body. To the amusement of the court, we continued a relationship of the mind in stark contrast with the clandestine couplings that others indulged in amongst the darkly lit corridors of the palaces of Paris.

As Anjou led me around the ballroom of the Louvre one humid August night, I noticed the Polish envoys standing awkwardly against a wall. "They look severe," I tried, but failed, to catch their eyes.

"They're more boring than the Protestants," he pulled his face into a scowl. His misery was palatable.

"Are you dreading your trip to Poland?"

"It tears me away from you, from my mother and France. How can I do anything other than resent it?"

His admission surprised me. Since hearing of his election to the throne, I had assumed he saw it as a stepping stone to power and the place that he and his mother had always hoped for him. Fate might not give him the throne of France, but it had delivered the kingdom of Poland.

"I hate to see you in such misery," I squeezed his hand, desperate to lighten his mood. "I hated leaving Navarre for Paris after I married Condé, so I can understand how much you will miss France."

He expelled a long sigh, never breaking in the steps of the intricate dance. "Oh, Marie—it is your compassion I think I will miss the most." He looked deep into my eyes as if preparing to say more. At that moment, the dance ended, and he led me from the dance floor to the dais where the king and Queen Elisabeth sat. The king's face was hard as a stone and he gave his brother a stern look. Anjou acted as if he was oblivious to the king's anger.

"Back so soon, brother?" Although the comment referred to his return from the dance, we all knew that the king referred to Anjou's continued delay in leaving France for his kingdom.

"It is my duty to return the Princess de Condé to the queen," he fixed a courtly bow to Elisabeth, who returned his gesture with a nod of her head.

"Ladies, would you like refreshment," opening his arms wide, he gestured to the queen and me. His charm was, as always, irresistible. As the king scowled at his brother, the queen gave him a warm smile.

"Brother, I believe that we have been here before. The only difference is that this time, I can see my feet." Elisabeth was right; it was almost exactly a year since the masquerade ball when Anjou sat attentively at our side. This time, however, I was not so determined to keep Anjou from me. I had grown to crave his company and the knowledge he would leave me as they had forced my husband to do scarcely a month earlier, filled me with a sudden sadness. There would always be the endless rounds of balls, receptions and masques of the court, but the person who made them all worthwhile for me would leave me. I spent the rest of the evening trying to keep my expression cheerful, but I knew that nights like this would soon be a thing of the past. France's loss was my loss, and I resented the Poles for taking Anjou from me.

17

Life without my husband and Anjou became very dull indeed. As much as I tried to make up for my loneliness by staying busy, it could not compensate for the hole in my heart. During the cold months of the fall and winter of 1573, Elisabeth and I grew even closer, and she did her best to make up for Anjou's absence in my life.

The melancholy and dissatisfaction were prevalent in court, even touching the Queen. Despite giving birth to a healthy daughter a year before, she was unsuccessful in conceiving another child. Adding to her misery, in October, Marie Touchet, the King's longtime mistress, announced that she carried the King's child. If the child were a boy, the humiliation for Elisabeth would be unbearable. Ever the princess, she soldiered on, not showing her unhappiness to the court.

As we walked amongst the gardens of the Tuileries one afternoon, Elisabeth's absentmindedly playing with the dog jumping at her feet. "I wonder if I am long for this court, Marie."

That had my attention, "Do you think that the King will divorce you?" I could not bear the thought that I would lose yet another friend and ally at court.

"No, I don't know if the King's health will last much longer." She spoke in low tones; to speak of the King's death was treason.

I lowered my voice, and we quickened our pace, so that we could walk together without being heard by her servants who trailed behind us at a discreet distance. "Is it his mind or his body; or both?" There had been rumors that the King was mentally unfit for the throne before his older brother's death, but of course, none of us would speak of it openly. Questioning the sovereign's fitness to rule could endanger both our lives. Yet, Elisabeth meant nothing of it; she spoke as a loving wife who feared for her spouse's health and happiness.

Her shoulders slumped, "Both, I think that his spirit broke on St. Bartholomew's Day. He constantly cries that he hears the screams of the dying. I don't know if it is out of guilt or some madness coming upon him." Throughout his life, the King had been known to experience convulsions and various fits, but none of them life-threatening. Given Elisabeth's concern, there was a real danger that they were becoming life-threatening. She was not a woman given to exaggerations. If she was concerned, then there was a genuine threat to the King's health.

"If I had a son, then at least we would feel safe knowing that there would be a regency. But as things are now," she shook her head.

"The King of Poland is his only heir," the death of the King was the only event that would bring Anjou back to France. I brightened at the thought of his return. As soon as I warmed to the idea, a worrying thought chased after it. As the new King of France, he would immediately need a Queen at his side.

Elisabeth must have noticed the clouds that crossed my face. Mistaking them for concern over the King, she patted my hand. "Don't worry, Marie; perhaps I'm just worrying too much. It is a wife's prerogative, after all."

I smiled at her, determined that she would not know the exact reason for my sudden change in mood. "I think that to be a good wife; one must worry incessantly."

"How is the Prince of Condé? Here I have gone on about my husband and you are here with yours so far away. I'm sorry—I am being selfish."

I shook my head, "Nothing of the sort. We are friends, after all. What worries you, concerns me." That was more than a little lie, but I swallowed the guilt that came with my saying it.

❦

I RE-READ THE LETTER IN MY HAND TO MAKE SURE THAT I understood my husband's request. Condé had readily agreed to entrust me with passing information amongst Protestants, but this was different. He expected me to use my relationship with my sister to spy on the Guise. My husband must have taken leave of his senses.

Furrowing my brow, I read his letter once again, slowly, as if that would help me absorb his instructions. "I have intercepted messages from Eu to Joinville," he began, naming the county my sister had inherited from our father and the chateau located at the heart of the Guise holdings. "Phillip of Spain plans to give the Guise gold to back a coup that will bar the Ducs d'Anjou and Alceon, as well as Navarre, from inheriting. They're tired of the Valois and want to do away with them. They plan to put the Cardinal Bourbon in their place. No concrete plans have been made yet, but I need you to learn what you can from your sister."

Catherine was due to give birth to her child in mid-December and I planned to accompany her to Joinville for the birth. My offer to join her was part of my plan to reconcile with my sister, not serve as a spy in her home. Even if no one discovered my activities, the guilt would show in my face and mar our reconciliation. We were so close to becoming genuine friends, and I resented my husband's plan to ruin that chance.

"Henry, you ask too much of me."

"Madame?" My page came into my study, ready to take a note at my command.

"I was musing aloud. It is nothing." I dismissed him with my hand. A thought came, unbidden to me: was it possible that either of my sisters had spies planted on me within their own homes?

"Forgive me, Madame, but I come with a note from the Queen

Mother." A letter from Catherine could not be ignored. Tearing open the seal, I read her missive.

I was commanded to journey with the King of Poland and his entourage across France to see him to his new kingdom. As the Queen Mother knew that I planned on traveling to Joinville with my sister, she and her son eagerly desired my presence when his progress across to the western border towards the Duchy of Lorraine. We would be within traveling distance to the court for a few weeks, a welcome distraction from the awkwardness I would feel while lodging at Joinville.

"Well, I suppose I will be going to Joinville after all." At least I would enjoy Anjou's company for a few more weeks. The despondency I felt at losing him lifted a little.

A COURT PROGRESSION IS MORE COMPLICATED AND EXPENSIVE THAN the moving of armies and this trip was no exception. Along with Catherine and her favorite son, Navarre and the Duc de Guise followed from Paris to Lorraine, where the Queen Mother's second daughter, Claude was the Duchess de Lorraine. Amongst the throng of nobles and retainers, the Duc d'Alceon and his retainers, Joseph Boniface de la Mole and Annibaile Coconnas were to accompany us. To Margot and Henriette's delight, they were allowed to stay behind in Paris as we started the long, arduous trip towards the border.

The court planned to stay in Lorraine for two weeks. Anjou had fulfilled his brother's wish in leaving Paris, but he was determined not to abandon the kingdom for the one he was to rule. At one of the countless banquets given by the leading men of Lorraine, Mole sat next to me, whispering in my ear.

"He thinks that if he tarries long enough, he will become King of France."

Mole's impertinence annoyed me, "Who?"

"Anjou. Did you not hear? The King has been diagnosed with consumption. It is only a matter of time before Anjou is recalled to France to become her King. If he dallies long enough, he won't have to become King of that barbarous court." A Polish noble walked by, close enough to overhear Mole's gossip. I flinched at the thought of him overhearing our conversation.

"I think you assign too many ill thoughts to the new King." I had no desire for Anjou or Catherine to believe I was disloyal to Anjou. My roles as a spy and courtier both depended on it. Mole had somehow determined that I was a likely ally and friend and had spent most of our trip trying to toady up to me. Despite my ongoing efforts to discourage him, he never stopped his efforts to ingratiate himself with me. In Paris, I heard whispers that Henriette carried on a flirtation with Coconnas, his friend. Perhaps Mole thought that relationship gave him unfettered access to me as well. The man was sadly mistaken; he only made me queasy. I wanted nothing more than to avoid him. When I returned to Paris, I would speak to Henriette about her relationship with Coconnas.

Luckily, I caught Anjou's eye at that moment and shot him a pleading look. Ever the gallant, he turned from his conversation and hurried to my side. "Thank you for keeping the Princess company, sir. I relieve you of your duty."

"Thank you," I hissed in his ear, my intimate gesture drawing the attention of the Poles in attendance. Half of Anjou's new subjects were said to be Lutherans and from what I had observed, they followed the strict moral code that Protestants in France did. Likely, they disapproved of my relationship with their new sovereign, but none of them had the courage to say so publicly.

"He's an odious man, that Mole. Mark my words; he will be trouble."

"He has attached himself to me like a leech." I shuddered, the image causing me to think of the King's illness. Was Mole correct? Was I in imminent danger of losing Elisabeth's presence at court? Tears stung at my eyes.

"Marie—I know! I hate the idea of leaving France. I cannot imagine how terrible it will be without you."

The tears spilled down my cheeks. Unwilling to hide my feelings, I let them fall. "I feel as if my entire world is shrinking. Every friend and ally I have in court is leaving me."

He stopped and took my hands in his. "You have my promise, that I will do everything in my power to ensure that you don't feel deserted. I will write to you every day and I will make sure that my mother continues to protect you like her daughter."

"I will hold you to that, Majesty." I curtseyed to him, as his due as a sovereign. He kissed the top of my head as if in a blessing.

LIFE WITHOUT MY HUSBAND AND ANJOU BECAME VERY DULL. As much as I tried to make up for my loneliness by staying busy, it could not compensate for the hole in my heart. During the cold months of the fall and winter of 1573, Elisabeth and I grew even closer, and she did her best to make up for Anjou's absence in my life.

As we walked amongst the gardens of the Tuileries one afternoon, Elisabeth absentmindedly played with the dog jumping at her feet. "I wonder if I am long for this court, Marie."

That had my attention, "Do you think the king will divorce you?" I could not bear the thought I would lose yet another friend and ally at court.

"No, I don't know if the king's health will last much longer." She spoke in low tones; to speak of the king's death was treason.

I lowered my voice, and we quickened our pace, so we could walk together without being heard by her servants who trailed behind us at a discreet distance. "Is it his mind or his body; or both?" There had been rumors that the king was mentally unfit for the throne before his older brother's death, but none of us would speak of it openly. Questioning the sovereign's fitness to rule could endanger both our lives. Yet, Elisabeth meant nothing of it; she spoke as a loving wife who feared for her spouse's health and happiness.

Her shoulders slumped, "Both, I think his spirit broke on St. Bartholomew's Day. He constantly cries he hears the screams of the dying. I don't know if it is out of guilt or some madness coming upon him." Throughout his life, the king experienced convulsions and various fits, but none of them life-threatening. Given Elisabeth's concern, there was a real danger they were becoming life-threatening.

She was not a woman given to exaggerations. If it concerned her, then there was a genuine threat to the king's health.

"If I had a son, then at least we would feel safe knowing that there would be a regency. But as things are now," she shook her head.

"The King of Poland is his only heir," the death of the king was the only event that would bring Anjou back to France. I brightened at the thought of his return. As soon as I warmed to the idea, a worrying thought chased after it. As the new King of France, he would immediately need a queen at his side.

Elisabeth must have noticed the clouds that crossed my face. Mistaking them for concern over the king, she patted my hand. "Don't worry, Marie; perhaps I'm just worrying too much. It is a wife's prerogative, after all."

I smiled at her, determined that she would not know the exact reason for my sudden change in mood. "I think to be a good wife; one must worry incessantly."

"How is the Prince of Condé? Here I have gone on about my husband and you are here with yours so far away. I'm sorry—I am being selfish."

I shook my head, "Nothing of the sort. We are friends. What worries you, concerns me." That was more than a little lie, but I swallowed the guilt that came with my saying it.

⁂

I RE-READ THE LETTER IN MY HAND TO MAKE SURE I UNDERSTOOD my husband's request. Condé had readily agreed to entrust me with passing information amongst Protestants, but this was different. He expected me to use my relationship with my sister to spy on the Guise. My husband must have taken leave of his senses.

Furrowing my brow, I read his letter once again, slowly, as if that would help me absorb his instructions. "I have intercepted messages from Eu to Joinville," he began, naming the county my sister had inherited from our father and the chateau at the heart of the Guise holdings. "Phillip of Spain plans to give the Guise gold to back a coup that will bar the Ducs d'Anjou and Alençon, and Navarre, from inheriting.

They're tired of the Valois and want to do away with them. They plan to put the Cardinal Bourbon in their place. I have made yet no concrete plans, but I need you to learn what you can from your sister."

Catherine was due to give birth to her child in mid-December and I planned to accompany her to Joinville for the birth. My offer to join her was part of my plan to reconcile with my sister, not serve as a spy in her home. Even if no one discovered my activities, the guilt would show in my face and mar our reconciliation. We were so close to becoming genuine friends, and I resented my husband's plan to ruin that chance.

"Henry, you ask too much of me."

"Madame?" My page came into my study, ready to take a note at my command.

"I was musing aloud. It is nothing." I dismissed him with my hand. A thought came, unbidden: was it possible that either of my sisters had spies planted on me within their own homes?

"Forgive me, Madame, but I come with a note from the Queen Mother." I could not ignore a letter from Catherine de Medici. Tearing open the seal, I read her missive.

She commanded me to journey with the King of Poland and his entourage across France to see him to his new kingdom. As the Queen Mother knew that I planned on traveling to Joinville with my sister, she and her son eagerly desired my presence when his progress across to the western border towards the Duchy of Lorraine. We would be within traveling distance to the court for a few weeks, a welcome distraction from the awkwardness I would feel while lodging at Joinville.

"Well, I suppose I will go to Joinville after all." At least I would enjoy Anjou's company for a few more weeks. The despondency I felt at losing him lifted a little.

A COURT PROGRESSION IS MORE COMPLICATED AND EXPENSIVE THAN the moving of armies and this trip was no exception. Along with Catherine and her favorite son, Navarre and the Duc de Guise followed from Paris to Lorraine, where the Queen Mother's second daughter, Claude was the Duchesse de Lorraine. Amongst the throng of nobles and retainers, the Duc d'Alençon and his retainers, Joseph Boniface de la Mole and Annibaile Coconnas were to accompany us. To Margot and Henriette's delight, they were allowed to stay behind in Paris as we started the long, arduous trip towards the border.

The court planned to stay in Lorraine for two weeks. Anjou had fulfilled his brother's wish in leaving Paris, but he remained determined not to abandon the kingdom for the one he was to rule. At one of the countless banquets given by the leading men of Lorraine, Mole sat next to me, whispering in my ear.

"He thinks if he tarries long enough, he will become King of France."

Mole's impertinence annoyed me, "Who?"

"Anjou. Did you not hear? The doctors diagnosed the king with consumption. It is only a matter of time before the Queen Mother recalls Anjou to France to become her king. If he dallies long enough, he won't have to become king of that barbarous court." A Polish noble walked by, close enough to overhear Mole's gossip. I flinched at the thought of him overhearing our conversation.

"I think you assign too many ill thoughts to the new king." I had no desire for Anjou or Catherine to believe I was disloyal to Anjou. My roles as a spy and courtier both depended on it. Mole had somehow determined that I was a likely ally and friend and had spent most of our trip trying to toady up to me. Despite my ongoing efforts to discourage him, he never stopped his efforts to ingratiate himself with me. In Paris, I heard whispers that Henriette carried on a flirtation with Coconnas, his friend. Perhaps Mole thought relationship gave him unfettered access to me as well. The man was sadly mistaken; he only made me queasy. I wanted nothing more than to avoid him. When I returned to Paris, I would speak to Henriette about her relationship with Coconnas.

Luckily, I caught Anjou's eye at that moment and shot him a pleading look. Ever the gallant, he turned from his conversation and hurried to my side. "Thank you for keeping the Princess company, sir. I relieve you of your duty."

"Thank you," I hissed in his ear, my intimate gesture drawing the attention of the Poles in attendance. They said half of Anjou's new subjects were Lutherans and from what I had observed, they followed the strict moral code that Protestants in France did. Likely, they disapproved of my relationship with their new sovereign, but none of them had the courage to say so publicly.

"He's an odious man, that Mole. Mark my words; he will be trouble."

"He has attached himself to me like a leech." I shuddered, the image causing me to think of the king's illness. Was Mole correct? Was I in imminent danger of losing Elisabeth's presence at court? Tears stung at my eyes.

"Marie—I know! I hate leaving France. I cannot imagine how terrible it will be without you."

The tears spilled down my cheeks. Unwilling to hide my feelings, I let them fall. "I feel as if my entire world is shrinking. Every friend and ally I have in court is leaving me."

He stopped and took my hands in his. "You have my promise, that I will do everything in my power to ensure that you don't feel deserted. I will write to you every day and I will make sure that my mother continues to protect you like her daughter."

"I will hold you to that, Majesty." I curtseyed to him, as his due as a sovereign. He kissed the top of my head as if in a blessing.

❧ 18 ❧

In late November, I had to take leave of both Catherine and Anjou as I settled into the Chateau Joinville to aid my sister in her lying in. "I only have one birth to recommend me," I smiled, referring to Princess Elisabeth, now a year old.

She waved her hand, "Don't worry—I usually go through the process quickly. More than likely, you'll be back in Paris in a few weeks."

"I have no plans to pack up and desert you." No matter what else, I wanted to use this time to connect with my sister. The months I spent as a guest at Henriette's home meant that our relationship overshadowed that of the one I had with Catherine.

I stood and walked over to the nightstand where Catherine's Book of Hours lay and I began to look through it. "The miniatures are beautiful." It was true, the artisanship of the saints was remarkable. As I continued to admire them, however, something seemed amiss. I glanced at my sister.

"Catherine, why do some of these saints look familiar? Do I know the models?'

A furious blush spread across her face and down her neck. I had to know what caused that blush. "Catherine? What is it?'

She bit her lip, "You do know a few of the models. I, on the other hand, have known all of them to a rather remarkable degree." A giggle escaped from her throat. She was up to some naughtiness.

"What do you mean?"

She cleared her throat. "It's a way of remembering them."

"Who?"

"My former lovers."

"Catherine! For shame!"

She waved her hands in the air, "Don't be such a prude, Marie,"

"Prude? Catherine that is sacrilege!"

"Why? All saints were at one time, sinners. I'm merely making that point private."

I couldn't help myself; a giggle burst out of me. "You should be ashamed."

"Marie, it is to your disadvantage that you grew up Protestant. Thank God you converted." She laughed, caught up in her joke. I tried to scowl at her, but failed. Her naughty behavior was appealing, especially because she felt so little guilt over it.

"I do still feel scandalized at court. I thought I would faint the first time I attended a card game."

"So did I, after I married Guise and converted. I had to stop gasping out loud every time I saw something that violated Calvin's teaching."

"How long did that take?"

She counted on her fingers, "Nine, ten months?'

"You are incorrigible, sister." I took her hand, squeezing it.

"It is good to have you here. The politics of court weigh me down. It's much easier to concentrate on one's lover than one's political leanings. Leanings that change by the day, if not the hour."

I thank God that I accompanied her for the birth of her child, because in early December, her labor pains began. Early on the morning of December 3rd, she gave birth to a girl. Although the child looked like an angel, she lived only for a few hours. My sister was despondent, dissolving into a deep melancholy. After giving birth to two sons, one who only lived for two years, the idea of having a girl was a dream that she desperately wanted to realize.

CATHERINE AND I SPENT THE REST OF 1573 CONSTANTLY IN ONE another's company, officially far from the maneuvering of the court. I continued to keep my eyes open for a sign of Spanish gold or the beginnings of a plot, but little came to my notice.

I was determined to make myself useful to her, doing everything within my power to help her mourn the child and work through her grief. Still, my promise to aid the Protestants could not be ignored for very long. Condé sent missives, asking me to come to Amiens to visit him. Winter in the easternmost reaches of France that year was mild, and I made plans to visit him at the end of February. Those plans changed abruptly two days after Christmas day when I walked past the door of the chateau's comptroller. Two excited voices, deep in a conversation caught my ear. Slowing my pace, I started to listen in on their conversation.

"Of course he's still a Protestant! The King was gullible to think that he was genuine and now he's installed himself as Lord of Picardy."

Picardy! They must have been referring to my husband.

"We have friends assembled in Matigny, far enough that he can't go running to his brother-in-law for safety."

I wondered which brother-in-law he referred to, Nevers or Guise? Did Catherine have a traitor in her home, or had a conspiracy been under my nose the entire time? My heart sank at the thought.

"Get this message to Nancy, as soon as possible. We don't have much time to plan."

Determined to avoid being caught, I rushed into a dark corner. With my sudden movement, I could not hear the rest of the conversation, despite the fact that I knew I desperately needed to. Condé would need to hear every precious word of the plot against him, but I could not risk being caught spying in my own sister's home.

As quickly as I could manage without arousing suspicion, I returned to my apartments and began writing to my husband. "Christmas was wonderful, but I cannot stand to be parted from you any longer. I will be there early and I fully expect you to make preparations for my visit."

Calling for my page, I sent the letter to Picardy, knowing that Condé would understand the coded message. Once again, my husband's life was in danger; and once again, I was the best hope for saving him.

In late November, I had to take leave of both Catherine and Anjou as I settled into the Chateau Joinville to aid my sister in her lying in. "I only have one birth to recommend me," I smiled, referring to Princess Elisabeth, now a year old.

She waved her hand, "Don't worry—I usually go through the process quickly. More than likely, you'll be back in Paris in a few weeks."

"I have no plans to pack up and desert you." No matter what else, I wanted to use this time to connect with my sister. The months I spent as a guest at Henriette's home meant that our relationship overshadowed that of the one I had with Catherine.

I stood and walked over to the nightstand where Catherine's Book of Hours lay and I looked through it. "The miniatures are beautiful." It was true, the artisanship of the saints was remarkable. As I continued to admire them, however, something seemed amiss. I glanced at my sister.

"Catherine, why do some of these saints look familiar? Do I know the models?"

A furious blush spread across her face and down her neck. I had to know what caused that blush. "Catherine? What is it?"

She bit her lip, "You know a few of the models. I have known all of them to a rather remarkable degree." A giggle escaped from her throat. She was up to some naughtiness.

"What do you mean?"

She cleared her throat. "It's a way of remembering them."

"Who?"

"My former lovers."

"Catherine! For shame!"

She waved her hands in the air, "Don't be such a prude, Marie,"

"Prude? Catherine that is sacrilege!"

"Why? All saints were at one time, sinners. I'm merely making that point private."

I couldn't help myself; a giggle burst out of me. "You should be ashamed."

"Marie, it is to your disadvantage you grew up Protestant. Thank God you converted." She laughed, caught up in her joke. I tried to scowl at her, but failed. Her naughty behavior was appealing, especially because she felt so little guilt over it.

"I do still feel scandalized at court. I thought I would faint the first time I attended a card game."

"So did I, after I married Guise and converted. I had to stop gasping out loud every time I saw something that violated Calvin's teaching."

"How long did that take?"

She counted on her fingers, "Nine, ten months?"

"You are incorrigible, sister." I took her hand, squeezing it.

"It is good to have you here. The politics of court weigh me down. It's much easier to concentrate on one's lover than one's political leanings. Leanings that change by the day, if not the hour."

I thank God that I accompanied her for the birth of her child, because in early December, her labor pains began. Early on the morning of December 3rd, she gave birth to a girl. Although the child looked like an angel, she lived only for a few hours. My sister was despondent, dissolving into a deep melancholy. After giving birth to two sons, one who only lived for two years, having a girl was a dream she desperately wanted to realize.

꧁꧂

CATHERINE AND I SPENT THE REST OF 1573 CONSTANTLY IN ONE another's company, officially far from the maneuvering of the court. I continued to keep my eyes open for a sign of Spanish gold or the beginnings of a plot, but little came to my notice.

I would to make myself useful to her, doing everything within my power to help her mourn the child and work through her grief. Still, I couldn't ignore my promise to aid the Protestants for long. Condé sent missives, asking me to come to Amiens to visit him. Winter in the easternmost reaches of France that year was mild, and I made plans to visit him at the end of February. Those plans changed abruptly two days after Christmas day when I walked past the door of the chateau's comptroller. Two excited voices, deep in a conversation caught my ear. Slowing my pace, I listened in on their conversation.

"Of course he's still a Protestant! The king was gullible to think he was genuine and now he's installed himself as Lord of Picardy."

Picardy! They must have been referring to my husband.

"We have friends assembled in Matigny, far enough he can't go running to his brother-in-law for safety."

I wondered which brother-in-law he referred to, Nevers or Guise? Did Catherine have a traitor in her home, or had a conspiracy been under my nose the entire time? My heart sank at the thought.

"Get this message to Nancy, as soon as possible. We have little time to plan."

Determined to avoid being caught, I rushed into a dark corner. With my sudden movement, I could not hear the rest of the conversation, although I knew I desperately needed to. Condé would need to hear every precious word of the plot against him, but I could not risk being caught spying in my sister's home.

As quickly as I could manage without arousing suspicion, I returned to my apartments and wrote to my husband. "Christmas was wonderful, but I cannot stand being parted from you any longer. I will be there early and I fully expect you to make preparations for my visit."

Calling for my page, I sent the letter to Picardy, knowing that Condé would understand the coded message. Once again, my husband's life was in danger; and once again, I was the best hope for saving him.

❧ 19 ❧

"Your Highness is most welcome!" The rotund rosy-cheeked man greeted me as I entered the small Chateau my husband used in governing Picardy. I was relieved to be there, my toes tingling from the early January cold. I had just managed to arrive in Amiens before a sleet storm and the disagreeable weather would keep me indoors for several days after my arrival.

When my sister Catherine heard of my sudden desire to leave for Picardy, she protested constantly. "You are mad to try to trek across the countryside this time of the year! What possible reason could you have to leave now!" Her recovery from the birth dictated that she stay in bed, but that did not bar her from regaling me with hundreds of reasons why I should remain in Joinville. I was relieved to see that none of Catherine's protests seemed to stem from her involvement in the plot against my husband. Apparently, she was completely oblivious to the scheming going around her. As much as I hated leaving my sister and the bond that we had recently formed, I could not allow my husband to be blindsided in the plot developing in Picardy. I had to do all that I could to Save him.

I half-ran to my husband's apartments, determined to speak to him without delay. Opening the heavy door without ceremony, I looked around the room to find him working at his desk. "Have you learned anything about the conspiracy?"

His face folded into a deep frown, "Yes—it goes even further than you had feared. Apparently, you were just in time. According to Princess Catherine, there was a plot to kidnap or assassinate her in Navarre. Her death would be the end of an independent Navarre, since her brother is unable to escape the French court. Without your help, we never would have made the connection." He looked up at me and gave me a rare smile. "Thank you, Marie. I cannot tell you how valuable you have been to me."

"I promised you that I would help you and our friends, and that is what I did." I returned his smile with a genuine one of my own. The Bourbons were our family, and I was more than willing to keep them safe. The idea of my cousin, Catherine in danger made me sick. Thankful for the new amity between us, I sat in the chair beside him. After so many months at odds in one another's company, peace between us seemed odd. Neither of us knew how to break the awkwardness between us. Unsure where to start, I tried to make conversation.

"My sister, Catherine is doing well. She is getting over the loss of her daughter."

He nodded, "Good."

Having mentioned Catherine, now I regretted doing so. What if Henry had found evidence that she was in on the conspiracy after all?

He squelched my fears with his next words, "There is no proof that Catherine was in on the plot against me. You can rest assured; your sister is most likely innocent."

My entire body shuddered with relief. Before I could stop myself, I crossed myself. "Thank God—we're just now beginning to speak to one another as sisters."

The longer that I spent in my husband's company, the more that the awkwardness between us lessened. That January became a kind of honeymoon for us; one denied us when during the wedding of Navarre and the subsequent massacre in Paris. We were still mismatched as husband and wife, but we developed respect for one another during my days in Picardy. During our nights, to my shock, we began to act as man and wife. Finally, I started to enjoy my status as Princess de Condé.

Our delayed honeymoon could not last forever, however; eventually, I was recalled to court to serve as a lady-in-waiting to Queen Elisabeth. Mole's words proved to be true, and the King was indeed suffering from consumption. Elisabeth and the Queen Mother wrote to me, begging me to return to serve Elisabeth during the King's illness. I could not refuse a direct missive from the Valois, so in February, I was forced to face the ice and cold to make the journey from Picardy to the Tuileries, where the court stayed. Bidding adieu to my husband, we promised to see one another again as soon as possible.

Several unexpected things awaited me at the Tuileries. For one, the Queen Mother assigned me apartments as close as possible to that of the Queen's. This housing assignment was fortuitous since The Hotel de Cleves had closed with Catherine's absence and I felt uncomfortable continuing to impose on Henriette at the Hotel de Nevers. The Hotel de Bourbon had never been my home, despite that fact that I had a right to establish a residence within the vast building.

The other surprise waiting for me came in the guise of a glut of letters from the Duc d'Anjou from Poland. Each letter came directly from the Polish court to the Queen Mother, who held them for me until my return from Joinville and Amiens. Untying the ribbon that held the fat stack of paper, I started to read each letter as Anjou poured his feelings out to me.

Poland and its court were a dull, uncultured wasteland, the worst possible place for Anjou. Virtually from the start, he was miserable and longing for home. Lost in his misery, Anjou began to confess deeper feelings towards me. For the first time, he told me that he loved me and that he had always hoped for a future between us. I had to fight the anger at reading his words; had Anjou professed his love for me before Condé and I had remarried, we could have been man and wife before he left for Poland. I could have stood by his side as his queen as he began his reign.

Anger soon gave way to longing and as I read his letters, I fell further in love with him. In March, I could not control my emotions, crying one moment and the next, screaming in anger at the vicissitudes of fate. Then I discovered that my warring emotions came from another source: I was pregnant.

Catherine and I sat together one evening as I tried to improve my card playing skills. "I have a confession to make."

She put her cards down and exhaled loudly, "Thank God! Finally! You and Anjou are lovers? Well, I must say, it took longer than I had expected." Since her return to Paris, her color returned, along with her spirits. I was thrilled to have my vivacious sister once again.

I shook my head furiously. "No! Anjou and I have never been intimate, but Condé and I were when I went to Amiens. And now I'm carrying his child."

She hastily tried to rearrange her face, but I caught her before she managed to do so. "Well, that's wonderful! You both need a legitimate heir. This is good news, truly. It is." She bit her lip nervously, unable to continue.

"You are a terrible liar, Catherine."

She shrugged her shoulders, "It's obvious to anyone that you and Condé are miserable and that Anjou would be a better match for you."

Too angry and embarrassed to look her in the eye, I laid a card down without looking at it. "I am a married woman and it's obvious now that our disaster of marriage was consummated. If I were to ask for a divorce, there would be no grounds. You know that as well as I do."

"If you were free, then would you marry Anjou?" I could feel her stare, yet I continued to ignore her.

"What exactly are you suggesting? You were only free to marry Guise once The Prince de Porcien was in his grave." As soon as the words were out of my mouth, I regretted them. Catherine had been innocent in the last plot against my husband. Was she really suggesting that I kill my own husband? Was she capable of forming a conspiracy of her own in the mistaken thought that she was helping me?

"Condé is very much like our Uncle Antoine," she said, referring to the former King of Navarre, who switched faiths at will unlike our stalwart Aunt Jeanne whose conversion to Protestantism was genuine. "He never wanted to become a Catholic in the first place. He could argue that you and the Queen Mother coerced him."

"If he chooses that tactic, he loses the King's protection and the governorship of Picardy. It's too important for him to lose." Particularly as it stood between two Guise territories, but I would not say that aloud to my sister. I had no desire to make her into my enemy.

"Catherine, we're talking about things that will never happen. There's no use in going over what could or could not occur." I rubbed my eyes, suddenly exhausted. Between the pregnancy and my sister's prying, I had had enough for one evening.

"YOUR HIGHNESS IS MOST WELCOME!" THE ROTUND ROSY-CHEEKED man greeted me as I entered the small Chateau my husband used in governing Picardy. It relieved me to be there, my toes tingling from the early January cold. I had just arrived in Amiens before a sleet storm and the disagreeable weather would keep me indoors for several days after my arrival.

When my sister Catherine heard of my sudden desire to leave for Picardy, she protested constantly. "You are mad to trek across the countryside this time of the year! What reason could you have to leave now!" Her recovery from the birth dictated that she stay in bed, but that did not bar her from regaling me with hundreds of reasons I should remain in Joinville. It relieved me to see that none of Catherine's protests seemed to stem from her involvement in the plot against my husband. Apparently, she was oblivious to the scheming going around her. As much as I hated leaving my sister and the bond we had recently formed, I could not allow my husband to be blindsided in the plot developing in Picardy. I had to do all that I could to save him.

I half-ran to my husband's apartments, determined to speak to him without delay. Opening the heavy door without ceremony, I looked around the room to find him working at his desk. "Have you learned anything about the conspiracy?"

His face folded into a deep frown, "Yes—it goes even further than you had feared. Apparently, you were just in time. According to Princess Catherine, there was a plot to kidnap or assassinate her in Navarre. Her death would be the end of an independent Navarre, since her brother cannot escape the French court. Without your help, we never would have made the connection." He looked up at me and gave me a rare smile. "Thank you, Marie. I cannot tell you how valuable you have been."

"I promised you I would help you and our friends, and that is what I did." I returned his smile with a genuine one of my own. The Bourbons were our family, and I was more than willing to keep them safe. The thought of my cousin Catherine in danger made me sick. Thankful for the new amity between us, I sat in the chair beside him. After so many months at odds in one another's company, peace between us seemed odd. Neither of us knew how to break the awkwardness between us. Unsure where to start, I tried to make conversation.

"My sister, Catherine is doing well. She is getting over the loss of her daughter."

He nodded, "Good."

Having mentioned Catherine, now I regretted doing so. What if Henry had found evidence she was in on the conspiracy after all?

He squelched my fears with his next words, "There is no proof that Catherine was in on the plot against me. Your sister is most likely innocent."

My entire body shuddered with relief. Before I could stop myself, I crossed myself. "Thank God—we're just now speaking to one another as sisters."

The longer I spent in my husband's company, the more that the awkwardness between us lessened. That January became a kind of honeymoon for us; one denied us when during the wedding of Navarre and the subsequent massacre in Paris. We were still mismatched as husband and wife, but we developed respect for one another during my days in Picardy. During our nights, to my shock, we acted as man and wife. Finally, I enjoyed my status as Princess de Condé.

Our delayed honeymoon could not last forever, however; eventually, I had to return to court to serve as a lady-in-waiting to Queen Elisabeth. Mole's words proved true, and the king was indeed suffering from consumption. Elisabeth and the Queen Mother wrote me, begging me to return to serve Elisabeth during the king's illness. I could not refuse a direct missive from the Valois, so in February, it forced me to face the ice and cold to make the journey from Picardy to the Tuileries, where the court stayed. Bidding adieu to my husband, we promised to see one another again as soon as possible.

Several unexpected things awaited me at the Tuileries. For one, the Queen Mother assigned me apartments as close as possible to that of the queen's. This housing assignment was fortuitous since The Hotel de Cleves had closed with Catherine's absence and I felt uncomfortable continuing to impose on Henriette at the Hotel de Nevers. The Hotel de Bourbon had never been my home, despite that fact I had a right to establish a residence within the vast building.

The other surprise waiting for me came in the guise of a glut of letters from the Duc d'Anjou from Poland. Each letter came directly from the Polish court to the Queen Mother, who held them for me until my return from Joinville and Amiens. Untying the ribbon that held the fat stack of paper, I read each letter as Anjou poured his feelings out to me.

Poland and its court were a dull, uncultured wasteland, the worst possible place for Anjou. Virtually from the start, he was miserable and longing for home. Lost in his misery, Anjou confessed deeper feelings towards me. For the first time, he told me he loved me and that he had always hoped for a future between us. I had to fight the anger at reading his words; had Anjou professed his love for me before Condé and I had remarried, we could have been man and wife before he left for Poland. I could have stood by his side as his queen as he began his reign.

Anger soon gave way to longing and as I read his letters, I fell further in love with him. In March, I could not control my emotions, crying one moment and the next, screaming in anger at the vicissitudes of fate. Then I discovered that my warring emotions came from another source: I was pregnant.

Catherine and I sat together one evening as I tried to improve my card playing skills. "I have a confession to make."

She put her cards down and exhaled loudly, "Thank God! Finally! You and Anjou are lovers? Well, I must say, it took longer than I had expected." Since her return to Paris, her color returned, along with her spirits. It thrilled me to have my vivacious sister once again.

I shook my head furiously. "No! Anjou and I have never been intimate, but Condé and I were when I went to Amiens. And now I'm carrying his child."

She hastily tried to rearrange her face, but I caught her before she did so. "Well, that's wonderful! You both need a legitimate heir. This is good news, truly. It is." She bit her lip nervously, unable to continue.

"You are a terrible liar, Catherine."

She shrugged her shoulders, "It's obvious to anyone you and Condé are miserable and that Anjou would be a better match for you."

Too angry and embarrassed to look her in the eye, I laid a card down without looking at it. "I am a married woman and it's obvious now that our disaster of marriage was consummated. If I were to ask for a divorce, there would be no grounds. You know that as well as I do."

"If you were free, then would you marry Anjou?" I could feel her stare, yet I continued to ignore her.

"What exactly are you suggesting? You were only free to marry Guise once The Prince de Porcien was in his grave." As soon as the words were out of my mouth, I regretted them. Catherine had been innocent in the last plot against my husband. Was she really suggesting that I kill my husband? Was she capable of forming a conspiracy of her own in the mistaken thought she was helping me?

"Condé is very much like our Uncle Antoine," she said, referring to the former King of Navarre, who switched faiths at will unlike our stalwart Aunt Jeanne whose conversion to Protestantism was genuine. "He never wanted to become a Catholic in the first place. He could argue that you and the Queen Mother coerced him."

"If he chooses that tactic, he loses the king's protection and the governorship of Picardy. It's too important for him to lose." Particularly as it stood between two Guise territories, but I would not say that aloud to my sister. I had no desire to make her into my enemy.

"Catherine, we're talking about things that will never happen. There's no use in going over what could or could not occur." I rubbed my eyes, suddenly exhausted. Between the pregnancy and my sister's prying, I had had enough for one evening.

20

"I can't tell you how happy I am for you," Elisabeth gave me a warm hug, uncharacteristic of royalty, but very much in line with the warm woman standing before me. "By all means, sit. You should take it easy until the child comes."

"Don't make too much of a fuss over me." I almost felt guilty for giving her my good news, given the dark circles that appeared daily under her eyes. The king's illness progressed despite an extensive list of physicians who tried to give him relief. Physically and mentally, his body was breaking down. The queen spent countless hours at his bedside, in prayer and tending to him, yet none of her efforts had come to anything.

"The Queen Mother sent to Italy for more experts to help my husband, but I fear that it's for nothing. He keeps telling me to send for Anjou, that he feels his end is near."

I took her hand, sitting with her wordlessly. A lone tear slid down her face. "I'm sorry—I should not have mentioned Anjou."

I shook her head, "Oh, don't be silly. You can talk about anything with me."

"I know that it's uncomfortable for you given the marriage negotiations."

My blood ran cold. "What marriage negotiations?"

Elisabeth looked horrified. Her face drained of color and she pursed her lips tightly closed. "Mein Gott, you haven't even heard?"

"No, Anjou said nothing." He wrote me daily, each letter more passionate and most written at least partially in his blood. He had said nothing about marriage in those letters.

"With the king's illness, he and the Queen Mother think it is prudent for him to marry a princess as soon as possible. If Anjou were to take the throne suddenly, he would need an heir," she looked up guiltily at my face.

I stood up ramrod straight, determined to breathe. The air came from somewhere, yet it did nothing to calm me. I had no right to expect Anjou to remain unmarried. It was selfish and unrealistic given his position. "I understand. A kingdom without a secure heir would be-" I stopped, suddenly aware of how thoughtless my train of thoughts sounded to Elisabeth.

"We've drifted from your happy news, Marie." The official royal tone in her voice told me she wanted to move our conversation from the heartbreaking news to something lighter. "Ladies," she raised her voice higher so that her attendants and maids could hear her, "we will all sew garments for the next Prince de Condé. We have little time, so we will have to work hard. Now, who will start on the embroidery?" She motioned her maid forward and directed us furiously in our needlework.

***

"APPARENTLY, HE WAS SET UP FROM THE BEGINNING," LOUIS WIPED his mouth, as we finished the final course of our supper. "Anna Jagiellon made her support of Anjou's election to the Polish throne contingent upon his marrying her. We were unaware of that fact, so I'm sure it came as quite a shock to Anjou," he laughed, earning a sharp look from Henriette.

"Still, few of the Polish nobles want her to be Queen of Poland. From their point of view, she's hardly a strong candidate for a consort.

Apparently, some of them thought he would reject her for marrying... Er, a French lady."

"Are you saying that Anjou wants to develop a relationship with me in order to rid himself of a Polish princess?" My head was spinning, and I tried to process all the new information.

"If Anjou has time to choose his wife yes—I believe that he would much prefer you to any other woman. As far as I can see, he earnestly loves you. But as you know, politics make marriages, not desire."

I snorted at his words. Out of the three of us, I probably understood that concept the most. "Does he have time, do you think, to consider his options?"

Louis looked torn; he had served the current king loyally since coming to France as a foreign prince. Even amongst family, it was dangerous to talk about the demise of a king. As one of Anjou's closest advisors, he would be well rewarded once Anjou took the French throne. "You know, I am no physician. Consumption has no cure; they can only manage it. Illnesses of the lung are often fatal to the sufferer. Besides his lungs, Charles suffered from emotional fits and convulsions since he was a child. His health was never that good. He may die before Anjou could even make the trip to France, much less secure a marriage of his own."

Henriette rose to her feet, breaking Louis' concentration and causing him to jump to his own feet. "Louis, I think that is enough talk of politics for one evening. Marie, I believe that I could go for some fresh air. Why don't you accompany me?" Thankful for the distraction, I followed her lead out of the room and towards the courtyard of the Hotel de Nevers.

"MARIE, I THINK YOU STILL HOLD TO THE CALVINISTS IDEAS OF morality and they hardly serve you in the real world of the French court. No, don't interrupt; listen to me. It is honorable to remain faithful to your marriage vows, but when that honorable behavior makes you and everyone around you miserable, you have the right to look for your happiness." Henriette had with no hesitation, started giving me advice about my situation with Anjou.

I could never understand how similar my sisters could be on their feelings of infidelity yet approach them in such wildly different ways. For Henriette, it was a calculated move while Catherine considered her dalliances to be a romantic adventure. No matter what their approach, they both counseled me to go for the same result.

I placed my hands on my hips, my pregnancy moods making me even more quarrelsome than ever. "If I understand you correctly, you are advising me to take Anjou as my lover. According to your husband, there may be a chance that I could take him as my husband. If I became his wife, I would be Queen of Poland and later of France. Would it not be smarter to hold out for a larger prize?"

"Remember the story of Anne Boleyn? She forced Henry VIII to wait for seven years, then got her king. Once she had him, she failed in her duty to give him a son and he cut her head off. Do you want the same thing to happen to you?"

I scrunched my face, "We aren't as barbarous as the English, Henriette. I hardly think Anjou would have me beheaded."

"You don't know what can happen in a month, a year, or whatever. None of us is immortal. You would be foolish to deny yourself some happiness. Having a devoted lover is a great source of joy."

"I happen to think that I have the time to see how this works out. I am carrying my husband's child and this is hardly time to contemplate a second husband. Once I give birth, I'll see if it's in my best interest to keep the husband I have or replace him."

She was silent, "You know, if you give birth to a healthy boy, your stock as a potential queen will rise. Elisabeth hasn't been able to give the king a son, but if you could prove that you can give a man sons..."

"All the more of a reason I should take it easy during this pregnancy. I've been remarkably healthy this past year and I want to pass that health on to the baby."

She nodded, "Fine, but remember what I told you about the rewards of having a lover."

21

Looking back on that evening, I should have taken the time to talk to Henriette more about her views on keeping a lover. I would find out later that she and Margot were playing a dangerous game, spending time with the odious Joseph Boniface de La Môle and his friend Annibaile de Coconnas. Henriette took the latter as her lover, either out of boredom or some unknown strategy. As the King's health steadily declined, plots and conspiracies abounded in the court, but I was determined to stay clear of them. Consumed with the determination to get what he considered his due, the young Duc d'Alençon plotted to take over the throne of France right from under Anjou's nose, in complete disregard of the line of succession. As his retainers, Mole and Coconnas formed the heart of the plot, with Margot allying with her youngest brother against Anjou.

"I don't trust Mole, not for a second." Catherine and I were in the Queen Mother's apartments, absentmindedly working on our embroidery well out of earshot of the rest of the retinue. Fear for her son's birthright showed with every movement that the elder Valois made within the court and I noticed that her entourage grew steadily larger as she kept her friends and enemies closer to her.

"What could Henriette be thinking, keeping Coconnas as her

lover? I thought you were supposed to be the impetuous one!" I
stabbed my needle into my finger, yelping at the pain. Catherine gave
me a sympathetic look and smiled warily.

"Henriette's loyalty, foremost, is to Margot, then to the rest of us.
You might think that she's just as calculating as Louis, but she can be
reckless." The two had yet to reconcile and their lawyers beat a steady
route from the Hotels Guise and Nevers as they fought over our
father's inheritance. The Guise were bleeding money heavily as Duc
Henri tried in vain to liquidate his father's and uncle's outstanding
debts. Catherine's financial problems failed to break Henriette's
resolve to fight her for her inheritance.

A messenger rushed into the Queen Mother's antechamber at that
moment, cutting off my response. "I must see the Queen Mother!" We
rose to our feet as Madame de Sauve rushed to gather her Majesty.

A rustle of skirts announced the Queen Mother's arrival, and we
sank to our knees in reverence. "Yes?" Her voice sounded stretched
thin as if expecting the worst.

"We have just received news from Picardy." At his words, my head
snapped up. My heart began to beat so loudly that I barely heard his
next words. "The Prince of Condé has abjured Catholicism and
escaped to Strasbourg."

A collective gasp reverberated across the room. I felt every eye
upon me, Save my sister's. To her credit, she grabbed my hand and
squeezed it to steady me.

"Condé has betrayed the King? So the kingdom is beset by conspiracies after all?" The Queen mother turned her face to me and for a
moment, I was sure that she would blame me for having a hand in his
betrayal. "Take the Princess de Condé home, Madame de Guise. She is
in no condition to hear this terrible news!"

"Yes, Madame." Catherine bobbed a quick curtsey, and all but
dragged me out of the room. I barely remember her efforts to bundle
me into her coach, or the trip to the Hotel de Guise. To her credit, she
never took the opportunity to say "I told you so" to me. She only held
my hand and placed my head in the crook of her neck as I sobbed.

THE SHOCK OF MY HUSBAND'S BETRAYAL WAS SO GREAT THAT I TOOK to my bed immediately. The stress of the pregnancy added to my misery and soon my chronic lung malady returned. That was perfectly all right with me; I had no desire to go back to a court rife with gossip about my treacherous husband and my marriage. Catherine hovered over me and she and Henriette made a temporary truce as they worked in tandem to take care of me while I laid in bed.

"It's best that you stay here. The King and his mother see spies and conspiracies everywhere." From the tone of Henriette's voice, I surmised that one of the conspiracies involved her and Margot's lovers.

"If I may offer a bit of advice, I think that you and Margot should stay clear of Mole and Coconnas." I exercised my prerogative as the patient and a pregnant woman to boss my oldest sister around for a bit. Henriette did not take kindly to my switching our roles.

She waved her hand, dismissing my concern. "Oh, Margot and I are fine. We've been at this game for far longer than you can imagine."

"I've lost enough these past few months and I have no desire to lose you as well." Her dismissive attitude grated on my nerves.

"Louis is Anjou's closest advisor and we have no plans to betray him."

"But does the King think that? The Queen Mother? How can you be sure?" Henriette's intransigence was giving me a headache.

A knock sounded at the door, startling us all. My nerves were frayed, and I was in no mood for more bad news. Catherine's young page stuck his head in the room. "Madame, a letter from the Polish court. Her Grace said that the Princess should receive it right away." He placed it in Henriette's hand, and she in turn gave it to me.

"I'll leave you to read it." She smiled and kissed my forehead, as if in apology. Bustling Henriette out of the room, she took her leave.

I looked down at the letter. Anjou's familiar hand made me smile. Opening the letter, I drank in his words.

"My dearest Marie, my heart breaks to hear of the betrayal you have just suffered. Condé is a villain and a fool. I have instructed my court to send word to the Pope on your behalf to annul your marriage. No believer in the true church should remain yoked with a heretic. And no faithful wife should suffer the agony of a feckless, faithless husband.

I await your reply,

🪷

Henri, by the Grace of God, King of Poland and Grand Duke of Lithuania"

🪷

Anjou's words comforted me more than anything and by the beginning of April, I felt recovered enough to return to court service. Despite Anjou's offer to help, I worried that the Queen Mother blamed me for Condé's behavior. I tried to avoid her as much as possible, but within days, she called me to her private chambers.

"My dear, my heart breaks for you. No one should have to suffer what you have had to endure! And in your condition. Rest assured, my son and I will do everything in our power to make your situation right." She rose and enveloped me in a motherly hug. My fear dissipated and I melted into her arms. Before I realized it, tears started to flow down my face.

"What is this? No, no tears! I have written to His Holiness and asked that your marriage to that heretic be annulled." She took a handkerchief and wiped my tears away. "All will be put right soon; you have my word on it."

Enveloped in the bubble Queen Mother's protective presence, I lost track of Henriette's dalliance with Annibaile de Coconnas. In mid-April, as I walked down the corridors of the Chateau St. Germain, I heard a horrible commotion directly in front of me. Unwilling to draw myself into another scandal, I hung back and tried to make myself as inconspicuous as possible. A continent of the King's guard rushed past me, swords unsheathed. My heart sank when I realized that they were heading straight for the chambers occupied by Mole. Within moments, their voices drifted into the hallway.

"We found something!"

"Witchcraft!"

"It's an attack on His Majesty!"

I prayed a fervent prayer that whatever the guards found, it had nothing to do with Henriette. Staying rooted to my spot away from the commotion, I could not hear what was transpiring. The courtiers who had rushed past me in a mad rush to see the commotion passed the information along the hallway.

"It's a wax figure of the King!"

"Mole meant to kill the King!"

"My God, he'll hang for this!"

Even in my hiding spot far down the hallway, I could hear Mole protesting his innocence. His words were useless, as the guards placed him under arrest and within the hour, both he and Coconnas were imprisoned. Fear rose within me and I had to get to my sister. If she were in danger, perhaps I could use my influence with Anjou and the Queen Mother to Save her.

LOOKING BACK ON THAT EVENING, I SHOULD HAVE TAKEN THE TIME to talk to Henriette more about her views on keeping a lover. I would find out later that she and Margot were playing a dangerous game, spending time with the odious Joseph Boniface de La Môle and his friend Annibaile de Coconnas. Henriette took the latter as her lover, either out of boredom or some unknown strategy. As the king's health steadily declined, plots and conspiracies abounded in the court. I was determined to stay clear of any plots. Consumed with the determination to get what he considered his due, the young Duc d'Alençon plotted to take over the throne of France right from under Anjou's nose, in complete disregard of the line of succession. As his retainers, Mole and Coconnas formed the heart of the plot, with Margot allying with her youngest brother against Anjou.

"I don't trust Mole, not for a second." Catherine and I were in the Queen Mother's apartments, absentmindedly working on our embroidery well out of earshot of the rest of the retinue. Fear for her son's birthright showed with every movement that the elder Valois made within the court and I noticed that her entourage grew larger as she kept her friends and enemies closer to her.

"What could Henriette be thinking, keeping Coconnas as her

lover? I thought you were my impetuous sister!" I stabbed my needle into my finger, yelping at the pain. Catherine gave me a sympathetic look and smiled warily.

"Henriette's loyalty, foremost, is to Margot, then to the rest of us. You might think she's just as calculating as Louis, but she can be reckless." The two had yet to reconcile and their lawyers beat a steady route from the Hotels Guise and Nevers as they fought over our father's inheritance. The Guise were bleeding money heavily as Duc Henri tried in vain to liquidate his father's and uncle's outstanding debts. Catherine's financial problems did not break Henriette's resolve to fight her for her inheritance.

A messenger rushed into the Queen Mother's antechamber at that moment, cutting off my response. "I must see the Queen Mother!" We rose to our feet as Madame de Sauve rushed to gather her Majesty.

A rustle of skirts announced the Queen Mother's arrival, and we sank to our knees in reverence. "Yes?" Her voice sounded stretched thin as if expecting the worst.

"We have just received news from Picardy." At his words, my head snapped up. My heart beat so loudly that I barely heard his next words. "The Prince of Condé has abjured Catholicism and escaped to Strasbourg."

A collective gasp reverberated across the room. I felt every eye upon me, save my sister's. To her credit, she grabbed my hand and squeezed it to steady me.

"Condé has betrayed the king? So the kingdom is beset by conspiracies after all?" The Queen Mother turned her face to me and for a moment, I was sure she would blame me for having a hand in his betrayal. "Take the Princess de Condé home, Madame de Guise. She is in no condition to hear this terrible news!"

"Yes, Madame." Catherine bobbed a quick curtsey, and all but dragged me out of the room. I barely remember her efforts to bundle me into her coach, or the trip to the Hotel de Guise. To her credit, she never said "I told you so". She only held my hand and placed my head in the crook of her neck as I sobbed

THE SHOCK OF MY HUSBAND'S BETRAYAL WAS SO GREAT I TOOK TO MY bed immediately. The stress of the pregnancy added to my misery and soon my chronic lung malady returned. That was perfectly all right with me; I had no desire to go back to a court rife with gossip about my treacherous husband and my marriage. Catherine hovered over me and she and Henriette made a temporary truce as they worked in tandem to take care of me while I laid in bed.

"It's best you stay here. The king and his mother see spies and conspiracies everywhere." From the tone of Henriette's voice, I surmised that one conspiracy involved her and Margot's lovers.

"If I may offer advice, I think you and Margot should stay clear of Mole and Coconnas." I exercised my prerogative as the patient and a pregnant woman to boss my oldest sister around for. Henriette did not take kindly to my switching our roles.

She waved her hand, dismissing my concern. "Oh, Margot and I are fine. We've been at this game for far longer than you can imagine."

"I've lost enough these past few months and I have no desire to lose you." Her dismissive attitude grated on my nerves.

"Louis is Anjou's closest advisor and we have no plans to betray him."

"But does the king think that? The Queen Mother? How can you be sure?" Henriette's intransigence was giving me a headache.

A knock sounded at the door, startling us all. My nerves were frayed, and I was in no mood for more bad news. Catherine's young page stuck his head in the room. "Madame, a letter from the Polish court. Her Grace said the Princess should receive it right away." He placed it in Henriette's hand, and she gave it to me.

"I'll leave you to read it." She smiled and kissed my forehead, as if in apology. Bustling Henriette out of the room, she took her leave.

I looked down at the letter. Anjou's familiar hand made me smile. Opening the letter, I drank in his words.

"My dearest Marie, my heart breaks to hear of the betrayal you have just suffered. Condé is a villain and a fool. I have instructed my court to send word to the Pope on your behalf to annul your marriage. No believer in the true church should remain yoked with a heretic. And no faithful wife should suffer the agony of a feckless, faithless husband.

I await your reply,

🙶🙷

HENRI, BY THE GRACE OF GOD, KING OF POLAND AND GRAND DUKE OF
Lithuania".

🙶🙷

ANJOU'S WORDS COMFORTED ME MORE THAN ANYTHING AND BY THE
beginning of April, I felt recovered enough to return to court service.
Despite Anjou's offer to help, I worried that the Queen Mother
blamed me for Condé's behavior. I tried to avoid her as much as possible, but within days, she called me to her private chambers.

"My dear, my heart breaks for you. No one should have to suffer
what you have had to endure! And in your condition. RM son and I
will do everything in our power to make your situation right." She rose
and enveloped me in a motherly hug. My fear dissipated and I melted
into her arms. Before I realized it, tears slipped down my face.

"What is this? No, no tears! I have written to His Holiness and
asked that your marriage to that heretic be annulled." She took a handkerchief and wiped my tears away. "All will be put right soon; you have
my word on it."

Enveloped in the bubble Queen Mother's protective presence, I
lost track of Henriette's dalliance with Annibaile de Coconnas. In mid-
April, as I walked down the corridors of the Chateau St. Germain, I
heard a horrible commotion directly in front of me. Unwilling to draw
myself into another scandal, I hung back and tried to make myself as
inconspicuous as possible. A continent of the king's guard rushed past
me, swords unsheathed. My heart sank when I realized that they were
heading straight for the chambers occupied by Mole. Within
moments, their voices drifted into the hallway.

"We found something!"

"Witchcraft!"

"It's an attack on His Majesty!"

I prayed a fervent prayer that whatever the guards found had nothing to do with Henriette. Staying rooted to my spot away from the commotion, I could not hear what was transpiring. The courtiers who had rushed past me in a mad rush to see the commotion passed the information along the hallway.

"It's a wax figure of the king!"

"Mole meant to kill the king!"

"My God, he'll hang for this!"

Even in my hiding spot far down the hallway, I could hear Mole protesting his innocence. His words were useless, as the guards placed him under arrest Fear rose within me and I had to get to my sister. If she were in danger, perhaps I could use my influence with Anjou and the Queen Mother to save her.

22

I found Henriette sitting in her salon, strangely quiet. "For God's sake, what is going on?" I searched her face, but I could not read her expression.

"We had to do it."

"Do what?" Confused, I tried to make sense of her words. "And who are 'we'?"

"Margot and I. The Queen Mother was right. There is a conspiracy. And it reaches far further than she suspected." Henriette's words were dull and emotionless. Even for my usually quiet and methodical sister, her behavior was a cause for concern.

"Henriette, tell me you weren't part of the conspiracy." The implication was too much for me to consider. I would not lose my sister. I would fall on my knees and beg the King for mercy before that happened.

She shook her head, "No. There are Bourbons involved, but I had nothing to do with it." Bourbons. She must mean Navarre. If he was indeed part of a conspiracy against the King and Anjou, his life was in danger more than during the days after St. Bartholomew's.

"What will happen to Navarre? For God's sake, tell me!" I searched her face, but she still sat as if in a trance. Our poor cousin,

Catherine in faraway Navarre would never recover the loss of her older brother.

"Margot took care of it. She penned a confession for Navarre. He will escape blame and so will Alceon."

I exhaled a deep sigh. "That's a relief."

"But someone had to take the blame." Snapping out of her reverie, she looked directly at me. "Margot had to sacrifice Mole and Coconnas. The King sentenced them both to die."

I had to know how deep this disaster reached. "Is this due in part to Condé's defection?"

She nodded, "These Malcontents are working together, Protestant and Catholic. Everyone knows that the King will die soon. Anjou is probably months away from becoming King of France. Alceon planned to raise an army and overthrow Anjou. Navarre was stupid enough to ally himself with Alceon. France cannot afford to lose the men who are second and third in line to the throne. So," she let out a long exhale, "Margot decided that Mole and Coconnas would take the blame."

"How exactly?" True, the Valois children could be cold and calculating, but would Margot allow two innocent men to hang?

"Margot penned a letter for Navarre, claiming that he had been 'led astray by unscrupulous people.'" Having implicated the hapless men, the only remaining task was to place the blame on them formally.

"The wax figure, where did it come from?"

"Mole claimed it was to win Margot's love, but the King would not listen to his explanation. He believes it was created to send him to his death. ,"

"Henriette, this is monstrous. These men cannot be held as scapegoats."

She shook her head. "This is the way of the French court, Marie. The ultimate goal is simply to survive."

GUILT ATE AWAY AT BOTH MARGOT AND HENRIETTE, AND THE TWO planned a daring rescue of their Condémned lovers. Years of clandestine affairs prepared them for their ruse, during which they would bribe the guards to see the Condémned men for a final time. Once their visit was over, the women planned to dress Mole and Coconnas as Margot and Henriette and allow them to walk out of the prison unmolested. When the guards came for the execution, the two would be far from Paris and Margot and Henriette would be in the cell to greet the guards.

Unfortunately, the King caught wind of a plot to free the men and after announcing the date of their execution, he quietly had them executed before Margot and Henriette could make their way to their cell. Henriette was despondent and the guilt she felt continued to eat away at her.

Unable to rescue their lovers, Margot and Henriette made one last romantic gesture. Under cover of darkness, they cut down their bodies and paid to have them buried in unmarked graves. The men's hearts were embalmed, in a sense saving them for all of Eternity. Margot would keep Mole's heart with her for the rest of her life, repaying him for her betrayal in a sense. Henriette's more practical nature meant that her mourning was not as melodramatic as the Queen's, but I knew that she felt her grief just as keenly.

Determined to return her kindness, I went to the Hotel de Nevers and marched into her bedchamber. Amongst the bedcovers, my resilient sister looked frail. Unable to think of anything better, I crawled into bed and held her as while she wept.

WITH MY MARRIAGE IN SHAMBLES, ANJOU DISPOSED OF ALL restraint and began writing to me on a daily basis. His words became more concrete and tender, reassuring me of his love for me. None of his letters contained a proposal of marriage, but given the fact that I was not legally free to marry, he could hardly do so for propriety's sake. Amongst his words of love, he wrote of his continued disenchantment with the Polish court. Upon his arrival in Poland, displaced Protestants from France assailed him, blaming him for the St. Bartholomew's day massacre. Despite his best efforts, he could not install the customs and manners that the French were so famous for. The women were woefully unattractive, "Especially this one ungainly fifty-year-old cow that is determined to make me her husband." I knew from his description that the "cow" he referred to was the hapless Anna Jagiellon. Perhaps his words were a bit mean and unkind to his subjects in Poland, but I was so grateful to have a lifeline to my confidant that I forgave any lapse of manners on his part. He did have a point, after all, in refusing a woman twice his age who expected marriage as her "thanks" for supporting his claim to the Polish throne.

At the same time, I was enraged to find letters from Strasbourg, sent from my wayward husband. He had the nerve to berate me for my correspondence with Anjou and in his letters, he began to accuse me openly of adultery. I do not know if he had heard of the work done on my behalf to annul our marriage, but his hypocrisy at using me to act as his spy and his subsequent betrayal was too much for me. I refused to answer his letters, and I threw each one upon the fire as soon as I finished reading it.

The court continued to be in shambles and within weeks of the executions of Mole and Coconnas, the King succumbed to his illness. Despite the fact that we all knew his death was imminent, the reality of losing the King and his sweet Queen was too much a blow for me. By tradition, Elisabeth was required to remain confined for a month following the King's death to ensure that she did not carry the royal heir. My heart ached for her, given the fact that I knew that nothing would please her more than to give her husband a posthumous heir. I knew more than most how hard she had tried to carry the King's son, but all of their work was to no avail. I had no desire to rub my pregnancy in Elisabeth's face and assumed that she would not want me with her during her confinement. To my surprise, she immediately sent word that she wanted me at her side for the duration of her stay.

"I don't think that there is anything that I can say to console you, Madame." Tears welled in my eyes and I wiped them away, determined not to make a spectacle of myself.

"Your presence here is all I need. I need a friend now, more than anything."

"Where will you go, after His Majesty is laid to rest?" There was no delicate way to ask, so I charged awkwardly ahead.

"I have loved being Queen of France, but I am tired of court life. Once my dower lands are settled, I will go home to Austria."

I had known that this would happen, but hearing her say it, made it all too real. The unbidden tears slipped faster down my face. "I can't imagine court without you."

"That is why I requested that you stay with me; I want my last memories of France to be of time spent with a true friend." Court life without the angelic presence of Elisabeth of Austria seemed like a miserable place indeed.

"What about Princess Elisabeth? Will she accompany you to Austria?"

She shook her head. "No, she will be happiest with her grandmother. I cannot ask for a better protector than Catherine de Medici."

My heart broke for her. My child had not yet been born, yet I could not imagine living without him or her. If Anjou and I were to marry, I had no doubt that the child would have a devoted stepfather in the new King of France. Impatience rose up within me and I suddenly wanted to see Anjou more than anything. But I knew that Anjou's arrival meant the permanent departure of Elisabeth and I did not want to lose the gentle woman who had been my friend for almost two years.

Elisabeth rose and walked to the dresser. Taking a small box from the dresser, she returned to her seat and placed the box in my lap. "I think that this should go to the next Queen of France." She gave me a knowing smile, and I blushed at the inference.

"I hope you don't mean me. It's presumptuous to think that I could be—"

"Just open it."

Inside the box, a beautiful carcanet, a necklace made to sit below a lady's ruff winked in the light. Rubies framed the delicate floral design of the piece. "It's beautiful. But I cannot take it. It's for too grand of a lady."

"It's perfect for the future Queen of France. And I insist that you take. Every time that you wear it, you will remember me and our friendship." She pressed the box into my hand, an uncharacteristically aggressive move for her.

"Thank you." I could think of nothing else to say.

I FOUND HENRIETTE SITTING IN HER SALON, STRANGELY QUIET. "For God's sake, what is going on?" I searched her face, but I could not read her expression.

"We had to do it."

"Do what?" Confused, I tried to make sense of her words. "And who are 'we'?"

"Margot and I. The Queen Mother was right. There is a conspiracy. And it reaches far further than she suspected." Henriette's words were dull and emotionless. Even for my usually quiet and methodical sister, her behavior was a cause for concern.

"Henriette, tell me you weren't part of the conspiracy." The implication was too much for me to consider. I would not lose my sister. I would fall on my knees and beg the King for mercy before that happened.

She shook her head, "No. There are Bourbons involved, but I had nothing to do with it." Bourbons. She must mean Navarre. If he was part of a conspiracy against the King and Anjou, his life was in danger more than during the days after St. Bartholomew's.

"What will happen to Navarre? For God's sake, tell me!" I searched her face, but she still sat as if in a trance. Our poor cousin, Catherine in faraway Navarre would never recover the loss of her older brother.

"Margot took care of it. She penned a confession for Navarre. He will escape blame and so will Alençon."

I exhaled a deep sigh. "That's a relief."

"But someone had to take the blame." Snapping out of her reverie, she looked directly at me. "Margot had to sacrifice Mole and Coconnas. The King sentenced them both to die."

I had to know how deep this disaster reached. "Is this due in part to Condé's defection?"

She nodded, "These Malcontents are working together, Protestant and Catholic. Everyone knows that the king will die soon. Anjou is probably months away from becoming King of France. Alençon planned to raise an army and overthrow Anjou. Navarre was stupid enough to ally himself with Alençon. France cannot afford to lose the men who are second and third in line to the throne. So," she let out a long exhale, "Margot decided that Mole and Coconnas would take the blame."

"How exactly?" True, the Valois children could be cold and calculating, but would Margot allow two innocent men to hang?

"Margot penned a letter for Navarre, claiming that he had been 'led astray by unscrupulous people.'" Having implicated the hapless men, the only remaining task was to place the blame on them formally.

"The wax figure, where did it come from?"

"Mole claimed it was to win Margot's love, but the king would not listen to his explanation. He believes someone created it to send him to his death. ,"

"Henriette, this is monstrous. They can not hold these men as scapegoats."

She shook her head. "This is the way of the French court, Marie. The ultimate goal is simply to survive."

᭢᭢᭢

GUILT ATE AWAY AT BOTH MARGOT AND HENRIETTE, AND THE TWO planned a daring rescue of their Condémned lovers. Years of clandestine affairs prepared them for their ruse, during which they would bribe the guards to see the Condémned men for a final time. Once their visit was over, the women planned to dress Mole and Coconnas as Margot and Henriette and allow them to walk out of the prison unmolested. When the guards came for the execution, the two would be far from Paris and Margot and Henriette would be in the cell to greet the guards.

Unfortunately, the king caught wind of a plot to free the men and after announcing the date of their execution, he quietly had them executed before Margot and Henriette could make their way to their cell. Henriette was despondent and the guilt she felt continued to eat away at her.

Unable to rescue their lovers, Margot and Henriette made one last romantic gesture. Under cover of darkness, they cut down their bodies and paid to have them buried in unmarked graves. They embalmed the men's hearts saving them for all of Eternity. Margot would keep Mole's heart with her for the rest of her life, repaying him for her betrayal. Henriette's more practical nature meant that her mourning was not as melodramatic as the queen's, but I knew that she felt her grief just as keenly.

Determined to return her kindness, I went to the Hotel de Nevers and marched into her bedchamber. Amongst the bedcovers, my resilient sister looked frail. Unable to think of anything better, I crawled into bed and held her as while she wept.

WITH MY MARRIAGE IN SHAMBLES, ANJOU DISPOSED OF ALL restraint and wrote me on a daily basis. His words became more concrete and tender, reassuring me of his love for me. None of his letters contained a proposal of marriage, but given the fact that I was not legally free to marry, he could hardly do so for propriety's sake. Amongst his words of love, he wrote of his continued disenchantment with the Polish court. Upon his arrival in Poland, displaced Protestants from France assailed him, blaming him for the St. Bartholomew's day massacre. Despite his best efforts, he could not install the customs and manners that the French were so famous for. The women were woefully unattractive, "Especially this one ungainly fifty-year-old cow that is determined to make me her husband." I knew from his description that the "cow" he referred to was the hapless Anna Jagiellon. Perhaps his words were mean and unkind to his subjects in Poland, but I was so grateful to have a lifeline to my confidant I forgave any lapse of manners on his part. He had a point in refusing a woman twice his age who expected marriage as her "thanks" for supporting his claim to the Polish throne.

At the same time, I was enraged to find letters from Strasbourg, sent from my wayward husband. He had the nerve to berate me for my correspondence with Anjou and in his letters; he accused me openly of adultery. I do not know if he had heard of the work done on my behalf to annul our marriage, but his hypocrisy at using me to act as his spy and his subsequent betrayal was too much for me. I refused to answer his letters, and I threw each one upon the fire as soon as I finished reading it.

The court continued to be in shambles and within weeks of the executions of Mole and Coconnas. Before long, the king succumbed to his illness. Although we all knew his death was imminent, the reality of losing the king and his sweet queen was too much a blow for me. By tradition, Elisabeth was required to remain confined for a month following the king's death to ensure that she did not carry the royal heir. My heart ached for her, given the fact that I knew that nothing would please her more than to give her husband a posthumous heir. I knew more than most how hard she had tried to carry the King's son, but all of their work was to no avail. I had no desire to rub my pregnancy in Elisabeth's face and assumed that she would not want me with her during her confinement. To my surprise, she immediately sent word she wanted me at her side for the duration of her stay.

"I don't think there is anything I can say to console you, Madame." Tears welled in my eyes and I wiped them away, determined not to make a spectacle of myself.

"Your presence here is all I need. I need a friend now, more than anything."

"Where will you go, after they lay His Majesty to rest?" There was no delicate way to ask, so I charged awkwardly ahead.

"I have loved being Queen of France, but I am tired of court life. Once my dower lands are settled, I will go home to Austria."

I had known that this would happen, but hearing her say it, made it all too real. The unbidden tears slipped faster down my face. "I can't imagine court without you."

"That is why I requested that you stay with me; I want my last memories of France to be of time spent with a true friend." Court life without the angelic presence of Elisabeth of Austria seemed like a miserable place.

"What about Princess Elisabeth? Will she accompany you to Austria?"

She shook her head. "No, she will be happiest with her grandmother. I cannot ask for a better protector than Catherine de Medici."

My heart broke for her. My child had not yet been born, yet I could not imagine living without him or her. If Anjou and I were to marry, I knew that the child would have a devoted stepfather in the new King of France. Impatience rose within me and I suddenly wanted to see Anjou more than anything. But I knew that Anjou's arrival meant the permanent departure of Elisabeth and I did not want to lose the gentle woman who had been my friend for almost two years.

Elisabeth rose and walked to the dresser. Taking a small box from the dresser, she returned to her seat and placed the box in my lap. "I think this should go to the next Queen of France." She gave me a knowing smile, and I blushed at the inference.

"I hope you don't mean me. It's presumptuous to think I could be--"

"Just open it."

Inside the box, a beautiful carcanet, a necklace made to sit below a lady's ruff winked in the light. Rubies framed the delicate floral design of the piece. "It's beautiful. But I cannot take it. It's for too grand of a lady."

"It's perfect for the future Queen of France. And I insist that you take. Every time you wear it, you will remember me and our friendship." She pressed the box into my hand, an uncharacteristically aggressive move for her.

"Thank you." I could think of nothing else to say.

❧ 2 3 ❧

Word traveled quickly from Paris to Krakow that the King of Poland was now the King of France. I had hoped that Anjou would come quickly in triumph, and we could once again be together as we had before he left for Poland. Alas, politics meant that things were much more complicated than that.

The Poles had no desire to allow their newly elected monarch to leave for his new kingdom. Anjou was virtually a prisoner in his own court and he was forced to create an elaborate plan to leave Poland under his own subjects' noses. In May, I began to show signs of my pregnancy and I did my best to take the edge out of my anxiety by adjusting my gowns and making plans for my life as a single woman. I decided to take up temporary residence at the Hotel de Guise, although both of my sisters insisted that I live with each of them until I gave birth. The truce between Henriette and Catherine would extend throughout the day that I gave birth, likely in mid to late October.

Without a King and Queen at court, the Queen Mother took over the activities of the court and she made a point to install me as the second lady of the court. She functioned as Regent as Anjou made his tortuously slow way towards France, keeping a low profile and successfully dodging his angry Polish subjects. Sensing my impending change in status, ambassadors began to court my favor, starting with the Spanish ambassador.

"Madame, it is our hope that with your guidance the French court will regain its luster." The man's toadying manner irritated me. I realized that this would be my life from now on, constantly trying to discern the real meanings under every person's words. It would be the price of life with Anjou, but it was a price that I was willing to pay for happiness.

Word also drifted slowly from Rome regarding the status of my annulment from Condé. I had assumed that his status of heretic and renegade from the French crown would make the process progress quickly, but as I was to learn, with the Vatican, nothing happens quickly. Money and influence carried the day, and despite the fact that the new King of France and his mother requested the annulment, Rome continued to delay.

"Look at it this way, Marie. By the time you get the annulment, you'll be fully recovered from the birth. The timing may be more fortuitous than you had thought." My sister, Catherine did her best to cheer me, but thanks to my pregnancy moods and the ongoing frustration, I was in no mood to listen to reason.

As he continued to flee from Poland to France, I heard virtually nothing from Anjou. Instead, he once again, commissioned Desportes to write to me, filling my desk with love poems. The elegies and sonnets were almost as dear to me as the man who commissioned them and I spent long hours rereading them and wishing that he would return to France as soon as possible.

My husband continued to stir trouble, traveling between the courts of the German counts and princes to raise an army against Anjou before he could even take the throne. When Louis told me of how much effort Condé had expended in building his army, I thanked God that the process of my annulment was already advanced enough to keep me from being implicated in my husband's schemes. As before, the Queen Mother bore me no ill will, instead of keeping me in her privy chambers at the Chateau Blois as she held onto the French throne for her favorite son. I had planned to remain in Paris at the

Hotel de Guise for the remainder of my pregnancy, but once we heard about Condé's duplicity, both my sisters and I decided that I would be safer directly under Catherine de Medici's protection. I spent that long summer at Blois, living very much like her beloved daughter as we waited daily for Anjou's return.

With Anjou's continued absence during the Summer of 1574, the Protestants in La Rochelle began to threaten to take advantage of his delay by once again revolting against the crown. Still stung by my husband's betrayal, I turned a deaf ear to the entreaties of Protestant lords at court who asked for my help and support.

In July, the Queen Mother summoned me to her presence. "I have good news, Marie. My son has managed to leave the Poles and is now safely in Vienna."

"Vienna! But that is nowhere near Paris!" I was horrified at the idea that he was so far away from me.

"The Poles refused to allow him to leave without permission from their Parliament. Imagine," she snorted in disgust, "they thought that they could order their King, the King of France, around as if he were a mere stable boy!"

"Will he return to us soon?" I would take any assurance from her that our long wait was finally over.

She nodded, "Have no fear, my dear. Anjou will come back to us." She pulled a letter from her desk, smiling at me. "This is from Elisabeth."

I was thrilled at her letter. I had not realized that Elisabeth would use the occasion to get a message to me. A smile lit up my face and Catherine nodded. "And these," she pulled out a large stack of letters," are also for you." There was no doubt who sent those letters. With an indulgent smile, she dismissed me from her chambers.

The letters were just the encouragement I needed during those hot, restless days. Anjou had spent each day writing to me, but he was unsure how his letters would eventually get to me. In them, he detailed his flight from Poland, from the day that he discovered of his brother's death. He told me about the clandestine meetings with his French lords to plan his escape, detailing the danger he faced. His words concluded by telling me of the day that he finally slipped safely from the Polish borders.

※

※

※

AUGUST CAME AND STILL, THE NEW KING HAD NOT RETURNED TO his kingdom. The Queen Mother spent each day working to balance the power factions of the cabinet and the Duc de Guise wasted no time in controlling the ultra-Catholic faction. This lead to more friction between them, but my sister and I were spared from the effects of their power struggle. Condé continued to gather more money and more German Protestant troops and he started attacking towns across Normandy. Without a King upon the throne and without a strong military commander to follow his directives, France once again faced civil war.

"This is ridiculous," I hissed to Catherine one day as we furiously stitched clothes for my baby. He's doing his best to tear the country apart." My hatred for my husband had never been greater.

"My husband is doing his best to gather the troops, but the Queen Mother is determined not to give him command of the royal army." The Queen Mother had good reason to distrust the Guise; before Catherine de Medici could assume the Regency for her eldest son King Francis II, the Guise took over the ruling of France and squeezed her completely out of power. The Queen Mother would be foolish to hand over power to the Guise, no matter how desperate the current situation.

"The King is safely in Italy. There's no danger of Spain or even the Austrians capturing him. What possible reason could he have for this delay?" By the end of my sentence, I was shouting and my sister looked at me in amazement.

"The King has to raise money to fight Condé. Your husband," she saw me flinch at the word, "got the better of him in gathering money and troops. Now as King, he has to beg for money from foreign rulers. It's the way of rulers." Once again, Condé stood in the way of my happiness. His self-centered nature truly knew no limits. France was without her King because of him. I could have killed him with my bare hands at that moment.

"I don't know how long his mother can hold on to the throne for him."

"Impatient to become Queen of France?"

"Don't even tease me about that. I've had no offer and I have no desire to curse my chances."

"Ah, so you do want to become Queen, then?"

I sighed. "I want to be happy."

Lost in our girlish teasing, we barely heard the knock at the door. "Come," Catherine beckoned the messenger, whose blanched face sent terror down my spine. Catherine sat with her back to the boy and it was not until she turned around that she noticed his expression. In his hand, he held a letter, edged with black.

She tore the letter open and read furiously. In minutes, she collapsed in tears. "It's from my husband's grandmother. My son, Henry," she could not say any more. Her second child, barely two years old, was dead. Catherine's grief filled the room. Within a year, my effervescent sister had lost two of her beloved children. Although losing a child was a regular part of life, the loss of even one was devastating to see. I could offer my sister little comfort, but I was determined to give her as much support as I could. My impending motherhood made me an emotional mess, yet it also made it easier to relate to the agony that a mother goes through when losing a child.

WORD TRAVELED QUICKLY FROM PARIS TO KRAKOW THAT THE KING of Poland was now the King of France. I had hoped that Anjou would come quickly in triumph, and we could once again be together as we had before he left for Poland. Alas, politics meant that things were much more complicated than that.

The Poles had no desire to allow their newly elected monarch to leave for his new kingdom. Anjou was virtually a prisoner in his own court and it forced him to create an elaborate plan to leave Poland under his own subjects' noses. In May, my body showed signs of my pregnancy and I did my best to take the edge out of my anxiety by adjusting my gowns and making plans for my life as a single woman. I took up temporary residence at the Hotel de Guise, although both of my sisters insisted that I live with each of them until I gave birth. The truce between Henriette and Catherine would extend throughout the day I gave birth, likely in mid to late October.

Without a king and queen at court, the Queen Mother took over the activities of the court and she made a point of installing me as the second lady of the court. She functioned as Regent as Anjou made his tortuously slow way towards France, keeping a low profile and successfully dodging his angry Polish subjects. Sensing my impending change in status, ambassadors courted my favor, starting with the Spanish ambassador.

"Madame, we hope that with your guidance the French court will regain its luster." The man's toadying manner irritated me. I realized that this would be my life from now on, constantly trying to discern the real meanings under every person's words. It would be the price of life with Anjou, but it was a price I would pay for happiness.

Word also drifted slowly from Rome regarding the status of my annulment from Condé. I had assumed that his status of heretic and renegade from the French crown would make the process progress quickly, but as I was to learn, with the Vatican, nothing happens quickly. Money and influence carried the day, and although the new king of France and his mother requested the annulment, Rome continued to delay.

"Look at it this way, Marie. By the time you get the annulment, you'll be fully recovered from the birth. The timing may be more fortuitous than you had thought." My sister, Catherine did her best to cheer me, but thanks to my pregnancy moods and the ongoing frustration, I was in no mood to listen to reason.

As he continued to flee from Poland to France, I heard virtually nothing from Anjou. Instead, he once again, commissioned Desportes to write me, filling my desk with love poems. The elegies and sonnets were almost as dear as the man who commissioned them and I spent long hours rereading them and wishing he would return to France as soon as possible.

My husband continued to stir trouble, traveling between the courts of the German counts and princes to raise an army against Anjou before he could even take the throne. When Louis told me of how much effort Condé had spent in building his army, I thanked God that the process of my annulment was already advanced enough to keep me from being implicated in my husband's schemes. As before, the Queen Mother bore me no ill will, instead of keeping me in her privy chambers at the Chateau Blois as she held onto the French throne for her favorite son. I had planned to remain in Paris at the Hotel de Guise for the rest of my pregnancy, but once we heard about Condé's duplicity, both my sisters and I decided that I would be safer directly under Catherine de Medici's protection. I spent that long summer at Blois, living very much like her beloved daughter as we waited daily for Anjou's return.

With Anjou's continued absence during the Summer of 1574, the Protestants in La Rochelle threatened to take advantage of his delay by once again revolting against the crown. Still stung by my husband's betrayal, I turned a deaf ear to the entreaties of Protestant lords at court who asked for my help and support.

In July, the Queen Mother summoned me to her presence. "I have good news, Marie. My son has left the Poles and is now safely in Vienna."

"Vienna! But that is nowhere near Paris!" It horrified me to think he was so far away from me.

"The Poles refused to allow him to leave without permission from their Parliament. Imagine," she snorted in disgust, "they thought they could order their king, the King of France, around as if he were a mere stable boy!"

"Will he return to us soon?" I would take any assurance from her that our long wait was finally over.

She nodded, "Have no fear, my dear. Anjou will come back to us." She pulled a letter from her desk, smiling at me. "This is from Elisabeth."

I was thrilled at her letter. I had not realized that Elisabeth would use the occasion to get a message to me. A smile lit up my face and Catherine nodded. "And these," she pulled out a large stack of letters," are also for you." There was no doubt who sent those letters. With an indulgent smile, she dismissed me from her chambers.

The letters were just the encouragement I needed during those hot, restless days. Anjou had spent each day writing, but he was unsure how his letters would eventually get to me. In them, he detailed his flight from Poland, from the day he discovered of his brother's death. He told me about the clandestine meetings with his French lords to plan his escape, detailing the danger he faced. His words concluded by telling me of the day he finally slipped safely from the Polish borders.

AUGUST CAME AND STILL, THE NEW KING HAD NOT RETURNED TO HIS kingdom. The Queen Mother spent each day working to balance the power factions of the cabinet and the Duc de Guise wasted no time in controlling the ultra-Catholic faction. This lead to more friction between them, but my sister and I were spared from the effects of their power struggle. Condé continued to gather more money and more German Protestant troops and he attacked towns across Normandy. Without a king upon the throne and without a strong military commander to follow his directives, France once again faced civil war.

"This is ridiculous," I hissed to Catherine one day as we furiously stitched clothes for my baby. "He's doing his best to tear the country apart." My hatred for my husband had never been greater.

"My husband is doing his best to gather the troops, but the Queen Mother refuses to give him command of the royal army." The Queen Mother had good reason to distrust the Guise; before Catherine de Medici could assume the Regency for her eldest son King Francis II, the Guise took over the ruling of France and squeezed her completely out of power. The Queen Mother would be foolish to hand over power to the Guise, no matter how desperate the current situation.

"The king is safely in Italy. There's no danger of Spain or even the Austrians capturing him. What reason could he have for this delay?"

By the end of my sentence, I was shouting and my sister looked at me in amazement.

"The king has to raise money to fight Condé. Your husband," she saw me flinch at the word, "got the better of him in gathering money and troops. Now as king, he has to beg for money from foreign rulers. It's the way of rulers." Once again, Condé stood in the way of my happiness. His self-centered nature truly knew no limits. France was without her king because of him. I could have killed him with my bare hands at that moment.

"I don't know how long his mother can hold on to the throne for him."

"Impatient to become Queen of France?"

"Don't even tease me about that. I've had no offer and I have no desire to curse my chances."

"Ah, so you do want to become queen, then?"

I sighed. "I want to be happy."

Lost in our girlish teasing, we barely heard the knock at the door. "Come," Catherine beckoned the messenger, whose blanched face sent terror down my spine. Catherine sat with her back to the boy and it was not until she turned around that she noticed his expression. In his hand, he held a letter, edged with black.

She tore the letter open and read furiously. In minutes, she collapsed in tears. "It's from my husband's grandmother. My son, Henry," she could not say any more. Her second child, barely two years old, was dead. Catherine's grief filled the room. Within a year, my effervescent sister had lost two of her beloved children. Although losing a child was a regular part of life, losing even one was devastating to see. I could offer my sister little comfort, but I wanted to give her as much support as I could. My impending motherhood made me an emotional mess, yet it also made it easier to relate to the agony that a mother goes through when losing a child.

❧ 24 ❧

By September, I finally understood Elisabeth's comment about waddling everywhere and the inability to see her feet. My own feet disappeared from my sight, seen only when I put my feet up to get some semblance of relief. The pregnancy stretched my body as well as my patience. I cursed Condé for putting me in this position, then abandoning me to it. During the past months, I heard not one word from him, which was probably just as well. I refused to play the part of an abandoned wife. I would not stand for someone to look at me with pity.

Although the King wrote me daily, I had long since given up hope of meeting him for his triumphant return to French soil. Instead of taking the journey towards Lyon to meet him, I settled in the Hotel de Guise to get ready to welcome my child. My sister, Catherine was determined to return the favor I paid her in helping her birth her child almost a year earlier. As we sat, sewing furiously to finish the baby's clothes, on the fifth of September, the new King of France finally returned to his kingdom. The majority successfully made the long trip to Lyon to meet him, foremost, Navarre and the Duc d'Alençon, the new Dauphin.

"You did send plenty of letters with the Queen Mother?'

A smile pulled at the corners of my mouth, "Of course. I told His Majesty that had he returned earlier I could have greeted him in person."

"Marie, it is unseemly to chide the King of France! You cannot afford to be spiteful now."

"I was only teasing him. He knows that I'm teasing him. He also knows that the first chance that I get, I will receive him with all of my love."

I hated the idea of having the man I loved so close, yet being separated by a condition that I brought on by my naivety. Had I not fallen for Condé's ruse, I could have been in Lyons, enjoying the fruits of my efforts these long months. We looked daily for word of my annulment and each day I knew that it was that closer to arriving. As I became less and less mobile, I used the lazy hours of napping to fantasize about the court that Henri III and I would preside over. My sisters, of course, would be my chief ladies-in-waiting. I laughed at that; how they would fuss at the idea of having to serve their youngest sister! Still, there was no one in the entire county that I trusted more to be at my side.

Before that long summer, I had thought that I was a patient woman. As the days passed, I realized just how difficult it was to wait for something that I had wanted for so long. Finally, I would have the loving husband and partner that I had wanted in Condé. All I had to do was sit and wait for him to come to me.

MY CHILD WAS LATE IN COMING. THE MIDWIFE CAME TO THE HOTEL de Guise and declared that we had miscalculated and that it should be here by now. This was not the news that I expected nor wanted to hear. My nerves had been rubbed raw from waiting, both for the birth and the return of the King. Neither seem in any rush to arrive and I had become the most irritable creature on earth. Catherine had borne the brunt of my anger, regretting her offer of hospitality during my laying in period.

"Marie, it always takes longer for the first child. It happened to both of us." In her frustration, Catherine had enlisted Henriette to keep me calm. Henriette was happy to stay in Paris and allow Louis to travel on to Lyon to meet the King. Despite their best efforts to keep me calm, nothing seemed to work. I became more frustrated by the day.

"How long will this child take? Will it ever come?" We all knew that the moment I had recovered from the birth, I would jump in a coach and make my way to Lyons. Nothing either of them said could stop me. Henriette and the King were experts in sneaking off unattended and I was determined to follow their example.

"Marie, the calculation was off. That happens often. Babies are hard to keep to a schedule, even after they are born." Catherine tried vainly to calm me down, but as always, it proved to be pointless.

"Can't we do something to make the child come earlier?" Frustration was wearing me out and I could not wait for the moment that I was relieved of my burden. At that point, I was willing to try anything.

My sisters exchanged glances, "Well, there are some folk cures."

As soon as October came, I was willing to try any unorthodox treatment, no matter how dangerous it seemed. Together, we walked across the courtyard of the Hotel de Guise in the misguided attempt to jostle the child into being born. When that failed, we consulted every maid and midwife in Paris for advice. Soon, we were plying me with copious amounts of wine, which only served to get me very intoxicated.

"Well, she is a bit calmer," Henriette remarked sardonically.

I flatly refused to try the squirrel broth that one midwife prescribed.

❦

FINALLY, ON OCTOBER 6TH, MY LABOR BEGAN. I SENT A QUICK prayer up to God that I was finally going to give birth. After our efforts, I started to fear that I would never have this child. Mixed with my relief came the sudden pain of my contractions. Terrified, I turned to Catherine for support.

"You will take care of this child if I don't survive, won't you? Don't let Condé raise it, for the love of God! Take it to Joinville and put it under the protection of the Guise."

My sister tutted, "Marie, every woman thinks that she is going to die when she is giving birth. This is your first time, so you haven't gone through it. You'll be fine, just try to calm down."

No matter how much she tried to reassure me, I spent the next nine hours in a complete panic. With each pain, I felt as if I were being torn apart. Henriette's confessor came and promised me that he would give me Last Rites if the midwife determined that they were needed. His assurance gave a little comfort, but until the baby was born, I would not be able to relax.

I did find comfort when a message arrived from Lyon, written in the King's hand. He eagerly awaited our reunion in Lyon and I reread the lines of his letter over and over, almost as a litany. His words came the closest to comforting me. Once this ordeal was over, I would finally be free of Condé and we could begin our lives together. I only had to endure the birth.

Finally, the midwife announced that it was time for me to start pushing the child from my body. After the grueling hours in labor, I barely had strength to sit up, much less push a baby from my body. Catherine set her jaw, and all but hauled me up to sitting. "Enough, Marie! It is almost over. You can handle a few more hours at most! Once the child is here, you can rest all you like."

Squeezing my hands as I pushed, we yelled and screamed almost in unison as the baby started to appear. For what seemed like hours, I managed to push until the umbilical cord appeared. "It's done; you can relax now!" Catherine kissed my hair, which by then, was dripping wet with perspiration.

The baby cried almost instantly, signaling to us that it was healthy. After the effort I expended, I would have been devastated to find that it was nothing, and that I had given birth to a stillborn. I fully understood the grief Catherine felt almost a year earlier when she learned of her daughter's death shortly after her arrival.

"It's a girl, Princess!" I slumped back onto the pillows in relief. A girl was fantastic news. Condé would likely never want to take custody of a girl as she could never become the next Princess of Condé. She was destined to live with me and the new King at the royal court. With her fortuitous birth, our plans would be easier to carry out now.

"Your daughter," the midwife handed the tiny newborn to me, her body pink with excretion and blood still clinging to her head. Atop her head was a sparse amount of dark brown hair. I took a moment to look at her. To my relief, she looked nothing like her homely father. This girl would be a great beauty, taking after the Cleves side of the family. A beautiful girl who deserved a beautiful name.

"Hello, Catherine." I smiled at her and touched her tiny pink fingers. She twitched them in response to my touch.

"You've already chosen a name?" Catherine looked at me, amused.

"Yes, for her aunt who helped me survive this ordeal." I smiled at my sister, who beamed back at the two of us.

"Not for the Queen Mother?" she teased.

"Oh, yes—that too. That's an incredible coincidence." We both laughed at that.

By September, I finally understood Elisabeth's comment about waddling everywhere and the inability to see her feet. My own feet disappeared from my sight, seen only when I put my feet up to get a semblance of relief. The pregnancy stretched my body and my patience. I cursed Condé for putting me in this position, then abandoning me to it. During the past months, I heard not one word from him, which was probably just. I refused to play the part of an abandoned wife. I would not stand for someone to look at me with pity.

Although the ling wrote me daily, I had long since given up hope of meeting him for his triumphant return to French soil. Instead of taking the journey towards Lyon to meet him, I settled in the Hotel de Guise to get ready to welcome my child. My sister, Catherine wanted to return the favor I paid her in helping her birth her child almost a year earlier. As we sat, sewing furiously to finish the baby's clothes, on the fifth of September, the new King of France finally returned to his kingdom. The majority successfully made the long trip to Lyon to meet him, foremost, Navarre and the Duc d'Alençon, the new Dauphin.

"You sent plenty of letters with the Queen Mother?"

A smile pulled at the corners of my mouth, "Of course. I told His Majesty that had he returned earlier I could have greeted him in person."

"Marie, it is unseemly to chide the King of France! You cannot afford to be spiteful now."

"I was only teasing him. He knows that I'm teasing him. He also knows that the first chance I get, I will receive him with all of my love."

I hated the thought of having the man I loved so close, yet being separated by a condition I brought on by my naivety. Had I not fallen for Condé's ruse, I could have been in Lyons, enjoying the fruits of my efforts these long months. We looked daily for a word of my annulment and each day I knew that it was that closer to arriving. As I became less and less mobile, I used the lazy hours of napping to fantasize about the court that Henri III and I would preside over. My sisters would be my chief ladies-in-waiting. I laughed at that; how they would fuss at having to serve their youngest sister! Still, there was no one in the entire county I trusted more to be at my side.

Before that long summer, I had thought I was a patient woman. As the days passed, I realized just how difficult it was to wait for something I had wanted for so long. Finally, I would have the loving husband and partner I had wanted in Condé. All I had to do was sit and wait for him to come to me.

MY CHILD WAS LATE IN COMING. THE MIDWIFE CAME TO THE HOTEL de Guise and declared that we had miscalculated and that it should be here by now. This was not the news I expected nor wanted to hear. It had rubbed my nerves raw from waiting, both for the birth and the return of the king. Neither seem in any rush to arrive and I had become the most irritable creature on earth. Catherine had endured my anger, regretting her offer of hospitality during my laying in period.

"Marie, it always takes longer for the first child. It happened to both of us." In her frustration, Catherine had enlisted Henriette to keep me calm. Henriette was happy to stay in Paris and allow Louis to travel on to Lyon to meet the king. Despite their best efforts to keep me calm, nothing seemed to work. I became more frustrated by the day.

"How long will this child take? Will it ever come?" We all knew that the moment I had recovered from the birth, I would jump in a coach and make my way to Lyons. Nothing either of them said could stop me. Henriette and the king were experts in sneaking off unattended and I wanted to follow their example.

"Marie, the calculation was off. That happens often. Babies are hard to keep to a schedule, even after they are born." Catherine tried vainly to calm me down, but as always, it proved to be pointless.

"Can't we make the child come earlier?" Frustration was wearing me out and I could not wait for the moment it relieved me of my burden. At that point, I was willing to try anything.

My sisters exchanged glances, "Well, there are some folk cures."

As soon as October came, I agreed to try any unorthodox treatment, no matter how dangerous it seemed. Together, we walked across the courtyard of the Hotel de Guise in the misguided attempt to jostle the child into being born. When that failed, we consulted every maid and midwife in Paris for advice. Soon, we were plying me with copious amounts of wine, which only got me very intoxicated.

"Well, she is a bit calmer," Henriette remarked sardonically.

I flatly refused to try the squirrel broth that one midwife prescribed.

FINALLY, ON OCTOBER 6TH, MY LABOR BEGAN. I SENT A QUICK prayer up to God that I would finally give birth. After our efforts, I feared that I would never have this child. Mixed with my relief came the sudden pain of my contractions. Terrified, I turned to Catherine for support.

"You will take care of this child if I don't survive, won't you? Don't let Condé raise it, for the love of God! Take it to Joinville and put it under the protection of the Guise."

My sister tutted, "Marie, every woman thinks she will die when she is giving birth. This is your first time, so you haven't gone through it. You'll be fine, just try to calm down."

No matter how much she tried to reassure me, I spent the next nine hours in a complete panic. With each pain, I felt as if I were being torn apart. Henriette's confessor came and promised me he would give me Last Rites if the midwife determined that I needed them. His assurance gave a little comfort, but until the baby was born, I could not relax.

I found comfort when a message arrived from Lyon, written in the king's hand. He eagerly awaited our reunion in Lyon and I reread the lines of his letter over and over, almost as a litany. His words came the closest to comforting me. Once this ordeal was over, I would finally be free of Condé and we could begin our lives together. I only had to endure the birth.

Finally, the midwife announced that it was time for me to push the child from my body. After the grueling hours in labor, I barely had strength to sit up, much less push a baby from my body. Catherine set her jaw, and all but hauled me up to sitting. "Enough, Marie! It is almost over. You can handle a few more hours at most! Once the child is here, you can rest all you like."

Squeezing my hands as I pushed, we yelled and screamed almost in unison as the baby appeared. For what seemed like hours, I pushed until the umbilical cord appeared. "It's done; you can relax now!" Catherine kissed my hair, which by then, was dripping wet with perspiration.

The baby cried almost instantly, signaling to us it was healthy. After the effort I spent, I would have been devastated to find that it was nothing, and that I had given birth to a stillborn. I fully understood the grief Catherine felt almost a year earlier when she learned of her daughter's death shortly after her arrival.

"It's a girl, Princess!" I slumped back onto the pillows in relief. A girl was fantastic news. Condé would likely never want to take custody of a girl as she could never become the next Princess of Condé. She would live with me and the new king at the royal court. With her fortuitous birth, our plans would be easier to carry out now.

"Your daughter," the midwife handed me the tiny newborn her body pink with excretion and blood still clinging to her head. Atop her head was a sparse amount of dark brown hair. I took a moment to look at her. To my relief, she looked nothing like her homely father. This girl would be a great beauty, taking after the Cleves side of the family. A beautiful girl who deserved a beautiful name.

"Hello, Catherine." I smiled at her and touched her tiny pink fingers. She twitched them in response to my touch.

"You've already chosen a name?" Catherine looked at me, amused.

"Yes, for her aunt who helped me survive this ordeal." I smiled at my sister, who beamed back at the two of us.

"Not for the Queen Mother?" she teased.

"Oh, yes—that too. That's an incredible coincidence." We both laughed at that.

❧ 25 ❧

our days after my daughter's arrival, I started to regain my strength. Catherine was correct; I did think that I would surely die from the birth, but I had survived despite my fears. I was sore, but I felt strong. As soon as I could, I wrote a letter to the King, giving him the news of my daughter. I told him of her beauty, how perfect she was and how she cooed when awake. Most of the time, she simply laid in my arms, content to doze off and make no noise whatsoever.

I talked about how he would love her as I did and that I could not wait until he beheld her for himself. I shamelessly told him that I had named her after the Queen Mother, not wanting to snub either of the senior Valois. It would not do to start our new relationship off with a royal snub and I was careful what I revealed to the King in my letters.

Although it was childish and spiteful, I did not bother to send word to my husband of our daughter's birth. He had cared not one whit for our welfare during my pregnancy and now that I had presented him with a daughter, I was sure that he cared even less. I think that he was suspicious that the child was not his, despite the fact that there was no evidence otherwise. How ironic if he felt I had betrayed him when he had betrayed my loyalty and trust by escaping to Strasbourg and later Geneva? He made his priorities quite clear to me months ago, and I felt no obligation to report my news to him.

Days later, the King wrote back to me, overjoyed at the news of my daughter's birth. He said that he hoped this would be the first of many healthy children and that my next child would most assuredly be a boy. "What a blessing for France that would be! Just think of it, Marie! And how we will love him!" His letters gushed with emotion and each day, I felt more restless at the thought that we could not see one another.

Flushed with excitement over his new reign, he made plans for the court that we would rule over. My sisters would be my Ladies of Honor and he agreed that they would be the perfect candidates. I could not help but laugh at the idea of both of them fetching my needlework as I had once done for Elisabeth. Pangs of guilt crossed my mind as I realized that I would soon take her place, despite her assurances that she thought I was the best candidate to become the next Queen of France.

I SPENT THE NEXT TWO DAYS RECOVERING, SLEEPING ON AND OFF while I recovered from the birth. So as not to worry the King, Catherine sent word to him that I had a slight cold and that I would join the court as soon as possible. I knew that new mothers were often exhausted, but I had no idea that I would feel that tired. I had expected to feel exhilarated, but other than my pride in my new daughter, I did not feel the euphoria that I had expected to feel. To my frustration, I started to feel dizzy when I stood, so I remained in bed as often as possible.

My sister hovered at my bedside, her face etched with concern. "You've been through a lot these past months. And your first birth is traumatic." She did her best to reassure me, but I could tell that her words were edged with concern.

The Guise's personal physician came to examine me and he determined that I had likely torn something during the birth. Hearing this, Catherine went ashen. "She will heal with rest, correct?"

He nodded slowly. "Given the right amount of rest, the Princess should recover. Her condition is serious, but I think that she can recover."

A week after the birth, I still felt tired and drained of all energy, but as if that were not enough, my old ailment came back to vex me. My lungs started to fill with fluid, choking me and causing me to cough constantly. I called Catherine to my bedside.

"Remember your promise; take her to Joinville and raise her under the Dowager Duchess. I have no desire for her to live with Condé."

"You're acting silly and that is what is wearing you out." My sister's voice was sharp, and I was annoyed. I was furious with her for suggesting that I was overreacting.

"I know my body and I know that it is weak."

She took my hand, "Marie, you are months away from becoming Queen of France. Right now you are being absurd. I won't have that behavior from you." Her tenderness was worse than her bossiness.

"Send in someone to dictate a letter; I want to write the King."

She shook her head, "That, I will not do."

A cough bubbled up in my throat, the rasping sound terrifying her. Without a word, she rose and walked out of the room. A few moments later, her personal secretary came in. "The Duchess said that you wished to send a letter to the King."

I nodded, "My sister thinks that I am silly, but I want to make sure that I can express myself to His Majesty while I am still able."

He nodded, kindness and understanding in his eyes. "Then I am ready."

◈

I HOPE THAT THE KING BURNED MY LETTER ONCE HE RECEIVED IT. I told him of my deepest feelings, those that I could not express in person for propriety's sake. I told him what I felt silly expressing to him in my previous letters. If I survived to meet him in Lyon, then I would arrive with his knowing just how much I loved him. He would know for certain that I had returned every desire he had had for me. We would begin our marriage with an understanding and full honesty, something that no other couple at the court could boast of.

If I were correct, and I did not have long, he would know from my own words how much he had meant to me. I told him how he filled a deep longing that my sullen and selfish husband refused to address. He would know for the rest of his life that even if no other woman genuinely loved him, I had done so. Even if every other person in his life were no more than a lying sycophant, I was not. He would have my entire heart and my mind, every last bit of both.

"Hold this letter; my sister will tell you when it needs to be sent." The young man stood, gave me a deep bow and gently walked out of my bedchamber. A few moments later, I was asleep.

MY SISTER IS SO STUBBORN THAT SHE ASSUMES THAT SHE COULD simply will me to live. If that were the case, I would have done so myself. No matter how strong my spirit, the ordeal of giving birth, combined with my weak lungs, meant that I simply did not have the strength to hold on to this life for much longer. Although my body was weak, I was hardly a weak woman. I had battled my condition for so long that I had finally used up my store of spirit.

Day by day, I could see myself slipping away from the world and feeling less like a part of mortal existence. The only thing that anchored me to this life was the sobbing woman who sat beside me. Every time I awoke, she was there. Most times, Henriette was also there, sadly resigned to the obvious fact that I must leave them both very soon.

I refused to send word to Lyon that I was fading. I would not cause the King grief when he was powerless to do anything to Save me. Even the King of France must bend his will to Providence. I was also worried that if he heard word of my condition, he would ride immediately to my bedside. I had no desire for our final moments together to be filled with tears and regret. I did not want to cast such a dark pall over his nascent reign. Catherine had promised to send my letter once I was gone, when he could not wring his hands helplessly in an attempt to help me.

On October 29th, I knew that the time for Last Rites had finally arrived. I spent as much time with my tiny daughter as possible, telling her things that she could not understand and would never remember. I was relieved that Catherine and the Guise would be there for her since it was obvious that I would not.

The priest came, and I confessed my sins before God and my fellow man. Unlike the public gossip sessions of my Protestant youth, our conversation was quiet and intimate. I was thankful for that, the mercy that the last time I spoke to a man of God, it would be without judgement and end in God's forgiveness. Although I felt no regret for leaving my husband and I had committed no adultery, the act of telling my worries to this man was a comfort to me. Once he left, I called Henriette and Catherine back to my bedside.

"You were strangers to me when I came to Paris and I thank you both for standing by my side when I needed you. I wish that we had more time together, but I can't do anything about that. My daughter will be in safe hands."

Henriette grabbed my hand and kissed it. Placing my palm to her wet cheek, she looked in my eyes. For a moment, Catherine was too overcome with emotion to come forward. Eventually, she sat by my other side, tears falling from her eyes.

"You would have been a splendid Queen of France." Henriette's voice was tender.

"We wouldn't have resented serving you a bit."

I laughed at that, "Yes, you would."

"Well, perhaps a bit."

We spent the next half hour quietly, simply enjoying one another's presence. Gradually, my strength left me and I had to close my eyes. The last sight I saw were their faces as they quietly sobbed and held me.

FOUR DAYS AFTER MY DAUGHTER'S ARRIVAL, I STARTED TO REGAIN my strength. Catherine was correct; I thought I would surely die from the birth, but I had survived despite my fears. I was sore, but I felt strong. As soon as I could, I wrote a letter to the king, giving him the news of my daughter. I told him of her beauty, how perfect she was and how she cooed when awake. Most of the time, she laid in my arms, content to doze off and make no noise.

I talked about how he would love her as I did and that I could not wait until he beheld her for himself. I shamelessly told him I had named her after the Queen Mother, not wanting to snub either of the senior Valois. It would not do to start our new relationship off with a royal snub and I was careful what I revealed to the king in my letters.

Although it was childish and spiteful, I did not bother to send word to my husband of our daughter's birth. He had cared not one whit for our welfare during my pregnancy and now I had presented him with a daughter; I was sure he cared even less. I think he was suspicious that the child was not his, although there was no evidence otherwise. How ironic if he felt I had betrayed him when he had betrayed my loyalty and trust by escaping to Strasbourg and later Geneva? He made his priorities clear months ago, and I felt no obligation to report my news to him.

Days later, the king wrote back overjoyed at the news of my daughter's birth. He said he hoped this would be the first of many healthy children and that my next child would most assuredly be a boy. "What a blessing for France that would be! Just think of it, Marie! And how we will love him!" His letters gushed with emotion and each day, I felt more restless at the thought we could not see one another.

Flushed with excitement over his new reign, he made plans for the court we would rule over. My sisters would be my Ladies of Honor and he agreed that they would be the perfect candidates. I could not help but laugh at the idea of both of them fetching my needlework as I had once done for Elisabeth. Pangs of guilt crossed my mind as I realized that I would soon take her place, despite her assurances she thought I was the best candidate to become the next Queen of France.

I SPENT THE NEXT TWO DAYS RECOVERING, SLEEPING ON AND OFF while I recovered from the birth. So as not to worry the king, Catherine sent word to him I had a slight cold and that I would join the court as soon as possible. I knew that new mothers were often exhausted, but I did not understand I would feel that tired. I had expected to feel exhilarated, but other than my pride in my new daughter, I did not feel the euphoria I had expected to feel. To my frustration, I felt dizzy when I stood, so I remained in bed as often as possible.

My sister hovered at my bedside, her face etched with concern. "You've been through a lot these past months. And your first birth is traumatic." She did her best to reassure me, but I could tell that her words were edged with concern.

The Guise's personal physician came to examine me and he determined that I had likely torn something during the birth. Hearing this, Catherine went ashen. "She will heal with rest, correct?"

He nodded slowly. "Given the right amount of rest, the Princess should recover. Her condition is serious, but I think she can recover."

A week after the birth, I still felt tired and drained of all energy, and if that were not enough, my old ailment came back to vex me. My lungs filled with fluid, choking me and causing me to cough constantly. I called Catherine to my bedside.

"Remember your promise; take her to Joinville and raise her under the dowager duchesse. I have no desire for her to live with Condé."

"You're acting silly and that is what is wearing you out." My sister's voice was sharp, and it annoyed me. I was furious with her for suggesting that I was overreacting.

"I know my body and I know that it is weak."

She took my hand, "Marie, you are months away from becoming Queen of France. Right now you are being absurd. I won't have that behavior from you." Her tenderness was worse than her bossiness.

"Send in someone to dictate a letter; I want to write the king."

She shook her head, "That, I will not do."

A cough bubbled up in my throat, the rasping sound terrifying her. Without a word, she rose and walked out of the room. A few moments later, her personal secretary came in. "The duchess said you wished to send a letter to the king."

I nodded, "My sister thinks I am silly, but I want to make sure I can express myself to His Majesty while I am still able."

He nodded, kindness and understanding in his eyes. "Then I am ready."

I HOPE THAT THE KING BURNED MY LETTER ONCE HE RECEIVED IT. I told him of my deepest feelings, those that I could not express in person for propriety's sake. I told him what I felt silly expressing to him in my previous letters. If I survived to meet him in Lyon, then I would arrive with his knowing just how much I loved him. He would know for certain I had returned every desire he had had for me. We would begin our marriage with an understanding and full honesty, something that no other couple at the court could boast of.

If I were correct, and I did not have long, he would know from my own words how much he had meant. I told him how he filled a deep longing that my sullen and selfish husband refused to address. He would know for the rest of his life that even if no other woman genuinely loved him, I had done so. Even if every other person in his life were only a lying sycophant, I was not. He would have my entire heart and my mind, every bit of both.

"Hold this letter; my sister will tell you when it needs to be sent." The young man stood, gave me a deep bow and gently walked out of my bedchamber. A few moments later, I was asleep.

MY SISTER IS SO STUBBORN THAT SHE ASSUMES THAT SHE COULD simply will me to live. If that were the case, I would have done so myself. No matter how strong my spirit, the ordeal of giving birth, combined with my weak lungs, meant that I did not have the strength to hold on to this life for much longer. Although my body was weak, I was hardly a weak woman. I had battled my condition for so long that I had finally used up my store of spirit.

Day by day, I could see myself slipping away from the world and feeling less like a part of mortal existence. The only thing that anchored me to this life was the sobbing woman who sat beside me. Every time I awoke, she was there. Most times, Henriette was also there, sadly resigned to the obvious fact I must leave them both soon.

I refused to send word to Lyon that I was fading. I would not cause the king grief when he was powerless to do anything to save me. Even the King of France must bend his will to Providence. It also worried me that if he heard word of my condition, he would ride immediately to my bedside. I had no desire for our final moments together to be filled with tears and regret. I did not want to cast such a dark pall over his nascent reign. Catherine had promised to send my letter once I was gone, when he could not wring his hands helplessly in an attempt to help me.

On October 29th, I knew that the time for Last Rites had finally arrived. I spent as much time with my tiny daughter as possible, telling her things she could not understand and would never remember. It relieved me that Catherine and the Guise would be there for her since it was obvious that I would not.

The priest came, and I confessed my sins before God and my fellow man. Unlike the public gossip sessions of my Protestant youth, our conversation was quiet and intimate. I was thankful for that, the mercy that the last time I spoke to a man of God, it would be without judgement and end in God's forgiveness. Although I felt no regret for leaving my husband and I had committed no adultery, the act of telling my worries to this man was a comfort to me. Once he left, I called Henriette and Catherine back to my bedside.

"You were strangers when I came to Paris and I thank you both for standing by my side when I needed you. I wish that we had more time together, but I can't do anything about that. My daughter will be in safe hands."

Henriette grabbed my hand and kissed it. Placing my palm to her wet cheek, she looked in my eyes. For a moment, Catherine was too overcome with emotion to come forward. Eventually, she sat by my other side, tears falling from her eyes.

"You would have been a splendid Queen of France." Henriette's voice was tender.

"We wouldn't have resented serving you a bit."

I laughed at that, "Yes, you would."

"Well, perhaps a bit."

We spent the next half hour quietly enjoying one another's presence. Gradually, my strength left me and I had to close my eyes. The last sight I saw were their faces as they quietly sobbed and held me.

EPILOGUE

C atherine, Duchess de Guise

I DELAYED SENDING THE LETTER TO THE KING AFTER MARIE LEFT us. I had no desire to admit to myself that she was gone. I knew that once the message left for Lyons, I was all but admitting to myself that my younger sister was dead. Eventually, Henriette convinced me that it was my duty to send word to the King that the woman he loved, the woman he wished to make his wife and queen, was gone forever.

We had sent no word to Lyon that she was fading after the birth because we naively believed that she would recover. With each day's passing, however, she faded more from us. Marie insisted that the King receive no word of her condition because she could not stand to have him sitting near her, feeling completely helpless. Until she told me this, I was unsure if she loved the King or if she was only flattered by his attention.

The Queen Mother broke the word to the King, telling him on November first, All Saints Day. After celebrating mass with Navarre and Alceon, the King was in the midst of writing to my sister and the

228

Pope of his desire to speed her annulment. He was determined to make her his wife as soon as possible and now that he was within his new kingdom, he was going to act with the influence of the King of France. The few who were present when the Queen Mother delivered the tragic news doubted the sincerity of his grief. He immediately fell into a chair and moments later dragged himself to a couch where he sobbed uncontrollably.

For three days, no one could approach him, even his worried mother. She began to fear that he would take his life in his grief. Finally, with the help of my husband and the King's favorite, Villequier, she barged into his chambers to ensure that her son had not ended his life in his grief. The three forced him to take food, as he had stead-fastly refused it during those three days. My husband related all of this to me and while their friendship was at that time non-existent, he genuinely felt compassion for the King's suffering. "When Henri reap-peared, no one would have recognized him in his melancholy and haggard countenance. The handsome features, which a few days previ-ously had dazzled his courtiers, were gone. The man who faced us was horrifying."

The entire court went into mourning, giving Marie the status due to a member of the Royal Family as if the two had indeed married as the King planned. The King and Queen Mother draped their private rooms in black and no one dared defy their order to wear mourning clothing. Whereas the King came to the frontiers of France as a buoyant and triumphant monarch, once he finally entered Paris there was little triumph. He entered behind two coffins, those of his brother and the woman he loved more than anyone else.

I kept my promise to Marie and personally took her daughter to Joinville, where my husband's formidable grandmother took over her rearing. To no one's shock, Conde never bothered to ask after her, due I think in part to his suspicion that she was Anjou's child. He had never been a favorite of mine, but his behavior after my sister's death disgusted me. He continued to neglect his firstborn child and I can think of no point when he bothered to meet my niece in person. When I heard of Conde's suspicious passing, I rejoiced in private. His death was no great loss to me.

People scoffed at the King when we married my husband's cousin Louise of Lorraine the following February. The whispers behind fans were that she looked too much like my sister. For myself, I felt a bit of triumph in that fact, because it proves that his love for Marie was sincere. Did it mean that his love for Louise was not real? I honestly do not know. My history and my husband's troubles with Henri III of France make it so difficult to be generous to him. As the years flew past, their relationship became so poisoned that I felt as if the King had always been my personal enemy. But that story is for another time.

I have envied Marie, mostly for the fact that unlike me, she experienced true love. She knew the feeling of being loved back, not the exhortation of being desired by a man for a short time. In that sense, she was the luckiest of all of us. Many bemoan the fact that she never realized her dream to become Queen of France, but I think that even without a crown, she was most deserving of one.

THE END

of

ALMOST A QUEEN

The story continues in **Lady of the Court. Tap here t**o get it now and start reading right away!

Join Laura du Pre's mailing list to receive a **free book,** the latest news about upcoming releases and special offers just for subscribers.

Read on for more books by this author, historical notes, and contact information.

ALSO BY LAURA DU PRE

Safe in My Arms: a FREE Three Graces short story

Lady of the Court: Book Two of the Three Graces Trilogy

Fate's Mistress: Book Three of the Three Graces Trilogy

Coming Winter 2017-18, The French Mistresses Trilogy

The Valois Mistress

The Uncrowned Queen of France

The Queen's Nemesis

WHO'S WHO AT THE FRENCH COURT

The Royal Family

Catherine de Medici, Queen Mother of France, wife of Henry II.
  Charles, King of France, Catherine's son
  Elizabeth of Austria, Charles' wife
  Henri, Duke of Anjou, Catherine's son
  Louise of Lorraine, Henri's wife
  Francis/ Hercules, Duke of Alençon, Catherine's youngest son
  Margot of Valois, Catherine's daughter

The Bourbons

Jeanne, Queen of Navarre, first cousin of Henry II, due to France's Salic Law, she cannot inherit the French throne, yet her descent through a male relative means any of her male decedents can.
  Antoine, King of Navarre. Jeanne's husband
  Henry, King of Navarre, Jeanne's only surviving son and heir
  Catherine of Bourbon, Henry's only sister
  Henri, Prince of Conde, Henry's first cousin

Marie of Cleves, Henri the Prince of Conde's first cousin and his wife

Henriette of Cleves, Duchess of Nevers, the eldest of the Cleves sisters and close friend of Princess Margot of Valois.

Louis Gonzaga, Duke of Nevers, an Italian who became a naturalized French due to his association with Catherine de Medici. He inherited the title Duke of Nevers from his father-in-law.

The Guise

[Descended from Claude, a younger brother of the Duc de Lorraine, the family retains the epithet "of Lorraine," and strong ties to their Lorraine cousins.]

Anna, Duchess of Guise and Nemours, a granddaughter of Louis XII.

> *Francis*, her deceased first husband and the second Duke of Guise
> *Mary of Guise*, Francis's sister and mother of Mary, Queen of Scots
> *Henri, Duke of Guise*, Anna's eldest son and heir to Guise dukedom
> *Catherine of Cleves*, Henri's wife and older sister of Marie of Cleves. Became Princess de Porcelian through her first marriage.
> *Catherine of Lorraine*, Duchess of Montpensier Anna's only daughter
> *Louis II, Cardinal of Guise*, younger brother of Henri
> *Charles, Duke of Mayenne*, brother of Henri

The Court

Simon, Baron de Sauve, Catherine de Medici's secretary who rose to become one of Charles IX's Secretaries of State.

Charlotte, Baronesse de Sauve and later Marquis of Noirmourtier, his wife.

HISTORICAL NOTE

Before we go any further, I want to introduce you to the "real" Marie of Cleves. This is a portrait painted by prolific court painter of the French court, Francois Clouet.

Marie of Cleves, Princess de Conde, by Francois Clouet

As much as I wanted to use this image of Marie for the cover, the dimensions are so small that it wasn't possible. Like most portraits by Jean Clouet and his son, Francois, the portraits were not meant to be large and hung on a wall. They were closer to today's yearbook photos, made to be exchanged by friends or other social uses. One of the most interesting uses for these portraits was a parlor game during which courtiers removed the name of the sitter and tried to correctly guess the name of the subject.

Marie's short life meant that her story was the easiest to write in terms of structure for this trilogy. I originally meant to use it as a free story to entice newsletter signups on my website. The lives of the three Cleves sisters closely paralleled that of Charlotte de Sauve, the subject of my upcoming novel *The Valois Mistress*.

Once I started my research on Marie, I realized that each sister had a story to tell, and that it would take much more than 20,000 words to tell them. That was the genesis of the Cleves Sisters Trilogy.

I did my best to stick with historical facts, as long as I could find a source that that gave dates and facts about Marie's life. The only gaping hole I found during my research was a logical reason for why she made a visit to her husband mere months before the Duc d'Anjou returned to France. Actually, I could not reason why she would bother sleeping with a husband she despised, which led to her only child, Catherine. Nothing in the historical record indicated that Conde was a marital rapist, and there are no indications whatsoever the she and Anjou ever had sexual relations with one another.

I fabricated the story of Marie volunteering to spy for Conde in order to try to save her failing marriage. There are no records that indicate she ever participated in any espionage. I hope that she did, and I certainly hope that she lost her temper and spoke her mind as often as she did in *Almost a Queen*.

Laura du Pre

ABOUT THE AUTHOR

Laura du Pre is an emerging author of historical fiction. Almost a Queen is Laura's first book and the first in the *Three Graces Trilogy*.

Laura holds a Master's Degree in History from Middle Tennessee State University. Before writing full time she worked as an archivist and a contributor for historical publications. She continues to live in the Deep South with her cranky elderly cat, Owen.

You can learn more about Laura at her website. Stop by there for a **FREE** copy of *Safe in My Arms: A Three Graces Story*.

You can download a FREE copy of the Three Graces short story *Safe in my Arms* at her website.

For more information
www.lauradupre.com
laura@lauradupre.com

A PREVIEW OF LADY OF THE COURT

I have to hand it to Claude Catherine; she's pulled off quite a gathering tonight. She packed anyone who is anyone in Paris into her salon, making it much warmer than the crisp October air outside. I slipped outside to take a break a few minutes earlier and by the time I returned; the festivities were in full swing. On this particular night, Claude invited painters, poets, sculptors, writers, everyone in Paris with an artistic bent, and amid everything Margot, Queen of Navarre holds court.

"Madame de Nevers," an undistinguishable woman whose name I cannot place nods at me, a trail of perfume following behind her. This may not be my party, but even the outliers of the court know I am a force to be reckoned with. They say I am the richest woman in France, and I would not deny tt. My wealth wasn't handed I worked hard for every crown and every sou I possess. Unlike most people at court, if I lost my entire fortune in an instant, I could build it back up with my own efforts. That is what they fear most about me. I rely on no one, not even the king himself.

I stand behind one of the elegant chairs Claude's servants pushed in from the ballroom and glance at the actor standing in front of the crowd. As the Duchesse de Retz, she has the money and taste to afford the furnishings that make her Hotel the envy of Paris. I pause for a moment to admire her décor, something she constantly threatens to tear down and replace with something new. Within a few seconds, I look in Margot's direction. She's bored but does her best to give the impression the man has not bored her sleep. Few people would suspect she is anything less than enraptured with his performance.

"God, he's terrible." A male voice slices into my ear and I turn to stare at him. I agree with him, but I don't appreciate the intrusion on my thoughts or my personal space.

Turning, I get a good look at him and lift one expertly plucked eyebrow. The motion never fails to intimidate a man foolhardy enough to go head to head with me. I enjoy the challenge of a good conversation and I want to know if the interloper is up to the task.

"You're an expert on actors, then?"

"Madame, I'm an expert on men, and this one can't muster up an authentic emotion to save his life." This was promising. He could keep up with me so far. I pressed further.

"Then, I suppose you're available to instruct someone on the finer points of acting?"

He gave me an elegant nod, "Madame, I am prepared to give you instruction, any time you wish. He wiggles his eyebrows suggestively. It would seem, however, the man standing in front of us needs my help more than you do." A good save, flirtatious, the invitation open. He was a bold one. I was about to respond when the performance blessedly ended and a round of polite applause erupted.

"Henriette, sit with me. We're about to have a song!" Margot could barely speak through her giggles. A second later and she had collapsed into them. "Excuse me, Monsieur," I rushed past him to see what had Margot all atwitter. I was disappointed I could not spar with him any further, but given his performance so far, I was sure I'd see him again soon.

"Aloysius, you must give us one of your poems tonight!" Margot pulled me next to her and threw her feathered fan to hide her face. "Help me, that actor was terrible! We have to do something, or the night is in jeopardy."

She pulled her fan down, her mask of gaiety back. Margot knew better than any thespian in France the benefit of showing an external face. *She could teach acting*, I thought to myself. The thought of Margot Valois, Queen of Navarre starting an acting troupe made me laugh almost as loudly as she had done a few moments earlier. A second thought followed, the realization that knowing Margot, starting a troupe of actors was exactly the kind of outrageous thing she would do. The thought had me in hysterics and I could not stop myself. Margot turned to me and pulled a face.

"What on earth is wrong with you? It wasn't that funny!"

I turned towards Margot and covered my mouth with my hand. "I'll tell you later. Aloysius, get up here now!" I gave him my most imperious look, and he bounded to his feet in seconds. Some men were so easy to intimidate.

I spent the rest of the evening at Margot's side, both of us determined to keep the actor from ruining the evening by returning to the makeshift stage in front of Claude's massive fireplace. Since her marriage, Margot was determined to enjoy every moment of Parisian society she had left until the king packed her off to the countryside to rule Navarre with her husband. I could barely blame her, given what I had heard about Navarre from my own sister Marie. The entire county thrived on misery and boredom. Navarre had converted to Protestantism, a strict flavor of heresy that encouraged a lifetime of dour behavior and sour faces. With their stark black clothing and stripped-down worship services, these men and women took everything enjoyable out of a religious service. Not only were their services dull, they were downright depressing. I shuddered at the thought of having to sit through one.

Thank God Marie was safe in Paris and away from the influence of the Protestants. Our Aunt Jeanne would have dragged us all into damnation with her heresy if given the chance. Margot had her work cut out for her, presiding over those humorless followers of John Calvin and his teachings. Presiding over a court that did not want them would intimidate most people, but Margot was not a woman to be intimidated because she was not wanted.

I found Margot the following afternoon in her privy chamber, lying on a divan, reading. She moved her lower legs to allow me to sit next to her. "Were you distracted last night at Claude's salon? Because I felt like something distracted you."

That was Margot, blunt when she wanted to be; and always perceptive. Many people saw her beauty and her glamorous facade and assumed she would be stupid, but they were quickly disappointed to find out she was quite the opposite. Margot never failed to notice anything.

"I was having a conversation before I sat down with you and I was still thinking about it." I hoped this small lie was close enough to the truth to satisfy her curiosity.

"About what?" She snapped the book closed.

"About starting an acting troupe here in Paris."

She snorted, "As if I had time for something like that. You had an entire conversation about an acting troupe? It sounds suspicious."

Margot then fell silent. She could wait me out until I confessed. She had done just that to me so many times before I knew it was useless to try to outsmart her. She might be a decade younger than I, but she could outmaneuver anyone.

"It wasn't the topic, it was the tone of the conversation." I sighed, giving unto her insatiable curiosity.

"The tone of the person speaking?" She was splitting hairs, trying to get at the truth.

I threw my hands in the air, "Were you watching me?" She bit her lip like a naughty girl. I had thought she sat engrossed in her own conversation, but she missed nothing.

"I saw you talking with a man and it looked animated. So," she tapped her fingers on the book lightly, drawing me in, "who was he?"

"You don't even know? There are men at the court you do not know?"

She shook her head, enjoying my discomfort. "No, wait—maybe I do. He's someone in my brother's household. Now, what was his name?" The tapping continued as she played with me like a cat and a mouse. "He's from Gascony and he has tropical sounding name."

"Coconnas." I was tiring of her teasing.

Sensing I tired of the game, she changed her tone. "Sorry, but as long as I've known you, you have never bothered to take a lover. That's," she waved her hands in the air dramatically, "a little odd for someone in your place. If I were I as rich as you, I'd have a line of lovers waiting outside my door."

"Are you saying I'm boring?" I looked at her with mock horror, which sent her into a fit of giggles. Margot was always up for a bit of fun.

"Yes, whoever heard of a woman who loved and was faithful to her husband?" She shuddered with mock horror.

"I've been quite pleased with Louis, thank you. He's never caused me a moment of trouble and I have no plans to cause him a moment of trouble, either."

"But you found Coconnas attractive?"

"Margot, I'm married, not a corpse." I gave her a thin smile, conceding her point.

❧

I returned home to the Hotel de Nevers, our Paris home, late that evening. Louis met me at the top of the stairs to our bedchamber. "He's not much better." The corners of his eyes creased, and I saw dark bags under his eyes.

I let out a long sigh. "Did the physician say anything about why he's losing so much weight?"

My husband shook his head, "He thinks it is a malignant tumor, or perhaps something in his blood. Without healthy blood, there can be no vigor."

A better mother would have rushed to her child's bedside to soothe her son. A better mother would know what to say to the boy who wasted away in front of our eyes. A better mother would not spend hours away from her own home because she could not stand the feelings of guilt and helplessness that came with caring for an ailing child. Since my son only had me for a mother, I hid at the Louvre for hours on end to keep from facing the apprehension that cast a dark cloud over our home.

"He's asleep; I would let him rest until tomorrow morning." Louis gently touched my shoulder, and I placed my hand on his. None of my money or his favor with the king could help us in this situation. We were two grieving parents who stood by and begged God to show us mercy. So far, God had decided not to do so, but we still hoped one day he would change his mind. Louis headed back to his study, and I drifted to my bedchamber like a wraith.

Frederick was our only son, and he had not even made it to his first birthday. When he came into the world, this past spring, he was pink and gave a lusty cry. Getting a child past the dangers of childbirth was dangerous enough and when we both survived the ordeal, I had thought he had survived the worst. At four months, when his older sisters put on pounds and become fat-cheeked cherubs, our son instead became thin and gaunt. We tried every remedy we could think of and consulted the midwives and wet nurses of Paris, but nothing worked. Soon the doctors arrived, including the most well-respected surgeons from Italy. Even they could not tell us for certain what was wrong with our son or whether he would survive.

We had two consolations that kept us from falling into total despair, our daughters Catherine, an opinionated girl of five and her sister, Marie who was all of two years old. Unlike her sister, Marie barely gave us any trouble as she was an obedient and quiet girl much like her father. While our daughters were proving to be healthy, we could not say the same for our only son.

Margot loves to tease me about my methodical nature, a quality that thankfully my husband shares. We both thought once we noticed a problem with our child if we attacked it hard enough we would eventually find a solution for it. Our inability to find any relief for his suffering has tried our faith in our own intellect.

Before, we could find solace in our shared ability to use reason, something that sustained our marriage for the past eight years. Louis and I have been very pleased with one another and along with our daughters, we formed quite a team. These days, however, my husband and I pass one another like specters. Faith and reason have deserted us, and I think we have forgotten how to manage the simplest communication with one another.

The noise and frivolity of the court somehow distracted me and each day I welcomed the opportunity to escape. While Louis and I engaged in strained pleasantries, the court at large was a haven for pointless and spiteful gossip. It's the perfect place to raise your spirits with its shallow pursuits. Therefore, I welcomed the opportunity to sit and watch a tennis game one mild afternoon in October.

"God help me, this is boring!" Charlotte de Sauve, the wife of the Chancellor and the mistress of Margot's husband, the King of Navarre, rolled her eyes. Although her own lover was one of the players, she frequently sighed as if she might well die of the boredom.

Navarre dropped the ball, and it rolled into the corner faster than he could run after it. "You stupid little beast!" Navarre ran after it, stumbling gracelessly as he did so. Navarre is my first cousin, although given how ungainly he is, you would not assume we shared any family ties. Stories abound that he spent his first eight years living in a mud hut and eating insects at his grandfather's insistence. Given how bad he smells, I think there may be a truth to the rumor. Charlotte de Sauve must be desperate to spend any time in his bed. But given the fact that she does so at the Queen Mother's behest, I'm sure she's paid well to do so.

"Baroness de Sauvé, perhaps you would be happier going inside?" Margot turned to look at her husband's mistress and arched an eyebrow. Margot has no ill feelings toward Charlotte, due in part to the fact that Margot has no hesitation in taking lovers of her own. Neither of them came into their marriage as innocent babes, or as virgins. They have an implicit agreement that each is free to take lovers. It's an agreement most royal brides would envy, and Margot enjoys the freedom it gives her.

"No, it's best I stay," Charlotte shot a wary glance at Catherine de Medici, who would no doubt berate her spy for failing to keep tabs on her assignment. No one could afford to anger the Queen Mother, especially someone as vulnerable as Madame de Sauvé. Her husband rose under the queen's patronage and she depends on the king's wishes to succeed her father as Vicomte de Tours.

I was once in Charlotte's place; eight years earlier, my brother James died and there were no brothers left to inherit my father's fortune. King Henry allowed me to become the Duchesse of Nevers, but on the condition I marry my second cousin, Louis and allow him to become the Duke of Nevers. Louis's mother was a Frenchwoman and came with the Queen Mother in her Italian retinue. Upon Louis' grandmother's death, the king allowed him to inherit his grandmother's estates. In France, a woman could inherit, as long as it suited the king's needs to do so. As long as Charlotte plays Catherine's game and willingly supplies her with valuable information, she will inherit as I did. The trick is in pleasing the Valois, not angering them too much, and remaining useful to them.

Navarre's opponent in the game was my striking brother-in-law, the current Duc de Guise. Duke Henri stood about a head taller than the rest of the court, towering above even the average-looking Valois princes. Guise's flowing blond hair and his rough good looks broke quite a few hearts in the court, mainly because Margot's. The two came dangerously close to marrying until the Queen Mother wrenched them apart. The result of that wrenching was that Guise quickly married my sister, Catherine in a wedding that raised every eyebrow in Paris.

Although Catherine sat only a few seats away from me, we could not even lock eyes. The Guise family was hemorrhaging money; and rather than face their creditors, they covered up that fact by demanding Catherine get more than her share of our father's estate. I refused to be bullied by a family of spendthrifts, so I refused to give Catherine a sou more than she was due. As a result, she refuses to speak to me.

"Navarre, if it's too much for you, you can call the game!" Guise gives him a courtly bow which would seem chivalrous if we did not know how much Guise despised Navarre. He hid his dislike of my cousin in the same manner he hid his financial situation. I'm sure Guise is putting Catherine up to this and I blame him for the greedy behavior more than I blame her. Catherine's passions have always swung from mood to mood and these days, she is more unpredictable than ever. She is due to give birth to their most recent child in

December and within a few days, she will travel to Joinville to give birth. Knowing how easy it is to lose a child, I feel guilty I am being unkind to her. I could lose my sister in childbirth and the thought upsets me so tears sting in my eyes. "Excuse me, I need to leave." I trip over two of the Queen Mother's teenage demoiselles as I stumble from the court and into the palace.

⁂

Headed for a quieter place and one far away from my pregnant sister, I entered the queen's presence chamber. The current queen is a quiet and unassuming Austrian named Elisabeth, who unlike the rest of the court prefers to stay out of sight. I found the queen and my youngest sister, Marie, stitching altar cloths.

"What did we miss?" Marie held a pin in her mouth, but she still spoke. Elisabeth smirked as she looks at her. Neither of them is a gossip, and it is slightly out of character for either of them to ask such a question.

"Just Navarre chasing tennis balls and Guise tossing his hair." Marie pulled her lips into a grimace at my bluntness.

"Is Catherine all right? Is she sitting comfortably?" Out of the three of us, Marie has no children yet, but she made up for that lack by accompanying our sister to her laying-in. She's hovered around her in anticipation of playing nursemaid.

"She's fine," I took a seat and tried to pick up a corner to start stitching. Marie's stitches are impressive. She's making up for lost time as she grew up a Protestant in Navarre with our aunt, the Queen of Navarre. Since converting to Catholicism, Marie wants to stitch every altar cloth in France.

"I don't miss the last months of pregnancy. I waddled everywhere, and I had to constantly sit down to catch my breath." We know the queen for her kindness and compassion, which is why she has no enemies in court. It is also why she has few friends because she has failed to supply the court with its lifeblood, scandal, and gossip.

"Marie, are you sure you want to go to Joinville? It's a long trip?" I'm being selfish, I know. I don't want to lose two of my sisters and remain alone in Paris. The court will leave next week to follow the Duc d'Anjou, the newly elected King of Poland and the king's younger brother to the French border to wish the new monarch well. Anjou is completely besotted with my sister and she spends as many hours as possible in his company.

"I promised Catherine I would help her out and I won't go back on my promise. Besides," she blushed a deep red, "I want to say goodbye to Anjou." After saying that, she suddenly became very interested in her embroidery and fell silent.

"My husband is happy to get the King of Poland to his subjects. I think France is a little too small with two kings." Elisabeth deftly summed up the sibling rivalry between king Charles and his younger brother. Anjou tarried despite the king's efforts to move heaven and earth to get him to the Poles. The news of Anjou's election to the Polish throne came while the royal army worked to subdue the city of La Rochelle and its rebellion against royal authority. The king faced a choice of continuing to fund the siege of La Rochelle or pay to have his brother conveniently out of the country for the foreseeable future. The price the king paid in ending a successful siege against Protestant rebels was too high and he regretted paying it immediately.

"Besides, Condé can't accuse me of immorality if I'm in a room with a woman giving birth." Marie rolled her eyes and stabbed the cloth with her needle.

"He's claiming that you're unfaithful? When the entire court knows the opposite to be true?"

"Yes, I can hear him drone on and on all the way from Picardy. Apparently, Paris is a bad influence on me and he thinks going to the countryside and away from bad influences will do me well."

I was the "bad influence" that had Condé so riled up. The rivalry between Anjou and the Prince of Condé stemmed from years of ill-gotten military appointments. The Queen Mother snatched command of the French armies from Condé's father, who was more qualified to lead troops than Anjou would ever prove to be. Condé ranted that Anjou flirted with Marie only to get under his skin. Louis and I had insisted Marie stay under our roof while Condé left to govern Picardy so her reputation would remain unsullied. Nothing could deter Anjou from writing amorous letters to my sister, however. Condé concluded that since I did nothing to stop those letters from coming into my home, then I must be encouraging my sister to cuckold him. Condé's paranoia was exhausting, but Marie wanted to follow her heart and remain loyal to her husband. How she juggled the two men was beyond me.

"How is your son, Madame de Nevers?" a polite and innocent question, asked by one without malice. Elisabeth of Austria simply meant to be polite, but her kindness caused me to tear up. I would prefer the cruelty and cutting remarks of the court to the bit of kindness the queen offered.

I shook my head, "No better. We've called in every surgeon we could think of, but no one seems to be able to help him." The tears overtook me, and I shook with sobs. Marie jumped to her feet and held me in her arms.

"Forgive me, Madame. I should not have upset you." Like her compassion, Elisabeth's remorse was genuine. "I can offer nothing other than my prayers, and you and your family are in them."

God had not deigned to answer my prayers, but maybe he would listen to Elisabeth's. I nodded and tried to mouth a "thank you" while Marie held me.

FURTHER READING ON THE FRENCH RENAISSANCE

I'm indebted to the historians and biographers who came before me.

- Borthwick, Robert Brown. *History of the Princes de Conde in the 16th and 17th Centuries*. Vol I &II, 1872.
- Carroll, Stewart. *Martyrs and Murderers: The Guise Family and the Making of Europe*. 2009.
- Goldstone, Nancy. *Rival Queens: The Rival Queens: Catherine de Medici, Her Daughter Marguerite de Valois, and the Betrayal That Ignited a Kingdom.* 2015
- Knecht, Robert J. *The French Renaissance Court*, 2008.
- —— *The Rise and Fall of Renaissance France*, 1483-1610, 2001.
- Freer, Martha Walker. *Henri III King of France and Poland*. Vol I-III. 1888.
- Marsh, Ann. *History of the Protestant Reformation in France*. 1851.
- Strange, Mark. *Women of Power: The Life and Times of Catherine de Medici*. 1976.
- Williams, H. Noel. *The Brood of False Lorraine: The History of the Ducs de Guise*. Volumes I & II.

Made in the USA
Monee, IL
09 October 2020